Tom Preschutti

A Lori Daniels Mystery

Pillow Talk

Black Rose Writing | Texas

The author grants the final approval for this literary material.

First printing

This is a work of fiction. Names, characters, businesses, places, events, and incidents
are either the products of the author's imagination or used in a fictitious manner.
Any resemblance to actual persons, living or dead, or actual events is purely
coincidental.

ISBN: 978-1-68433-265-6
PUBLISHED BY BLACK ROSE WRITING
www.blackrosewriting.com

Printed in the United States of America
Suggested Retail Price (SRP) $18.95

Pillow Talk is printed in Plantagenet Cherokee

I want to give a special thank you to my daughter, Jessica, who always has faith in me.

Thank you Roseann D. for your inspiration to write this novel and for your continued friendship through some difficult times.

Much appreciation to the trio of editors, Jessica, Roseann, and Katie E., who gave their time generously, without complaint, doing this tedious work.

Pillow Talk

CHAPTER ONE
First Raid

"You picked the wrong guy again, ..."

Police detective sergeant Lori Daniels droops her shoulders on her tall, athletic body, puts her head down, and shakes her short ash blonde hair.

"...but you'll survive as you always have," consoles Detective Sergeant Brenda Cervetti, Lori's best friend.

Having first met at the Police Academy, Brenda and Lori have shared a lot of experiences. Helping each other through the bad times and celebrating each other's joys, but mainly just being there as close friends do.

When in a crisis situation, they both seem to know how the other will react. Lori looks over at Brenda and thinks, "Is it the fundamental urge of self-preservation as to why she has Brenda by her side when being the lead going into a bad situation?"

The police van they are riding in hops on the uneven pavement as it goes through an intersection on the way to the raid of a suspected hideout for the Irish Boys Gang.

The jolt helps Lori get into her professional mode. Straightening herself, she starts reviewing the last minute instructions. "Heads up Red Team, as you are aware, we expect about a half dozen perps at the warehouse, but be advised there may be more. Reports indicate they are well armed. Use caution."

In the pre-raid meeting, floor plans, gotten from city building codes department, were used to plan the operation. Lori continues, "I will be point on the entry. Ramirez you will take up the rear to guard our backs and hold the door. Taylor will stay with you..."

Police Corporal Jason Taylor is a tall African American man with a muscular physique, sharp eyes and an angular face, looking much younger than his 45 years of age. He is the oldest and most experienced member of the team. A half-hour earlier, during the pre-raid squad conference, he took Lori aside to say, "With all due respect Sergeant I think I should be with you in the lead squad."

Lori had taken no offense at this questioning of her judgment. Smiling she said, "There is no doubt you are the best in the squad at this sort of thing, Jason, but you take too big a share of the risks. The younger members have to learn and to do that they must be put in harm's way. This time you will be on defense."

"...Lingle and Stetzler will fan out to the right, Morgan and Riccini will go left. Cervetti, Hayden, and Boris will join me pushing forward. The other doors are being covered by Blue Team. "

The van stops a block from the warehouse and Red Team exits the rear then jogs into position. They quickly assemble in a defensive formation near the warehouse door.

A message on the earbuds confirms that Blue Team is also in position. A rush of adrenaline hits Lori. She looks at her cell, 3:00 AM; then she gives the go.

The report from the 13th precinct gave a detailed layout of the warehouse, including the location of the lab and where the drugs are stored. Usually, the info on a target is not that precise, but this raid is initiated by Police Lieutenant Detective Mike Costner, recently promoted hot shot of the 13th. Costner has built up a reputation over the past year of finding good leads that reap big caches of drugs. His rep also says he has an ego to match.

Officer Taylor inserts the pry bar between the jamb and door yanking it open. Red Team rushes into the warehouse, fanning out across the floor. The large expanse is dimly lit by overhead lights. Crates and boxes of all sizes cover the vast floor area. Because of this, the officers will have to be extra careful in their sweep. A perp could be hiding anywhere.

Guns drawn, Lori takes point, followed by Brenda, Officer Bill Hayden and Officer Regina Boris. Lori quickly, but deliberately, moves down the main aisle that is wide enough to be used by forklift drivers during the day. The squad encounter no resistance and the four get to the back of the warehouse before the other two squads. The aisle ends at a "T," intersecting with a similar wider aisle.

Lori silently signals the squad to a halt. Moving slowly ahead, she then peers down each direction of the cross aisle. Again silently, she directs Boris and Hayden to the left. She and Brenda go right toward the suspected location of the lab.

Lori and Brenda advance about fifty feet down the aisle. Even through the dim lighting, Lori sees a closed door that leads to the suspected lab location. She tries to keep her anxiety and excitement in check as they carefully approach. Turning to give instructions, Lori sees Brenda's eyes widen. Suddenly a blast from behind breaks the silence. Brenda's shoulder jerks sideways and she is spun around with force. Immediately another blast rings out and the chest impact throws Brenda to the floor.

Horrified by her friend being hit, a blind rage fills Lori. She wields around and starts squeezing off rounds in the direction of the gunshots. Even in a rage, Lori's keen senses allow her to pick out details. A tall, overweight figure wearing jeans and a gray hoodie now turns his 45 automatic towards her. Because she is still in motion, Lori's first two shots go wide, but the third round hits the perp in the lower abdomen. The fourth, fifth and sixth rounds shatter his upper chest. The guy is dead before he hits the floor.

Lori immediately moves to Brenda, who is still prone on the concrete floor. As she reaches down to tend to her friend, the door to the lab bursts open. Three figures rush out and quickly scatter into the maze of crates and boxes.

Talking rapidly into her shoulder mike Lori shouts commands, "Morgan, Riccini, three perps are headed your way! Officer down!

Officer down! Get a bus here now! Blue team, perps on the move, enter the building."

Boris and Hayden arrive at Lori's side and quickly set up a defensive position to protect Brenda and Lori.

Brenda shakily raises herself on one elbow, "The vest took both slugs, I'm okay." Lori signals to Hayden to stay with Brenda. "Regina, you come with me to go after the three rabbits."

As Lori turns, an explosion rips through the warehouse. The lab door flies off its hinges with debris and boxes hurling across the floor. A rank chemical smell fills the air as smoke starts pouring from the lab. They all feel their lungs begin to burn. Lori points at Boris and Hayden, "You two help Brenda out of here, now! I'm going after the rabbits."

While following the trail of the three perps, Lori hears up ahead a single shot that is answered by automatic weapons. She recognizes the automatic fire of the police rifles. Slowing her pace, she cautiously moves forward.

Rancid smoke keeps billowing from the lab trailing Lori as she moves up one of the aisles. Suddenly, a voice calls from her left, "Daniels."

Lori whips around to the sound of the voice. Out of the shadows, a tall figure emerges. "You certainly got that perp. Where is it in the procedural manual about pumping four slugs into a suspect's chest? I don't recall that chapter," Lieutenant Mike Costner whispers sarcastically.

Facing Lori is one of the most handsome men she has ever seen. Mike Costner is tall with brown hair cut a bit long for a cop, well built, all muscle. By the grin on his face, she can tell he's used to high-pressure situations. His swaggering approach tells her he's extremely full of himself. "Lieutenant Costner, I'm guessing," she replies. Then adds, "Why weren't you at the pre-raid conference?"

More automatic fire erupts.

Pointing down the aisle, Costner smiles saying, "Let's finish this first. Then we'll talk about how you are going to convince me not to testify about you using excessive force." He moves off towards the gun fire. Lori follows.

As they get to the end of the aisle, the scene before them presents itself. The converging of Costner's Blue Team from Precinct 13 with Lori's Red team has cornered a half a dozen perps behind a pile of large crates. Sergeant Earl Shahidi of the Blue Team meets them and gives a quick sitrep of their position.

Costner then says, "I want to try something that may save a lot of shooting. Tell Blue and Red Teams to hold their fire and make no advance on the perps. "

Shahidi rises from behind the crates to survey the area before giving the order. Suddenly, a torrent of bullets blankets their position. Splinters of wood from the crates fly in all directions. Lori instinctively jumps up and pulls Shahidi out of harm's way, dragging him behind a large wooden crate. Now in a sitting position, Shahidi, wide-eyed and breathing heavy, nods to Lori in thanks. After a few seconds the barrage stops as the Red and Blue Teams answer the salvo, then Shahidi radios to both teams to hold their fire.

As the rancid smoke from the lab explosion starts to reach their position, Costner calls out, "This is police Lieutenant Michael Costner. You men are cornered with no way out. Throw out your weapons, walk out slowly with your hands in the air and you can avoid dying. You've got 30 seconds to comply. Because in 31 seconds, we are exiting the building and locking the doors. You'll either die from the smoke or get burned alive."

"Hope it works," Lori says smiling at the ploy used by Costner. She is starting to like this guy.

Several silent seconds pass, then a voice, "Alright, here are our guns." Weapons start being tossed from the makeshift barricade. "We're coming out. Don't shoot," the voice is a pleading command.

"No one will shoot if your hands are empty and in the air," Costner yells.

One by one the trapped men start coming out with arms raised. The smoke from the lab fire is starting to cover the entire warehouse and approaching sirens can be heard. Fire can be seen engulfing the crates and boxes along the aisle that Lori and Costner just came down.

The suspects are quickly cuffed and led out to awaiting vans. The firemen are running into the warehouse to try to control the blaze.

On the outside, with police and firefighters scrambling about, Lori can sense Costner behind her, a little too close.

"I'll need to consult with you about this operation before making my report. Especially, the possibility of excessive force being used," he whispers.

They both know that he has no authority to evaluate her performance. Lori would have normally told the guy to take a hike, but something about Costner makes her smile. She answers, "A consultation before submitting reports sounds okay. Is there any other reason for your request, lieutenant?"

He smiles and says, "After this raid's debriefing session, would you like to get a cup of coffee?"

Lori finds that she can't stop smiling and says, "I would, but I want to check on Brenda to see how she is doing."

"Brenda?" Costner asks.

"Sergeant Brenda Cervetti, she took one in the vest during this raid. Could I get a raincheck on the coffee?" Lori explains.

"No problem with the raincheck." Handing her his card, he adds, "Call me to let me know how she is doing and to set up coffee."

As she turns, Sergeant Shahidi walks up to her saying, "You took a chance jumping up like that and pulling me behind the crate. You saved my life in there sergeant. Thanks."

"We watch each other's backs. That's what good cops do," Lori replies humbly.

Shahidi smiles, then looks directly at Lori and says, "I have been in combat, before being a cop. What you did was very brave."

The raid de-briefing is at the Precinct 13 squad room. Lori is a bit surprised that Mike Costner does not sit next to her. She feels a twinge of jealousy that he is sitting in the back between a female officer from the 13th and Regina Boris of her squad. It surprises her that she feels even more jealous when Costner leans towards Boris and says something to her. Boris smiles and nods.

"Maybe it's wondering about her friend Brenda that is messing with her," Lori thinks.

When Captain Richard Lefler enters the squad room to begin the debriefing session, Lori immediately gets into her "professional" demeanor, including blocking out any thought of Costner.

As team leaders, Costner and Lori are eventually left alone with Captain Lefler to evaluate some details of the operation.

Upon leaving Costner reminds Lori, "Definitely let me know when you can meet up. Okay?"

Lori gets that same warm feeling again and can't stop smiling. "Okay," she says.

Double Date

Lori pulls her SUV into a guest parking spot at the tall apartment building. Taking the bag from the front seat, the contents clink as she gets out of the car. The Halon parking lot lights cast an orangey glow as she walks to the back door of the building. Pressing the button on the microphone to the right of the door, she says, "It's me," after a voice says "hello."

The lock clicks and Lori swings the glass door out as she enters. The brightly lit corridor leads to a bank of two elevators. She gets one quickly and goes to the sixteenth floor. At the door numbered 1645, Brenda greets her after a "shave-and-a-hair-cut" knock.

Once inside, Lori holds up the paper bag saying, "Thought we should double date tonight." She walks over to the kitchen island and places the bag on the counter. Pulling out a bottle of Pinot Grigio, Lori announces, as she looks at Brenda, "For your pleasure, let me introduce you to Mr. Timberlake." Taking the second bottle of Moscato out of the bag, Lori announces, "And for my date, meet Mr. DiCaprio."

With a big smile, Brenda applauds saying, "A perfect double date! We have not done this since we used to smuggle wine into the dorm at the academy. Great idea!"

Lori looks at Brenda with a bit of concern. "You seem a bit stiff from that shot to your vest. Take a seat. I'll get us a couple glasses," Lori tells Brenda.

Brenda takes a seat at one end of the large sofa in her living room.

Lori momentarily follows carrying two large stemmed glasses brimming with wine. She also sits on the sofa.

Looking directly at Brenda, Lori asks, "You doing okay?"

Brenda takes a sip of wine. "Just a little sore. That's all. It's nothing. This wine will quickly ease that condition."

They both salute with their glasses and take a much bigger sip.

"I'll tell you one thing that was definitely more fun when we were at the academy, dating," Brenda declares.

Lori nods her head in agreement. "Dating <u>was</u> fun back then. Now it's a big hassle."

Brenda smiles and they clink glasses. "Thank you for coming over. This is great! Why haven't we done this more often?" she ponders.

Lori thinks about this for a few seconds, then says, "I know. We get caught up in so much stuff now…" She lets the thought fade.

A few minutes go by with neither saying anything. Because they are such close friends, the silence is not awkward, but natural. They each take a few more sips of wine.

Brenda says, "Getting through the academy was so much easier because of our friendship."

"Yeah, the instructors called us the three musketeers… or was it stooges?" Lori jokes.

"Have you heard from him? I haven't," Brenda says as she gets up to pour herself more wine.

Lori looks up at Brenda. "No." She also gets up and walks to the kitchen island.

"It's been years." Brenda re-fills both their glasses.

Lori takes another sip of wine. "I treated him badly. Back then I wanted excitement, not commitment. Ellis seemed too…"

"Nice," Brenda finishes Lori's thought. "Commitment and loyalty don't seem so bad now. So many of the guys are such assholes," Brenda adds.

"Yeah, I've certainly met my share of those," Lori agrees.

As Brenda opens a kitchen cabinet door, she says, "I've been saving these for the right moment." She then holds up a family size bag of Cheetos[10] and adds, "We need these."

"Wine and Cheetos, why didn't I think of that!" Lori applauds.

They return to the sofa. Brenda takes two DVDs out of the end table drawer and holds them up to Lori. "Which way we heading tonight? 'Friends with Benefits[11]' or 'Titanic[12]'?" Brenda asks.

Lori pretends she is in deep thought, then says, "Friends. After all, it's your place, and he's your date tonight."

While Brenda prepares to put on the DVD, she says, "Oh, by the way. While I was at the emergency room getting checked out, the good Sergeant Shahidi of the 13th dropped in to see if I was okay."

"He's a good man. Handled himself very professionally today," Lori adds.

"He had very good things to say about you... like you saved his life! Girl, why didn't I hear about this from you?" Brenda kiddingly chides.

Lori deadpans a stare at Brenda. "All in the line of duty. Nothing more."

Brenda continues, "Mmm hmm, well, the fine Sergeant and I are going on a date Saturday. So thank you for saving his ever-so-nice butt."

They both laugh. Each takes a sip of wine and a handful of Cheetos as the movie credits begin to roll.

Lori and Costner

The sky is just starting to get dark as Lori walks to the Dining Car[1] diner. Costner is waiting outside at the front steps.

"Glad you good make it, Lori," Costner greets her with a broad smile.

"I was looking forward to it," Lori replies smiling.

"So, you've replaced Bartok as Red Team leader," Costner asks.

"Yeah, Ed decided he had enough of the rough and tumble. With two of his kids in college, he moved into a desk job that became available," explains Lori.

"So, when Precinct 11 conducts a solo raid, you'll be leading it."

Lori is a bit puzzled by the question, "Uh huh, ...why such interest?" she asks.

Costner takes his time answering, "It's Mark Turgeson. I have a personal reason to try to nail him. He has most of his operations in the jurisdiction of the 11th."

"Oh, so that is the reason you wanted to have coffee! You know I'll be leading the raids against his syndicate." Lori jokingly chides.

As Costner opens the diner door for Lori, he whispers, "No. The reason I asked you out is because you have a body like mortal sin."

Lori can't help smiling, even as she thinks, "What an ego on this guy!"

Mark Turgeson

A heavy set man is sitting on a sofa at his home watching a football game on television. He has a wide face and gray hair with a bald spot on top. Mark Turgeson, head of the Fifth Street Gang, is a very ruthless, very suspicious and at times a very cautious man. These traits have served him well in his 45 year career in the rackets. At the age of fifteen, he was recruited by none other than the head of the Gambini crime family, Tessaro Gambini.

The story goes that Turgeson had the audacity (or stupidity) to "boost" the car of Tessaro. After driving it around he intended to take it to a chop shop, but he first stops to get a burger at a drive-through. After picking up his order, he parks in a lot next to the burger joint.

While eating his burger, he decides to rifle through the center console and then the glove compartment of the car. In the plastic case holding the maintenance manual, he finds the owner's card. The owner is a company named Down State Disposal Enterprises, which means nothing to Turgeson. Continuing to eat while idly searching, under the passenger's seat Turgeson finds an empty envelope addressed from St. Patrick's Church to Mr. Tessaro Gambini. Turgeson stops chewing then almost chokes, coughing up bits of food on the dashboard.

Even with his very limited exposure to crime, Turgeson knows who Tessaro Gambini is. Being now too scared even finish his burger and not knowing what to do, in an act some in the mob later thought as completely stupid, Turgeson drives the car to the address on the envelope. He parks the car in the driveway of Tessaro Gambini's home, cleans off the dashboard with the sleeve of his sweatshirt, then walks up to the front door and rings the doorbell.

A short, heavyset woman, with dark hair that has turned mostly gray answers the door. It is Tessaro's wife. She asks Turgeson what he wants. While sobbing and shaking, he confesses what he has done. After saying multiple times that he is sorry, so sorry, she tells him to calm down. Taking the boy by the shoulder, she leads him through the house into the kitchen.

Sitting at the kitchen table in front of a glass of milk and a cannoli, neither of which he touches, he and Mrs. Gambini wait for Tessaro to come home.

When Tessaro arrives, Mrs. Gambini leaves the kitchen. Turgeson can hear her greet Tessaro; then he can hear them whispering. By this time Turgeson is sweating and almost in tears again. He is just about to bolt out the back door when Tessaro walks into the kitchen and sits at the other end of the table.

In a thick-accented voice, Tessaro asks, "You wanna tell me what you just told Lizetta?"

Trembling while telling the story, Turgeson is surprised when Tessaro starts roaring with laughter. As penance, Tessaro makes him wash the car, inside and out. After the chore is completed, he lets the boy finish the milk and cannoli because by this time Turgeson is calmer and hungry.

Tessaro later introduces him to a capo who will recruit Turgeson into the organization and teach him the ropes.

At the age of 30 Turgeson splits with the Gambinis and with several ex-Gambini capos starts his own organization, the Fifth Street Gang, away from the Gambini territory. When Tessaro dies, Turgeson easily takes over the rackets controlled by the Gambinis.

Today Turgeson holds reign of over half the illegal operations in the city. His goal is to run all of it.

"I have to go out for about an hour," he yells to his wife who is in the kitchen, "Do you need anything?"

"No, don't be late. Katie is bringing home her boyfriend. I told her we would be eating at six," his wife reminds him.

Mark Turgeson pulls his car out of the garage and starts driving. His route takes him around the streets on the outskirts of the city. Over the decades in his profession, he has learned that it pays to be very cautious. His dark green late model sedan keeps under the speed limit, stops at all stop signs and obeys all traffic signals.

His procedure is to drive around when discussing business, whether on the phone or in person. He knows it is difficult for anyone to listen in on a conversation in a moving vehicle. He is extremely paranoid about having a conversation recorded. Several of his business associates are in prison due to a recorded conversation. He keeps this car locked in his secure garage when not in use. He is the only one who drives it, and he personally uses a detector to scan the car for bugs before he takes a drive. The detector was purchased in Germany through one of the companies he controls. He is confident that his vehicle does not have any listening devices hidden in it.

He is now talking on a cell phone. The phone is a pre-paid disposable type that can be purchased with cash. No identification is necessary. It is almost impossible for law enforcement officials to trace the calls or usage on this type of phone. These types of phones are often called burners. The exact reason for the term "burner" is now vague, but most think it is because you can literally burn the phone to dispose of it.

Turgeson's driving seems random as he meanders through the streets, but the route is calculated to have his call "ping" off several cell phone towers, making the call that much more difficult to trace. He communicates directly with very few people. He is actually a very, very cautious man.

He is not wanted for any crime in the Commonwealth of Pennsylvania. Although, he does have a criminal record and served time at the State Correctional Institution in Chester 35 years ago. However, since then he has not been arrested or indicted for any infraction of the law. Regardless of his clean record, it is known to every law enforcement agency in the country that Mark Turgeson is the boss of the largest crime syndicate in the state, the Fifth Street Gang,

Due to Turgeson's pristine public record over the past decades, law enforcement agencies have had no success getting court orders to do surveillance on his home or tap his communications. Turgeson also has many connections in the government who inform him of any potential legal trouble coming his way. He has become a very wealthy man through his business dealing. He is not shy about spending money bribing officials. Of course, all the bribes are paid indirectly. Nothing can be traced directly to him.

"Did we come out alright, Bernie?" Turgeson asks over the phone as he slows down then stops for a red light.

Bernie Tontas is the man to whom Turgeson is talking. Tontas has been working with Turgeson for over 20 years. "Clean as a whistle, boss," Bernie replies.

"Good, good, make sure she gets her money today. I don't want any delays. We get the info quickly; we pay quickly. That's how I do business." Turgeson commands.

Bernie has heard this same statement from Turgeson at least a thousand times over the years. "Yes, the cash is being given to her as we speak. No delay," Bernie says as he rolls his eyes.

"Did you pass on the information about the Crimson Blade?" Turgeson asks.

Bernie pauses before answering, takes a deep breath then replies, "There is a slight issue again, boss. He wants more money."

There is a pause before Bernie hears, "That fucking arrogant prick. He is always upping the price. What is it this time?"

Bernie answers, "He wants $3000 more."

Another pause, then Bernie hears, "Pay the son-of-a-bitch. He is always nickel and diming, …well, in the end, he'll get his," Turgeson says resolutely. "Anything else, Bernie?"

"Nah, that's it, boss."

"Okay, you take care and give my best to the Mrs." Turgeson hangs up.

Lori and Brenda at Precinct 11

Brenda is already at her desk when Lori arrives. Their desks face each other. Lori puts her purse in the bottom drawer and asks, "You feeling okay?"

"The vest did its job. A couple of small bruises, that's all." Brenda continues, "Anything come up at the de-briefing I should know about?"

"Nothing special. Forensics is investigating the explosion. Seven perps were nabbed. I'll be stuck on desk duty until the Shooting Incidence Report process is completed. Standard stuff." Lori says.

Brenda gives Lori a sly smile, "Standard stuff, huh. Well, that's not what I heard. Diner, Costner, Breakfast."

"There are no secrets in this place," Lori says with a tinge of frustration, "Mike and I had breakfast after the de-briefing. That's all."

"Well, it's good, if it helps you get your mind off of Tom Exeter," Brenda tells her.

"You're going to be seeing Exeter in a couple days, aren't you?" Lori asks.

"Yep, I've completed all the paperwork to transfer to IA. Exeter's office set up an initial interview on Thursday," Brenda explains.

"I'm gonna miss you around here," Lori says with a bit of melancholy.

Brenda smiles and says, "I don't have the job yet. Anyway, we'll still see each other a lot. Just not every day at work."

Brenda & Tom Exeter at Internal Affairs

Brenda Cervetti, her shoulder length hair tied back in a ponytail, is wearing a gray dress suit over a white blouse and black shoes with one-inch heels. She walks into the five-story building of police headquarters and enters a large foyer with terrazzo flooring which is emblazoned in the center with a 10 foot diameter depiction of the department logo. A twenty-five foot high domed ceiling spans the foyer. On three sides the walls are painted light green with dark green accent striping. The exterior wall is all glass and aluminum. It is designed to give the impression of authority and security.

Showing her badge and ID to one of the two armed guards, Brenda avoids passing through the metal detector. Crossing the floor, she stops at the reception desk which has a spiral staircase on one side and a bank of elevators on the other. "Brenda Cervetti, I have a two o'clock with

Captain Exeter," she states to the officer at the desk.

The officer, a tall woman in her twenties with light red hair and green eyes, scans an unseen monitor. Handing Brenda a visitors badge on a lanyard, she directs her matter-of-factly, "Take an elevator to the third floor. Office number 301, give your name to the assistant at the desk."

Brenda thanks the officer and places the lanyard around her neck. She walks to the elevators. After pressing the "UP" button, she waits for the next car to arrive. Several seconds go by which results in other officers and civilians converging in the area to also wait. When the doors open, they all enter. A man in a suit generously asks for floors numbers. All, but Brenda, are going to level two.

Brenda gets off at three, checks the signage showing the range of office numbers going left and right. Turning right, she walks down a long corridor. It is painted in the same light and dark greens. She arrives at double doors adorned with POLICE INTERNAL AFFAIRS DIVISION and the division logo. Opening the right door towards her, she enters a small antechamber. There a plain clothed officer, a balding man in his late thirties with a face that perpetually looks like he smelled something awful, is sitting. The little sign on his desk displays the name Sgt. Lucas Faschnaght. He looks up as she approaches.

"Brenda Cervetti, I have a two o'clock with Captain Exeter," she states.

He picks up the phone, punches in two numbers, waits a moment and says, "Your two o'clock is here sir...Yes, sir."

Faschnaght then tells Brenda, "You can go in." Pointing right, he continues, "Go to your right. Make a left at the first corridor. Captain Exeter's office will be straight ahead."

Brenda nods, then follows the instructions. As she opens the appropriate door, Captain Tom Exeter, a tall, blonde haired man with the body of someone who was once very fit, but now is showing signs of prolonged desk work, stands and walks around his desk. He shakes Brenda's hand saying, "So glad you applied to our division. We can use your caliber of police officer." He shows Brenda one of the two chairs in front of his desk, then returns to his leather chair.

Looking around, she can see that the captain is a sports buff. Plaques depicting various sporting events decorate the eggshell white painted walls. The wall behind his desk is painted an accent color of mauve. A low table along this wall displays more sports memorabilia, including a football and baseball each with several flamboyant signatures.

"I see you've noticed my sports plaques. I get them specially made by my contact in Lemoyne, Mel Osterman. Perhaps you've heard of him. In fact, I have an idea for a special feature on a sports plaque. I got the inspiration from the promotion of a major university to restore the image of their football team. I won't divulge the university's name, of course, because the notion is in its infant stage. I ran the idea by Mel. He was taciturn in his enthusiasm and comments, but I could see in his eyes he liked the idea. It will be a big feather in my cap with the commemorative plaque industry."

Brenda smiles saying very flatly, "That's wonderful Captain Exeter."

A bit disappointed that Brenda is not more impressed, Exeter goes on, "Thank you… Brenda. What I have consistently demanded from my staff at Internal Affairs is nothing that I have not demanded from myself, high moral standards and dedication to service…"

After another minute of self-aggrandizement, he finally gets to the point, "As with the police academy, you finished the courses and testing for joining Internal Affairs with the top scores, especially, your psychological profile for honesty and integrity. For your first assignment, you will need all of your abilities. I am referring especially to your integrity and loyalty, because that is what will be most tested…"

"I am prepared for any assignment, sir," Brenda interrupts.

Obviously not accustomed to being interrupted, Exeter pauses a beat and looks blankly at Brenda, then he explains, "Good, the first thing is for you to complete the orientation into Internal Affairs. This should take no more than a week. Then you will be assigned to a very important case. That is all for now. You may go."

Brenda rises from the chair and nods to Exeter. She retraces her steps back to the elevator. On her way down to the ground floor, Brenda wonders if she made the right career move.

Celia Bouton meets Tom Exeter

Tom Exeter pulls the unmarked police cruiser off of Elmerton Avenue into the entrance drive, then turns looking for a parking spot. He finds one near the back. Locking his car, he proceeds to the entrance of the expansive three-story brick and concrete building. Double glass and aluminum framed doors lead to a foyer with guards and metal detectors. After showing his credentials and walking through the scanner, he is allowed into the headquarters of the State Police.

Being familiar with the layout, he continues to the bank of elevators, presses 3 and waits. He is fifteen minutes early for his 2:00 PM meeting with the head of the state police task force fighting drug trafficking, Captain Celia Bouton. He would normally have just talked on the phone with Captain Bouton, but this matter involves a very sensitive situation in the City Police Internal Affairs division, his own department.

The elevator car is empty when it opens. Exeter enters and rides up alone. Getting off on the third floor, he takes a left. The corridor walls are painted blue and gold, the official state colors. He walks down until he reaches the door labeled "Special Section 3" and goes in.

He enters a twenty foot by thirty-foot room. In it are nine desks occupied by male and female plain-clothes state troopers. Section 3 is an unusually large task force which speaks to the importance placed on corralling the drug epidemic. Walking past the desks, a few of the officers recognize Exeter. He returns their waves with a nod and a smile.

Exeter continues to a door, partially ajar, labeled "Captain Celia Bouton," knocks twice then enters.

The ten foot by ten-foot office has a bank of filing cabinets at one end and a utilitarian metal desk at the other. Seated at the desk is an overweight middle-aged woman with short brown hair, wearing a white blouse. Exeter shuts the door. "Come on in Tom," Captain Bouton says in greeting while motioning him with a wave to have a seat at one of the two chairs in front of her desk.

After a few pleasantries are exchanged about family and acquaintances, Tom says, "Thank you for meeting me on such short notice Celia."

Never having liked or respected Exeter very much, Celia gets down to business and replies, "On the phone, you sounded like it was a very serious matter. What's up?"

"Just this, I would like to have access to all the information being compiled by the Section 3 task force…"

Celia with a frown interrupts, "The task force is not part of your authority…but let's say I agree. What is so important that you had to come half-way across the state to meet me?"

To create a dramatic effect Exeter pauses before answering, "Have you noticed that all the raids made in Precinct 11 have resulted in very little contraband recovered and no arrests? I believe there is a gang informant in Precinct 11."

Celia's face reddens with anger thinking, "Of course we have noticed. Do you think we're idiots?!!?" This time it is she who pauses before speaking. After a moment she regains her composure and asks, "You've obviously thought about this before deciding to come to see me. What have you got in mind?"

Thinking he has given Celia new information and, in effect, one-upping her, Exeter straightens his back to strike a more professorial posture. His tone is as a lecturer instructing his class, "Because, in our monthly meeting of department heads, I spoke with Captain Richard Lefler of the 13th and Captain Tony Petracelli of the 11th. I asked both of them who is going to be the lead members from their precinct for the task force. Brown is using Lieutenant Mike Costner, and Petracelli is using Sergeant Lorraine Daniels."

Celia is getting impatient, "Costner has been getting good press about the successful raids he is leading. Daniels has a good rep as a cop's cop. Tell me something I don't know, Tom."

Annoyed at the interruption, Exeter continues, "Yes…, Costner seems to have developed some very good informants in the gangs. Not just low-level informants."

Celia interrupts again, "Has he identified these informants to you or Captain Lefler?"

Again, annoyed at the questioning by Celia during his explanation,

Exeter replies, "Lefler said he pressed Costner on this. He said that Costner didn't want to risk the names being leaked, which would jeopardize their safety. Lefler didn't press him anymore."

"Okay, …" Celia relents, "now about the mole at the 11th, who is it?"

Exeter looks at Celia, "I have reason to believe it's," he pauses for effect then continues, "Detective Sergeant Lorraine Daniels."

Celia pauses for a second then coolly asks, "Do you have any evidence?"

"The evidence is only circumstantial, so I don't want to share it yet," he says sheepishly.

Visibly frustrated Celia asks, "Are you asking that Daniels not be allowed to continue in the task force?"

Exeter looks down at his feet, then raises his head. Wearing a sly smile and in a slow cadence he says, "That is exactly what I don't want."

Celia raises her eyebrows while staring directly at Exeter. She picks up her phone, punches three numbers, waits a few seconds, then says, "Barbara, come to my office, Tom Exeter is here. I want you in on this."

Exeter sits back in his chair, and with an air of triumph, he smiles.

Less than a minute later, Lt. Barbara Maylars, a petite, attractive blonde, walks in. What is immediately obvious about Maylars is her well-toned body and how she carries herself with confidence. "Nice to meet you, Captain Exeter," she says while extending her hand.

Tom rises and shakes her hand, saying, "Nice meeting you, too." Maylars takes a seat next to Exeter.

Celia says, "Lt. Maylars, as the head of the task force in the city, you should hear this." Celia asks Exeter to repeat what he just said about the suspected mole.

When he is finished, Maylars asks, "Have you discussed this with Captain Petracelli?"

"No, I have not. I don't want a slip up at the 11th to put Daniels on to my brilliant plan," Exeter explains. "Sergeant Brenda Cervetti, a former member of Daniel's team, has applied for a transfer to Internal Affairs. After Cervetti does her orientation with IA, I've arranged with Petracelli to have her rejoin Daniel's squad. Eventually, through Cervetti, we'll give Daniels some false information which will allow us to catch her and the syndicate boss she is helping."

With a blank expression, Celia responds tactfully, "I think your plan has a… very low probability of success, Tom, but that is your business. Who Petracelli puts on Daniel's squad is his business. I have no control over that. I do have control of the task force." Celia adds fervently, "No officer is going to be blacklisted by me without hard evidence. If you mess with the operation of the task force, I'll come down on you hard. I'll expect updates from you on any information you acquire, or I'll go directly to the city police commissioner to complain to her."

Exeter's face reddens as he rebukes Celia's threat, "The last person to speak to me that way regretted it. As for the police commissioner, I plan on gaining that post for myself. My investigation will proceed and you better not interfere with it, or I'll contact the governor and complain about you."

Celia then asks, "Is there anything else?"

"No." Exeter gets up and leaves.

After he leaves, Celia looks squarely at Barbara saying, "Well, Exeter is right about one thing. There is a rat in the city police department helping a gang. Although I think he is way off base, run the financials of Lori Daniels. See if anything pops."

"Does he always act like he is superior to everyone?" Barbara asks.

Celia smiles, "Every time I have met him he does," she pauses, then continues, "…However, there are some parts of his plan that may eventually help us."

Barbara nods in agreement, then asks, "How is the crack-down in Pittsburgh moving along?"

Celia replies, "The latest indictments and arrests against the Muzi gang are ferreting out their top people. A plea deal with their second in command, Craig Zdonskova, ensures his cooperation." Celia then starts to rub her hands nervously.

Barbara notices Celia's anxiety and asks, "Are we going ahead with the plan?"

Celia takes a deep breath before answering, "Yes, he wants to do it."

"It will be extremely dangerous for him," Barbara adds.

"I know," is all Celia says.

Later in the day

Barbara Maylars prints out the information on the screen of her PC and takes the printed copies over to the office of Celia Bouton. She knocks on the door frame then walks through the open door.

Celia looks up from her desk, "What have you got for me?"

Barbara says, "I requested a copy of Lorraine Daniels personnel file from the city PD. That usually takes a few days to receive. However, here is a copy of the printout of her financials. The house she lives in was inherited from her mother, and so was the mortgage, which Daniels is up to date on the payments. She bought a used 2008 Subaru in 2011; it's paid off now. She has a checking and savings account, a couple hundred in checking, four grand in savings and no other investments or accounts. She owns no other properties. Typical financial statement for an underpaid police sergeant."

Celia says with sarcasm, "We both know as public servants, our reward is ministering to the public good." She looks over the financial report and adds, "Just as I thought. ...Well, we were told Sergeant Daniels is a good cop and can be relied on if we need her. This makes no sense. I wonder what Exeter is up to."

The Pittsburgh Contact

Celia Bouton presses the speakerphone on her desk. When she hears the dial tone, a number in Pittsburgh is called.

A pleasant voice answers, "Thank you for calling Pinter Insurance; we help keep you safe. Gail Amendola speaking. How may I help you?" While saying the standard greeting, Amendola gets a readout of the phone number that is calling and the name "Pennsylvania State Police" appears below.

Celia answers with the prearranged response, "Hi, I'm Gloria Denton, I spoke with another agent before about my fender bender."

"Right, Ms. Denton, I'll transfer you," Amendola says politely.

All of this exchange is part of the precautions set up by the State Police. The call is being routed to a safe house near Washington Township, just east of Pittsburgh. After a few seconds, Celia hears the phone ring twice, then State Police Corporal Joseph Maniford answers,

"Celia you are always punctual. I'm here with Craig Zdonskova, his attorney, P. J. Defolio and our attorney, Bryan Oleska. We've worked out the plea agreement, and all parties have signed on. Mr. Zdonskova said he is willing to cooperate."

Celia says, "Great, I'm glad we could come to an agreement. As we previously discussed, Mr. Zdonskova, you will contact Mark Turgeson with the information we provided to you. Are you ready?"

"Now that we will be working together, please, call me Craig," Zdonskova says with a touch of sarcasm.

Liking Zdonskova less and less every time they talk, Celia controls her anger and says with a professional tone, "The terms of the agreement are specific on this matter. Fail to comply, and the deal is off. Are you ready to contact Mark Turgeson?"

Defolio replies, "My client will cooperate."

Celia continues, "Mr. Zdonskova, even though we know where he lives, Turgeson is very very difficult to reach. How are you going to contact him?"

Zdonskova smiles and says, "Mark and I worked together many years ago for Tessaro Gambini. I know a sure way to contact him. Ya see, cops always think they are so smart with their surveillance. Body mikes and wiretaps… Now they think they're even smarter with drones, phone apps, and tracking devices."

Trying to control her impatience, Celia asks, "So how are you going to get word to Turgeson?"

"Mark and I always used the old fashion methods. Have one of your people run to the store and buy me a birthday card. Make it a nice one, too," Zdonskova says with a bit of sarcasm. "You see, back in the day, that is how Mark and I contacted each other without any worry about cops intercepting a message. Even when he and I were under strict surveillance, every Christmas card, Hanukah card, and birthday card made it through the US Postal System unopened. I'll use the return address with the fake name we used all those years ago, Mr. J. E. Hoover. Mark will know it is from me," Zdonskova says with a bit of triumph in his voice.

CHAPTER TWO
One on One Training

Lori leaves the women's locker room and enters the gym wearing dark gray sweatpants, a white tee shirt, and athletic shoes. A few days ago she and Mike Costner met over a cup of coffee. Lori really felt a connection with Mike. They agreed to meet this evening at the 11th Precinct gym.

A few seconds later Mike Costner comes in from the men's locker room at the other side of the gym.

As expected at this hour, no one else is there. The gym is a large rectangle room. Weight training equipment is clustered at one end of the gym. Treadmills and stationary bikes are at the other end. Several large blue wrestling mats fill the center.

Lori and Mike approach each other and meet at the center mat, standing about 6 feet apart.

Mike is wearing black athletic shoes, light gray sweatpants and a tight dark blue tee shirt that shows his lean muscular frame and tight abs. His hands are in workout gloves that have holes cut out for the fingers. Lori is wearing similar gloves.

"Ready," Lori says as she rises on the balls of her feet getting into her fighting stance.

Mike smiles, nods, then does the same, as they both close the gap between them.

Both throw some jabs which the other easily parries. Mike feints with his left, then lands his right fist on Lori's shoulder. She reels from the blow. Mike moves in to attempt a takedown.

In a single motion, Lori falls to the mat avoiding Mike's maneuver while swinging her right leg at the left ankle of Mike. He is off balance due to the blow and falls on his side to the mat.

Lori immediately pops up and returns to her fighting stance hopping on the balls of her feet.

Mike lays there for a few seconds blinking. The smile is no longer on his face.

"Have you quit already," Lori asks in a slightly sarcastic tone.

Mike immediately hops into his stance. He waves both hands in a "come and get me" gesture. This time Lori smiles then nods. They close the gap again. Costner again feints with his left, but quickly brings up his right foot towards Lori's abdomen. Lori swings her left leg back to avoid the blow and at the same time grabs Mike's right ankle. With this leverage, she hops him backwards two times then flips his leg up. Mike slams to the mat on his back.

Smiling while reaching down to help him up, Lori says, "You spend a lot of time down there, don't you!"

Mike's face flushes with anger. He takes her hand, but instead of rising with her assist, he pulls her down and swings his left leg just below her right knee. She crashes to the mat violently.

Lori immediately rolls away from Mike and returns to her stance. Mike gets up and resumes his stance.

"That is a bit underhanded for a friendly workout." Lori comments.

Lamely he answers, "Just playing. No harm meant."

After another 30 minutes, both are sweating and panting. "That's enough for today," Lori ends the session. "You're really good," she compliments.

"You're not too bad yourself," he replies.

She gives him a hug and a peck on the cheek. "Wanna get a drink later?"

Mike grabs her ass cheek and says, "Sure."

Lori walks back into the women's locker room. No one else is in the gang showers, and the hard tile surfaces echo the opening of her locker door. She grabs body wash, shampoo, conditioner, and loofah, then walks up to a shower head and turns on the water waiting a few seconds for it to turn warm.

She steps into the stream to wet her hair and naked body. The warm water feels comforting against her skin. She shampoos her hair, rinses out the soap and applies the conditioner, combing her fingers through her hair. She pours some body wash into her hands to wash her face and ears. Taking the loofah, she squirts in more body wash, and massages herself starting at her neck then moving across her chest and abdomen.

"Need some help?"

Lori turns to see Mike standing naked a few feet away. She can see he already has a partial erection. He steps to her. His body inches away. Caressing she can feel his dick against her leg becoming harder. Her nipples are firm rubbing his chest. His hands easily glide over her wet body.

He turns her around and pulls her to him with her back against his chest. His hard dick is rubbing her ass. His hands start exploring, traveling from her stomach to her breasts, then down to her vagina.

She reaches her hands back to feel the sides of his thighs and ass. Separating herself slightly, she gropes for, then finds, his dick and begins to stroke it.

A slight moan comes from him as he turns her again. Lori puts her arms over his shoulders with her hands behind his neck. The water covers their bodies with warm streams. He raises her off the wet tile floor. She separates her legs and wraps them loosely around him.

Her back is against the tile wall when he penetrates her and begins to pump in slow rhythmic motions. Lori responds with pelvic thrusts in syncopation with his pumping. Inevitably their movements quicken as their desire increases. His hands squeeze tighter on her ass as she clings desperately to his neck while he pumps faster and faster.

Her body shutters as she gives a series of slight moans. His body seems to spasm, and she can feel the warm fluid filling her vagina. He continues almost frantically with his pumping becoming more exaggerated as he starts to ejaculate. Her vagina feels warm and wet.

Their syncopation gradually recedes, leaving them both panting heavily. His hands ease their tension on her ass, while his head leans on her right shoulder. Her head on his right shoulder. The water running down between the tile wall and her back cools and refreshes her body.

"Well, I don't know about you, but I'm ready for that drink," Mike declares.

Lori gives a little laugh and agrees, "Me too."

After getting dressed, they walk the one and a half blocks to JD's Whiskey Buffet, a favorite haunt of the cops. The place is busy as usual, but they are able to find a booth. Lori slides into a seat, and Mike sits beside her. Over the next few minutes, several officers approach and congratulate them on the successful raid of the previous week. When the waiter arrives, they both order an IPA.

Mike says with a smile, "I liked that. I liked that a lot. We should spar again, real soon."

Lori can't help grinning like a school girl and says, "I'd like that a lot, too."

"Are you doing anything this weekend?" Mike asks.

"Nothing I can't break. Why, what have you got in mind?"

"I have a friend who owns a condo along the river on Columbus Boulevard. He owes me big time, so he lets me use it. I told him I'd be needing it this Friday and Saturday nights. You could be the lucky one to join me." Mike offers.

"That sounds like fun. What should I wear? Is there someplace you want to go?" Lori asks.

Mike smirks, "Most of the time you won't be wearing much. We'll hit a couple of bars and restaurants that I have connections with. They always treat me fine."

"Where should we meet?"

"You can pick me up at my place. I'll text you the address. The condo has its own parking stall." Mike explains.

"It's a date!" Lori agrees. She is excited to be able to spend a weekend with Mike. She is also beginning to feel that he likes her as much as she likes him.

First Task Force Meeting

Troop K is the name of the state police barracks operating in the city. State Police Lieutenant Barbara Maylars has chosen the Belmont Street headquarters for the initial meeting of the joint state/city task force to combat the drug trafficking in the city.

The three-story brick and glass building is located in a rural section of the city limits. City and state parks are within walking distance. The two block area immediately surrounding the building is flat and open. Several state police cruisers are assigned to continually patrol the area looking for parked vehicles that may be used for surveillance and eavesdropping during the task force meeting.

Thirty minutes prior to the meeting, unmarked police cars start arriving in the parking lot at the rear of the building. All four precincts stationed in the North section of the city are represented for today's meeting.

Police Sergeant Lori Daniels pulls into a parking stall three rows from the door at the rear of the building. For security purposes, because this door is the least observable from the surrounding area, all the police officers on the task force will use it to enter the state police building.

Lori is wearing a black skirt, a green buttoned blouse, and black pumps with an inch and a half heel. Walking towards the door, she is met by two other officers from the 7th and 9th precincts.

Sergeant Jim Umile of Precinct 7 and Lieutenant June Brown of Precinct 9 both have on civilian clothing. All participants were instructed to wear only civilian clothing to the task force meeting. Another security precaution to avoid anyone noticing the gathering of police.

Lori nods to the two saying, "It's been a long time June. How are Henry and the kids?"

"They're good. Henry got a promotion. Cynthia is entering first grade, and Zach is starting fourth grade," Brown answers.

Playfully, Lori asks Umile, "Are you finally gaining some weight, Jim?"

Umile smiles saying, "I wish. I am the only person I know that eats ice cream every day, but can't gain a pound."

Both Lori and Brown say simultaneously, "I wish I had that problem," then all three laugh.

As they go through the double doors, they are met by a state police corporal sitting at a desk behind a bulletproof glass window. Through the mike in the middle of the window, he says, "Welcome to K troop; the meeting is in conference room 201. Go up the flight of stairs. At the top take a right. First door on the left."

They get to the door marked 201 and walk in.

Conference Room 201 is a large rectangular room. The exterior wall is mostly windows. Two video projectors protrude below the ceiling. A one-person podium with a microphone sits in a corner. The room is dominated by a large oval oak table.

Already in the room are five police officers from different precincts also of the North and Northeast Districts of the city. Lori instantly recognizes Mike Costner and gives him a smile. He nods back and returns her smile. Greetings and handshakes are shared by all. Within minutes two other police officers arrive and the same scene repeats. Then they all take chairs around the table and exchange small talk. Mike sits next to Lori.

•   •   •   •   •

As they walk to the conference room, Sergeant Bentley asks Maylars, "Are you going ahead with the announcement?"

"Yes," Maylars replies.

Bentley continues, "This type of thing will get leaked, somehow."

Maylars looks at Bentley and says, "We'll plan for multiple outcomes."

Promptly at 10:00 AM Lt. Barbara Maylars enters the conference room along with two uniformed aides. Each of the aides is carrying a small stack of folders.

They sit at one end of the table near the end wall where the video projector faces. Maylars begins, "Thank you for coming and for being on time. We have a lot to cover. My name is Lieutenant Barbara Maylars.

I will be leading all the task forces in the city. My immediate deputies for this endeavor are to my right, Sergeant Tanya Bentley and to my left Sergeant Edward Kosinich. Some of you may know or have worked with Ed when he was a member of the city police."

Several of the police officers smile and nod to Kosinich in recognition.

Maylars continues, "As you already know, the state police department is setting up task forces throughout the state in conjunction with local municipalities to facilitate a joint effort to combat the rampant opioid and cocaine addiction epidemic. Social and medical agencies are working to help the victims, who have become addicts, and their families. Our job is to eradicate the gangs and organizations profiting from the illicit sale of these substances.

This is the first meeting of the task force for your city. Subsequent meetings will be held monthly. For security reasons, and to keep the meeting to a manageable number of attendants, there will be a total of five tasks forces in your city. The other task forces will have precincts representing the East, Central, Southwest and South Districts.

This task force designated "City North," will be represented by Sergeant Jim Umile of Precinct 7, Lieutenant June Brown of Precinct 9, Sergeant Lori Daniels of Precinct 11 and Lieutenant Mike Costner of Precinct 13. I'm glad you are part of this task force, Lieutenant Costner. You have made quite a name for yourself, and rightly so. Several drug distribution centers have been successfully raided because of the intel you gathered. You should be proud."

Costner smiles and nods to Maylars.

Maylars says something to each of her aides who then start handing out the file folders to each of the attendants. Then she continues, "The folders being given to you hold information we will cover at this initial meeting. However, before we get into the folders, some new information has come up that is important to address. The efforts of the state police and the Pittsburgh police have resulted in major disruptions to the distribution of both cocaine and opioids by the Muzi gang.

Due to this disruption, it has just come to our attention that a major supplier to the Muzi gang will be looking for new buyers here in this city. What we are going to show you is top secret. Officers put their lives on the line to get this. Do not share this with anyone outside this room."

Maylars asks Kosinich to turn on the projector. He gets up and stands at the podium, taps some buttons, and the overhead projector makes a humming sound. An image appears on the projection screen behind Maylars.

Turning towards the screen, Maylars explains, "This photo was taken at the Newark Airport last night. The man is Ellis Taramelli. He used to be one of us, a police officer. Taramelli has been identified as the front man for the Canonero organization. They are a major grower and manufacturer of drugs coming into the country.

He is here to set up a direct distribution link with major gangs. Canonero wants to by-pass the drug cartels, who are middlemen for distribution. As you can see from the photo, he is Caucasian, tall, slim build, no identifying scars or tats. His standard operating procedure is to personally meet with the heads of major distributors to negotiate a deal. We don't know which gang or gangs he will contact in the city. This man must be taken alive. The information we can gain from interrogating him is vital to our mission and to the Feds. To date, he has not been charged with any crime. This means we can only bring him in as a person of interest. That does not help us. We have to catch him in the act with one of the heads of a gang. Once again, I have to stress, do not discuss this man's identity with anyone outside this room."

Lori is struck dumbfounded by the image on the screen… the man walking past the baggage carousel on the photo, Ellis Taramelli, is the same man with whom she went to high school and the police academy.

After her initial hesitation, Lori raises her hand to interrupt Maylars report saying, "Lieutenant, Lieutenant Maylars…"

Maylars stops, looks directly at Lori, then down to the attendance sheet saying, "Yes, what is it…Sergeant Daniels?"

By this time the entire room is staring at Lori. She scans the faces looking at her, then continues, "…I know this man, Ellis Taramelli…"

Now it's Maylars turn to interrupt Lori saying, "How well do you know him, from where do you know him?"

"I went to high school with him, and we attended the academy together..., the police academy, I mean."

Maylars presses on, "And how well do you know him?"

Lori squirms a bit and shows some discomfort when she adds, "We became close friends our senior year in high school and continued being friends in the academy."

"How close of a friendship did you have with Taramelli?"

The room becomes dead silent with the question. Lori can feel her face heat up from embarrassment; she averts her eyes from Maylars and everyone else at the table. She composes herself as best she can then admits, "We were very close friends."

Lori can see smiles forming on the faces of all the people in the room, making her more embarrassed.

Maylars takes a few seconds, before saying, "Hmmm...please, see me after this conference. We have more to discuss."

Lori turns her head towards Mike Costner, who shows no emotion when he looks back at her.

When the meeting adjourns, Mike says to Lori, "You turned red talking about this Taramelli guy."

Not wanting to damage her relationship with Mike Lori pleads "Believe me, it was just a thing we had for a short time. Not a big deal. We are still going on the trip, right?"

For a split second, Lori notices a flash of what could be construed as triumph on Mike's face which is then quickly followed by satisfaction. He turns to her saying, "Of course we're going. Who you went out with before we met doesn't bother me." He then squeezes her knee before getting up to leave.

Almost at the door, Costner is stopped by Maylars and Tanya Bentley. Both women are smiling and openingly gushing while talking to him. He smiles back and, during the conversation, at different times he leans close to the women and touches each on a shoulder.

Lori finds herself feeling very jealous. She gets up and quickly approaches Maylars, Bentley, and Costner. "You wanted to talk to me," she says a bit too loud, interrupting their conversation.

Maylars says, "Yes, thank you for staying. Please, take a seat."

Maylars then turns back to Costner. She touches him on the forearm while saying, "Please, excuse us, Mike. I look forward to working with you."

"I do as well," Mike says. He then walks out of the room.

Sitting down next to Lori, Maylars, getting back to her professional manner, says "We have some questions for you about Taramelli if you don't mind."

Lori nods and a bit testily says, "Ask anything. The last time I saw Ellis... ah, I mean Taramelli, was years ago. It was *not* on good terms."

CHAPTER THREE
High School

"Okay, 5 minutes left in the quiz, once I say time, put your pencils down," says Mrs. Hunter, the math teacher. Ellis Taramelli has already completed the quiz and is waiting for the time to expire.

Hunter stands and starts to stroll through the aisle between seats scanning the progress. She silently mouths to Ellis, "Are you done?"

Ellis nods yes. He is usually the first to complete a math test and usually gets the highest score. He is also the teacher's pet.

After walking around the classroom again, Mrs. Hunter instructs, "Time, put your pencils down. Ellis, please, collect the quizzes from the class."

Ellis stands and starts to gather the sheets being handed to him by each student. At the back of the room, David Botts is still working on the quiz. Ellis says in a low voice, "Dave, Hunter wants the quiz paper."

David Botts is a 6 foot 5 inch tall, 250 lb. linebacker for the Cougar football team. He has a problem with math and won't be playing football in his senior year unless his grades improve. That is why he is still working on the quiz. As Ellis waits at Botts' desk to collect the quiz, he notices that Botts' face is turning red. Botts is deliberately not looking up and ignores Ellis.

"Dave, I gotta have the paper," Ellis explains quietly.

Botts continues to ignore Ellis.

Ellis, in a very low voice, so that only Botts can hear, says, "Come on

Dave."

Botts jumps to his feet in a rage and slams the quiz into Ellis' hand. Then in a loud, threatening voice says, "You and I are gonna meet after school."

The room turns completely silent as everyone stares at the two of them.

Mrs. Hunter shouts to Botts, "None of that talk in my class, Dave. Behave yourself."

After facing Hunter, Ellis turns to Botts and whispers, "Why you're pissed at me, I don't know. If you need to get something off your chest, I'll walk home down Lane Street. You can catch me then if you want," Ellis turns away from Botts and delivers the quiz sheets to Hunter.

Karyl Botts, the twin sister of Dave, hears the entire exchange as does the whole class. She is determined to stop her brother from beating up Ellis and, maybe, getting himself expelled.

Word spreads quickly through the school about the incident. During the remainder of the day, several students approach Ellis with jokes about how he is going to take a beating from Botts. Ellis just smiles and says, "Maybe."

Karyl Botts tries to get out of her last class early to intercept her twin brother, Dave, before he confronts Ellis. The class is chemistry lab. She and Lori Daniels are lab partners.

So when Karyl explains to Lori, who already heard about the incident, that she needs to get out of lab class early, Lori says, "We'll get this done quickly, and both of us will stop this fight."

"Thanks, Lori, you are the best," Karyl says with a smile.

Because they are trying to rush through the experiment, the formula mixture gets screwed up. The instructor, Mr. Dingaman, is unsympathetic to Karyl's plea that she has to leave early and makes them do the entire experiment over which results in them being the last ones to leave.

Because he has a bad temper, Karyl is very worried about her brother. His chance of getting a scholarship to play football in college will be screwed up if he gets expelled for fighting. Also, she has a crush on Ellis and having her brother pummel him is definitely something she wants to avoid. Karyl and Lori hurry out the front door of the school and run down the street trying to catch up to Ellis and Dave.

When the last school bell rings, Ellis gathers up his books, but does not go to the lot where his friend, Tony Laberonte, who usually gives him a ride home, has parked the car. Instead, Ellis walks out the front door of the building and starts to head home.

After walking a couple of hundred yards down Lane Street, Dave Botts steps out from behind some shrubs and calls to Ellis. Ellis turns to face him. Dave Botts stands 4 inches taller and weighs 55 lbs. more than Ellis. All of the extra weight is muscle.

Ellis casually walks over to Botts, eyes him up and down then says, "Dave, I know you are falling behind in math. So, I'm going to give you a choice. Do you want me to help you with the class or should I just whip your ass here and now and leave you bleeding on the pavement?"

As Karyl and Lori run down Lane Street, they can see the guys standing face to face. As they approach, they can hear Ellis make the threat. Karyl almost stumbles while gasping in shock, "Dave is going to kill him!" she thinks, but before she can say anything.

Dave is shaking his head and laughing. Then he says, "You got some pair of balls Ellis." Still smiling he adds soberly, "Sorry, I acted like that in Hunter's class. I wanted to meet you here so I could apologize." After a small pause he adds, "So, you're really willing to help me with math?"

"Yep, we can start this week, if you like. I'm sure we can bring your grades up," Ellis replies.

Karyl is almost in tears from stress, and then the relief that her brother will not be beating up Ellis. Lori just stands and smiles, amazed that these two "dopes" could behave so maturely. Ellis and Dave finally notice Lori and Karyl and look their way. Karyl catches her breath and walks over to them. With mock scolding, she says "Well, Ellis, if you won't beat the crap out of him, I will." She gives her brother a feigned punch in the stomach.

The four of them have a good laugh.

Later that Year

While carrying his books, Ellis Taramelli enters the main corridor to the school's administrative offices. Ellis is not familiar with this building, having only been in it during initial enrollment three years earlier.

He sees a girl holding her books standing near a locker. While approaching, he recognizes her as Karyl Botts, "Hi Karyl."

Karyl turns from her locker, "Hi Ellis, what are you doing here?"

"I have to see Connors, something about tests," he says that last part in a deep voice, feigning an ominous overtone.

"Do you think you're failing a class?" Karyl asks with a bit of concern.

"I hope not," he then asks, "Do you have a locker here?"

"I take the community service classes they give here... Extra credits. They let attending students use the lockers during classes," Karyl explains.

Ellis moves a bit closer, "So why haven't you and I ever gone out?"

Karyl smiles, "Maybe because you have not asked me."

"Three years attending classes together and I have never asked a beautiful girl like you out. I must be a dope!" he mockingly chastises himself.

She smiles again, "Well, we agree on one thing, you must be a dope... unless you are asking now," then she adds with an accusing tone, "...but aren't you going out with Barbara Shimonski?"

"No, we broke up over a month ago. It seems she likes the football quarterback types," Ellis confides.

"You're a nice guy Ellis; it _is_ a shame we did not go out together earlier. Now with only three weeks until we graduate..." She shrugs and asks, "What college are you going to?"

He says, "I'm taking law enforcement classes at the Community college and attending the police academy. So, would you like to go out Saturday?"

Putting her head down a bit, she says, "I already have a date for Saturday."

"With who?"

"Ralph O'Neill"

"The president of the Junior Business People of America, that nerd?"

Defending herself, Karyl retorts, "He's not a nerd."

Ellis makes a sly look on his face, then says thoughtfully, "You aren't the type of girl to break a date are you?"

Karyl looks up, then mimicking Ellis' demeanor, she says, "And you aren't the type of guy to ask me to break a date, are you, Ellis?"

"Is seven o'clock a good time to pick you up on Saturday?" Ellis asks smiling.

She smiles back, "Seven is great."

Karyl turns her attention down the hall.

Lori Daniels approaches them, "Hey you two, you look rather cozy."

Ellis turns, sees Lori, immediately his books slip from his hands. The largest landing on his foot. "Ow!" he yelps.

The girls laugh, and Lori adds, "You high on something Taramelli?"

He quickly picks up his books, after dropping the largest one for a second time.

Visibly flustered, Ellis says, "I have to see Mrs. Connors. Where is her office?"

Lori tells him, "Down the corridor, third door on the left."

Ellis quickly walks away with the giggling of the girls in his ears. He travels to the third door on the right and tries to open it, but it's locked."

"The third door on the left, Ellis. Not the right," Lori shouts. Both girls start giggling again.

Ellis crosses the hall and enters the office door.

Lori looks at Karyl saying, "He is such a klutz!"

"I don't think so, he's cute," Karyl replies.

Lori shrugs, "Well, anyway, I have been called to Connors' office, too. See ya later."

Lori walks down the corridor and enters the student counselor's office. Mrs. Connors is seated at her desk. She is a thin woman in her forties with a kind face. Ellis Taramelli is at one of the chairs in front of Mrs. Connors desk. They are chatting about the football team.

"This is a great year for the Cougars. One more win and we're in the semis." Mrs. Connors says enthusiastically. "Oh, here's Lori. Please, have a seat."

Lori, in blue jeans and yellow polo, walks around Ellis to sit on his right. On Mrs. Connors' desk rests a notepad in blue, gold and white (the school colors) a gold pen set with the school logo, an intercom box, a pair of reading glasses, and two folders, one each with the names of Lori and Ellis. The blinds on the large window behind the desk are open, putting the counselor in partial silhouette.

"Ellis would you mind closing the blinds; the cord is on the right side of the window."

Ellis walks around the desk going immediately to the left side looking for the adjustment cord. "...ah...Ellis your 'other' right," Mrs. Connors says with a slight smile.

Lori smiles as Ellis goes to the right side and closes the blinds, then returns to his seat with a sheepish look on his face.

Connors begins, "Although I will be speaking with each of you separately, I wanted to let you both know that you are in a similar situation, so feel free to discuss this with each other after this meeting."

The buzzer on the intercom sounds. Connors presses a button and scolds, "I am in session with some students and should not be disturbed."

"My apologies Mrs. Connors," comes the voice of Mrs. Farkas, Connors' assistant, "I realize you are with students, but this requires your immediate attention. It's the Gallas brothers..."

Connors frowns, "Not again, okay I will be right out." Facing each of them, she apologizes, "Please, stay here a bit. I'll be right back." She hurriedly moves around her desk and walks out the door to her office.

A few seconds go by then Lori says, "I saw the sign-up sheets. It seems you and I are taking the Law Enforcement courses at tech."

Ellis looks at Lori and smiles, "Yes, I noticed that too. Do you think that is what this meeting with Connors is about?"

"Could be."

Ellis smiles slyly and says, "Well, the most intriguing part of Law Enforcement is investigations. Let's take a look at our student folders." He leans over the desk and opens both.

Jokingly Lori reprimands in a deeper voice, "You can get expelled for that."

Ellis, not realizing she is kidding, immediately tries to shut the folders, but inadvertently knocks Lori's file off the desk spewing papers across the floor. He turns red with embarrassment.

Lori laughs, "Don't worry Ellis. I wish I had thought of looking through our files. I'll help you gather up this stuff." After straightening the folders, they immediately start comparing records. Then Lori lets out a giggle while pointing to a line on each of their files. "Hmmm… well, we now know who is the most intelligent one in the room!" she says.

Ellis glances to where she is pointing and bursts out laughing. There on the files are their IQ scores. Lori 120, Ellis 119. The two look into each other's eyes and laugh again. Lori puts her hand on his shoulder. "A lot of guys would not take this as well as you. That says buckets about you Ellis Taramelli."

They hear someone approaching the office door. Lori quickly closes the files and arranges them back to where they were on the desk. They sit back on their chairs trying to look casual.

Mrs. Connors returns and, as she is going to her chair, says, "Sorry about that. As the whole school knows, the Gallas brothers are a constant problem and today is no exception. Good thing at least one of them is graduating this year. Well, where was I? …oh yes, as I was saying both of you are in similar situations, but it is up to you if you want to discuss this with each other after our meeting. Ellis, I want to talk to Lori alone right now."

Ellis pushes himself off the chair and starts to leave the room.

"We'll only be about ten minutes. Please, wait in the outer office." Mrs. Connors asks.

When the door closes, Connors continues, "Lori, I wanted to talk to you about choosing Law Enforcement for your senior year studies. This is your file which includes your IQ Test results. You score well above average, but that is not the entire story. From input by your teachers and an examination of the results of your classroom quizzes and tests, it has come to our attention that you may have, oh, how shall I put it, a slight learning disability. Your contribution in the classroom is excellent, yet your test scores are below average. With this in mind in all probability, your IQ test scores are actually artificially low. In other words, you are probably a whole lot smarter than you have been led to believe."

A bit perplexed, Lori interrupts, "Thank you for this information, Mrs. Connors, but what does this have to do with anything?"

Connors frowns and says, "That is what I was coming to. I am not trying to belittle you, Lori. I want to help you reach your full potential. There are some remedies you can use on your own to overcome some of the symptoms." Reaching into the top drawer of her desk, Connors takes out a pamphlet and hands it to Lori. "Read this and keep it handy. There are some helpful tips for overcoming some of the difficulties you may have experienced. As an example, do you sometimes read something and get the completely wrong idea about what the author is saying?"

Lori at first does not say anything, but eventually nods, "Yes, sometimes."

"Listening to an audio version of the text while reading could help with comprehension," Connors recommends. "You are a very intelligent girl. I am aware of the ridicule you have taken from some students because reading can be difficult for you. Don't let them define you."

After a long pause, "Thank you again. I will definitely look through it," Lori says, but she still has a hint of skepticism.

Picking up on Lori's doubt, Connors pushes on, "Take this to heart, Lori, some of the methods in the pamphlet will dramatically improve your life."

Holding up the pamphlet, with a change of tone Lori replies, "Ya know, I will Mrs. Connors, I'll give this a try."

With a satisfied smile, Connors adds, "Thank you, Lori. Now about your decision to enroll in Law Enforcement classes at tech. With your potential, an academic course of studies at a university seems much more appropriate."

"I know you have my best interest in mind, but I want to be a cop, more precisely a detective." Lori explains, "After my brother was killed…, well, helping people get justice is what I want to do."

A few days after the meeting with Mrs. Connors, Ellis sees Lori sitting on the low stone wall that lines one of the walkways into the school. It is a warm clear day, and she is enjoying being in the sun. There is a book on her lap and earbuds connected to a CD player.

Ellis taps her on the shoulder and, after she removes the earbuds, he comments, "Wow, reading a book and listening to music at the same time. I couldn't do that."

"Hey, Ellis," holding up the player she answers, "This isn't music. It's an audio version of the novel I am reading for English Lit. Connors suggested I try this. Reading and listening at the same time really helps me. Before, I'd often get the meaning of a sentence wrong."

Sitting down next to her, Ellis adds, "Yeah, she gave me a list of ways to improve my studying, too." He catches a whiff of her perfume, and his mind goes blank for a few seconds. During this awkward silence, Ellis tries to think of something else to talk about, but with no luck. Lori keeps looking at him. Finally, he sighs and says, "Well, see ya around."

As Ellis rises to leave, he inadvertently trips on Lori's foot and tumbles. While reaching for Ellis, Lori calls out, "Are you all right?" in a half laughing/half concerned voice.

Picking himself up and not looking at Lori, Ellis brushes his pants and says, "I'm okay." He walks off without turning around.

At the Academy

Carrying her suitcase, Lori walks down the corridor of the police academy looking at door numbers. She sees 224 on an open door and walks in. Bending over a bunk bed, sorting clothes from a suitcase, is a well-toned Latina sporting jeans and a pullover sweatshirt. Her black hair falls just below her ears.

"Hi, my name is Lori Daniels. I guess we're roommates."

"My name is Brenda, Brenda Cervetti, nice to meet you. I hope you don't snore."

Lori laughs, "No I don't, at least no one has told me I do."

"Come to think of it, I hope I don't snore," Brenda laughs.

Lori puts her suitcase on the other bed, opens the zippered pocket and takes out the campus information brochure. Reading it, she smiles and tells Brenda, "This is what I was looking for." Brenda turns from her unpacking to look at Lori. Lori continues, "… the cadet ratio is ten males for every female on campus. It'll be like shooting fish in a barrel."

"I hear ya girl!" Brenda agrees while bumping fists with Lori. "So when do we start?"

• • • • •

Ellis leaves his room. Finds the stairwell door. Goes down a flight to the second floor. Walks through another door into the corridor and, checking out the numbers on the dormitory doors, finds 224, then knocks.

Wearing a tee shirt, gym shorts and athletic shoes Brenda Cervetti opens the door.

Eying Ellis up and down, Brenda says, "Well, hello hello! Hope you're not lost. I love getting surprise presents."

He smiles while trying not to be noticed glancing at Brenda's ample breasts, saying, "My name is Ellis, Ellis Taramelli. Lori and I have a study date."

"Hi Ellis, come on in. Don't mind Brenda; she doesn't bite," Lori calls to him while sitting on her cot and tying her shoes.

"Only when I have to…," Brenda says, glancing at Ellis' butt as he walks into the room. Then Brenda turns to Lori with mock scolding, "You didn't mention Ellis to me. Now I see why."

All three smile. Lori says to Brenda, "Get going to your workout. There'll be plenty of guys at the gym."

With a celebrity style wave of her hand, Brenda walks out and makes a dramatic point by locking the door as she leaves.

"She seems nice," Ellis says.

Lori looks at him and with a wry smile and answers, "I saw you checking out her boobs."

The books in Ellis' hand almost slip to the floor before he catches them. Quickly recovering, he answers, "I like that size, yes." Then he quickly changes the subject, "I dictated the next lesson on this." He hands Lori the flash drive.

"Thanks, Ellis, all kidding aside, I do appreciate you doing this, really." She opens her desk drawer and takes out another flash drive. Handing it to him, she says, "This is the one you gave me last week for Tactics class."

He puts it into his pocket, then he sits on her bed and opens a book.

Lori sits next to him on the bed, and they start to review a lesson. After about 30 minutes, Lori asks Ellis if he wants anything. "Just a glass of water, no ice," he says.

Lori gets up and goes to the mini-fridge. Taking out a jug, she unscrews the top and pours some water in a large plastic mug saved from a previous purchase of a convenient store slurpy drink.

As she brings the cup over, Ellis, who is not paying attention, gets up to stretch his legs. His shoulder hits the bottom of the cup spilling water down the front of the white tee shirt Lori is wearing. Her breasts become visible through the tee shirt and thin wet fabric of the bra.

Ellis' eyes widen as he stares.

Lori looks down at herself then up to Ellis. Feeling a little horny, she moves up to Ellis, then wrapping her arms around his neck, she gives him a kiss.

He reacts by holding her tight and giving her a more passionate kiss.

She reaches her tongue between his lips. They both open wider and entangle their tongues together.

Lori unbuttons Ellis' shirt and helps him quickly remove it. She then pulls off her tee shirt. Ellis fondles her breasts while she reaches back to unclip her bra. When it falls away, he is all over her breasts with his mouth. Licking and sucking gently on her nipples, his hands then work their way down until they are squeezing her ass, as she rubs his back.

Her hands reach down to unbutton and unzip her jeans. He pulls away and does the same with his jeans. Each struggles because their shoes are still on. Overcoming this inconvenience, they both quickly slip out of their underwear and immediately fall into the bed. She slides her hand down his stomach and takes hold of his cock which is warm and hard. He shutters from anticipation.

He turns on top of her while she opens her legs and guides his cock into her. He begins to stroke in and out in a controlled pumping motion. Her breasts are tight against his chest. She responds to his strokes. Ellis pushes up with his arms and knees. This raises his body inches above her stomach to allow room for her thrusting movement. Lori's nipples are now barely touching his sweaty chest.

Searching for somewhere to place her hands to increase the enjoyment, she slides her hands down the sides of his torso and squeezes as the enjoyment increases.

Sensing her excitement, Ellis slightly increases the frequency of his strokes while she willingly responds in kind. They both close their eyes as waves of pleasure engulf them while their bodies move in unison. His rigid member rhythmically penetrating and retracting. Her pelvis thrusting up and down. Each increases the speed of the motions as if they are one.

Her hands claw his torso, while to her surprise uncontrollable animal sounds come from deep within her. Ellis is breathing heavily as he too groans in pleasure. Sensing a climax both pump frantically reaching a crescendo of feral ecstasy. She feels warm liquid gushing inside her. He gives a few final thrusts, and she does the same.

Lori grabs Ellis by his ass cheeks pulling him closer in an attempt to keep his cock in her for a few moments longer feeling the warmth. They make slight pumping motions to prolong the pleasure both just experienced.

While breathing deeply from the exertion, Ellis laughs while saying, "I heard music."

Breathless, Lori questions, "What?!!?"

"I swear I heard music in my head while we were screwing," Ellis confesses.

"Well, I didn't hear music… but good for you," Lori says in a matter of fact way while sitting up. "Grab me a couple of tissues from over there in the box. You seem to be running down my leg."

After cleaning herself, she continues, "Brenda should be coming back soon. We should get dressed, and I have to make up the bed."

"Oh yeah, sure," Ellis stands to put his clothes back on.

Lori does the same, then while straightening the sheets, she says, "That was nice Ellis. I would not mind doing it again sometime… not mind at all." She smiles and gives him a kiss on the cheek.

Ellis can't help smiling. In fact, he grins like an idiot the entire way back to his room.

Brenda enters the dorm room returning from her workout.

Lori has her earbuds in, while reading a textbook. She waves "hi" to Brenda, takes out one bud and asks, "How did it go?"

"Real good, I felt very sharp today. Hit all my positions perfectly...I passed Ellis walking down the corridor; he looked like he won the lottery. What went on in here, young lady?" Brenda asks playfully.

Lori grins then replies with mock scolding, "Mind your own business. We were just studying."

"Uh huh," is all Brenda says before leaving to take a shower.

Celebrity Training

A black limousine with tinted windows pulls into the entrance to the Police Academy followed by a small van. A very well built tall African American man, dressed in a fitted button down silver shirt and black slacks, gets out of the limousine without waiting for the chauffeur, who is hurrying around the car to open his door. "Thank you, Greg, but no need here," he says.

"Very good sir," the chauffeur replies.

Behind him, a short, overweight Caucasian man in a blue business suit with a white shirt and red, white & blue striped tie also gets out of the limousine.

The tall man is television star Jason Henry of the long-running detective series, "Torrence for Hire." The chubby man accompanying him is producer Ted Feldman. Out of the trailing van is a contingent of the production crew.

Through an arrangement with the Mayor's Office and the Commissioner of Police, the production crew will spend two weeks at the academy to shoot some scenes and follow a set of chosen cadets through a typical day to add authenticity to the production.

The main building of the police academy is a single story tan brick building, bland in appearance. Small windows are evenly spaced around its perimeter. The main foyer has a green and white terrazzo floor with an 8 ft. diameter academy logo in the center. The walls are painted light green with dark green border stripping.

They are met at the entrance to the academy by a liaison for the mayor, the commandant of the academy and Jimma Koustafus, an instructor, a slightly overweight man of medium height wearing the uniform of a police sergeant. The three shake hands and exchange pleasantries with Henry and Feldman.

Koustafus finally says, "Well, I'm sure you want to get right to it, so if you and the crew will follow me."

The entire entourage follows Koustafus into the building, and he continues, "I was told you wanted to start in the lounge. Your crew can go right through those double doors and set up. Mister Henry, at the academy the cadets are divided into teams of four. This familiarizes the cadets with having to depend on accomplishing tasks as a squad instead of individually. I'd like to introduce the cadets you will be teamed with for the next few days."

As Koustafus escorts Henry towards one of the side offices, he says, "These cadets are among the top in the class. You have your best chance to learn the proper methods of police procedure and the true cadet experience with these three."

Upon entering Koustafus introduces them, "Mr. Henry, this is cadets Daniels, Cervetti and Taramelli." Each cadet is at attention, and one by one stiffly extend their hands to Henry as he presents himself in front of them.

After shaking each hand, Jason Henry adds, "Please drop the Mr. Henry. Call me Jason. May I call all of you by your first names?"

"Jimma, my name is Jimma. This is Lori, Brenda, and Ellis," Koustafus introduces.

Jason smiles and says, "The reason for this visit is to recreate the cadet experience. Please, treat me like another cadet, especially you, Jimma. When in front of the camera I want to make it as real as possible, so don't hesitate to let me know if something is not being done correctly."

Koustafus replies, "Will do."

Jason turns to the three cadets, "Lori, Brenda, and Ellis, please, treat me like just another team member. I will be here for a week of training before shooting starts. I'd like to get the real feel of the academy experience."

"Will do, sir," Lori says.

Jason looks at Lori and smiles. "Remember, no 'sir,' my name is Jason," he reminds her. Turning to Koustafus, Jason adds, "So, I'd like to get started if that is okay with you Jimma."

Koustafus quickly corrects Jason, "That is "sergeant" to you cadet."

Jason and the cadets smile at the first rebuke from Koustafus. They have heard many in the past months.

"Yes, sergeant," Jason corrects himself. He then adds, "Thank you all for this opportunity and, please, don't be easy on me. I want a genuine experience."

The cadets and Jimma are struck by the lack of ego and genuine friendliness of Jason. In answer to his request, surprisingly in unison, they all reply, "Will do," then all five break into laughter.

•   •   •   •   •

The next day, after two classroom sessions in the morning, Jason Henry, Koustafus and the three cadets go to the gym for hand to hand fighting practice. Jason starts to learn some elemental moves to incapacitate an assailant.

Koustafus begins, "Jason, this first move will be to stop an assailant who attacks you head on. Lori, go to the center of the mat. Jason, you will be the assailant."

Jason walks up to Lori and places his hands on her shoulders. "You're not asking her to dance," Koustafus yells, "Go back to the edge of the mat and grab her by the sweatshirt, like a perp would."

Jason walks back to his starting position then moves at a brisker pace and grabs Lori's sweatshirt with his two hands. She immediately swings her arms up and through the center of his arms. Then in one fluid motion sweeps her arms outward. This breaks his grip and pushes his arms up and away. Before he can bring his arms back down, Lori grabs his sweatshirt and collapses her body into a kneeling position with her left knee on the mat and her right knee upright. This pulls Jason down as well. Lori stops the move with Jason's chin inches from her upright knee.

"As you can see, if Lori kept moving, your chin would have been smashed into her rigid knee," Koustafus explains.

Lori then slowly raises Jason until they are face to face. They stare at each other, a bit too long for Ellis not to notice.

"Want to try again cadet," Lori teases.

"Okay," Jason says with a smile. "Let's see what you got."

Koustafus instructs, "This training is for real-life situations. This time, don't be so timid in the attack, cadet."

Jason stands up and returns to the starting position. This time he approaches Lori more quickly, but more cautiously. He grabs Lori's sweatshirt much tighter and braces his arms for the upward motion of her arms. Lori's first motion is the same, but this time she grabs his sweatshirt and falls backward. Using her strength and his forward momentum, Jason flies over Lori and hit the mat on his back with a loud thud. Immediately, Lori is on top of him with her knees on his shoulders, pinning Jason to the mat. Lori looks down at Jason and tweaks his nose with her right index finger. Jason stays on the mat and does not struggle to get up.

Again it seems to Ellis that Lori holds that position a bit too long.

"Okay, now it's your turn to learn these moves, Jason. Ellis, this time you're the assailant," Koustafus says.

•   •   •   •   •

After the week of training and the next week of shooting, Jason meets alone with Lori, Brenda, and Ellis. "I want to thank you all for helping me and being so patient with my fumbling. This is much tougher than I expected. I have to confess, Ellis, on the first day we trained I thought you didn't like me, but apparently, I was wrong. You gave me some very good pointers throughout the weeks."

Jason shakes Ellis' hand and gives Brenda and Lori a hug. "Listen I'm having a party at my place. It happens to be the day after you graduate from here. I would love for all of you to attend," Jason adds.

The three smile and assure him they will be there.

The Party

Lori, Brenda, and Ellis arrive at the gated entrance to the mansion of Jason Henry. All three are amazed at what they see. Leading in each direction, black iron fence about twelve feet high travels far into the wooded landscape where it disappears from their view. There are two stone pillars each holding large iron gates. A speaker similar to the ones in a drive-thru lane at a fast food restaurant is on the left. From the driver's seat, Lori rolls down her window. A voice from the speaker asks their business. Lori gives their names and says they were invited to a party. A few seconds later a buzzer sounds and the gates retract.

They travel about 400 feet up through a tree-lined paved driveway where the mansion comes into view. Lori stops the car and gazes. The three of them are struck by the size and beauty of the estate. The architecture is modern resembling huge garment gift boxes stacked so that the upper boxes overlap the lower ones with the impression of an upside-down staircase. The front side of each floor is all glass and gray metal frame.

Moving forward again, the drive ends in a u-shape in front of an eight-foot-wide walk leading to ten-foot-high double glass doors. On each side of the walk, perfectly manicured lawns hold no shrubbery. Two attendants, wearing matching black pants and shirt, wait at the entrance to greet the guests and park cars.

The three get out of the car dressed to the nines. Lori is wearing a red wrap around style dress, with red shoes. Brenda has on a form-fitting turquoise dress showing every curve of her body. White shoes with two-inch heels complete her outfit. Ellis has on brown slacks, black shoes and a blue polo style shirt with black horizontal stripes. An attendant escorts them to the front door.

Dance music can be heard coming from one of the upper floors. Another attendant directs the three to a white marble staircase leading to the second floor saying, "The party is upstairs, do you have any items you want checked into the cloak room?"

The three shake their heads and Ellis thanks the attendant.

Upon arriving at the top of the staircase, they can see that the front half of the second floor is one large room, the entire south wall is completely made of glass which overlooks the driveway and woods through to which they had just passed. In one corner several people are seated at a large L shaped bar. More people are standing at the bar talking among themselves.

In another corner, a corridor with six doors leads further into the house. In front of the window wall, a DJ wearing headphones is standing at a control panel and turntables moving to the beat of the music and adjusting controls. About ten couples are dancing in front of the DJ on the ecru colored marble floor that stretches throughout the room.

The three can recognize several actors and actresses from the television series in which Jason Henry stars. Other recognizable celebrities are present along with people they have never seen. Lori, Brenda, and Ellis look at each other like it is a dream. Brenda says, "Let's enjoy this moment while we can. I have a feeling it will never happen again." Lori and Ellis smile and nod in agreement.

Jason Henry sees the three, says something to a man and woman next to him, and walks over smiling broadly, looking even more impressive than on television. He immediately gives Lori and Brenda a hug then shakes Ellis' hand.

"Thank you for coming. I have been telling my guests about how gracious you all were to take the time to help me. Especially, you Lori, your insights into the challenge of initially adapting to life at the academy is critical to the story plot," he says with sincerity. Jason seems just as much a class act in real life as he portrays on television.

Ellis becomes a bit annoyed at the attention given to Lori. Then when Brenda and Lori start gushing over Jason, Ellis excuses himself and heads to the bar.

Arriving at the bar Ellis orders a beer and a shot of whiskey. Immediately several people approach him; two are from a popular television attorney show. One is an actress in her 30's, Jill Collins, petite, wearing a low cut green dress. Her small waist enhances the size of her larger than average breasts. The other is an actor in his late 40's, Bart Exton. The makeup he is wearing is an attempt to look younger. His hair is black and cut long. His dress shirt has the top three buttons open. He wears the shirt untucked over his khaki pants, trying to hide the extra weight he is carrying.

They begin to question him about being a police cadet and his motivation for joining the force. Ellis is surprised about how cordial and genuinely friendly these people are. His concern about going to a party where everyone is egocentric and full of themselves is dissipating with each new person he meets.

After a few minute lull, the DJ starts another song. Jason, Brenda, and Lori are joined by Eric Tanns, the latest in a long line of cinema comic book superhero portrayers. Eric wears his hair combed back with gel. His tall, muscular body shows no trace of fat. To Eric's request for a dance, Brenda, looking at Lori with astonishment, says, "Absolutely!" and leaves Jason and Lori alone.

Jason asks Lori, "Would you mind dancing with me? I have to warn you; I'm not that good."

Lori smiles even more broadly and says, "Absolutely!"

At the bar, Ellis is enjoying the attention he is getting.

"What are the requirements for enrolling in the police academy?" Jill asks.

Ellis answers, "Well, it depends on your career goals. To be placed on the track for detective work or administrative work. Some college courses are required for both. The academy courses last six months."

"What drew you to police work?" Bart asks.

Ellis explains, "I have always been drawn to solving puzzles. So detective work, especially undercover assignments, is what I hope to get into. Our graduation was last week, and now we are waiting for our placements."

Bart asks, "How do you get placed? Do you have any say about where you will go?"

Ellis continues, "When initially enrolled, the academy has you list three career preferences in order of importance. With the stipulation that, of course, you might get assigned to none. Brenda finished first in the class, so she will definitely get her preferred assignment. Lori, although she did not finish near the top of the class, will probably get her preferred assignments because she is so good at the tactical level, street smarts."

Jill asks, "Are Lori and Brenda the two women who accompanied you?"

"Yes…let's see, where are they… oh, there they are dancing…" Ellis stops in mid-sentence and sees Lori and Jason Henry dancing very close. He sighs, turns to the bar, and asks for another beer.

After the dance, Brenda chats with Eric, Lori comes to the bar and stands next to Ellis. "Whew, I can use a glass of wine," she nonchalantly says.

Ellis waves to one of the bartenders, "A glass of dry white wine for the lady, please."

"Right away sir," the bartender replies.

"Thanks, Ellis, I did not mean for you to get me the wine," Lori explains.

Ellis, who is looking straight ahead and avoids looking at Lori, responds, "No big deal."

The wine is delivered. Taking a sip, Lori asks, "This place is amazing, isn't it, and the people are so nice. Nothing like I expected."

"Yeah," Ellis keeps looking straight ahead and not at Lori.

"You feeling okay?"

"Yeah"

Lori shakes her head, picks up her wine and leaves to find Brenda. She sees Brenda still dancing with Eric. Lori smiles watching them circling each other with suggestive dance moves. When the music stops, Brenda says something to Eric. He smiles and nods; then she walks over to Lori. "I need a cold drink. That man is pure sex. Girl, take me where you got that wine."

Lori laughs, "Follow me."

At the bar, Lori avoids standing near Ellis. She and Brenda immediately strike up conversations with several people just coming off the dance floor, who are also heading to the bar.

Drinks are quickly served, and Brenda asks Lori, "Where's Ellis?"

"He's at the other end of the bar. Somehow, he is not in a good mood." Lori comments.

Brenda looks at Lori, "Uh huh, you know he's into you girl. You dancin' with Jason is what is bothering him."

Lori sighs, "I know but he should know we are not a couple. We had a few good times, nothing serious though. He has to grow up."

"I agree, but that is Ellis."

The two of them wander over to one of the buffet tables. While in mid-mouthful with an hors-d'oeuvre, Brenda is approached by Eric. "There are a couple people I would like you to meet." Touching her elbow, Eric asks, "Do you mind coming over to the bar?"

Brenda has to take a couple of seconds to finish chewing while she nods to Eric. She then faces Lori, "Want to come?"

"No, you go ahead. I'm still hungry."

Brenda smiles as she puts her arm in Eric's, "Take me away!"

While she is trying a few more hors-d'oeuvres, Jason returns, "Hope you are enjoying yourself, Lori."

Lori touches Jason on the arm saying, "This place is fabulous. The party is great, and you are really nice. Yes, I am having a wonderful time."

"So, why are you becoming a cop?"

Lori pauses, then answers, "Puzzles. I am good at figuring out things."

Looking a slight bit incredulous, Jason asks, "Is that the main reason?"

"No, not the main reason. While walking to his car, after a Philly's game, my older brother was killed when he was caught in the crossfire of two rival gangs. The killers were never caught. It has always haunted me. This is sort of a chance to get some justice…It's funny; I never told that to anyone before."

"Geez, Lori, I am so sorry." Jason consoles. "It is very touching you shared that with me."

Lori half smiles and touches his arm again saying, "I did not mean to bring a downer story to your party. I'm sorry."

Jason says while smiling, "No need to be sorry. Would you like to dance again?"

She smiles and nods yes. He puts his arm around her, and they walk onto the dance floor.

Ellis joins Jill at a buffet table. After trading some small talk, Ellis asks her for a dance, and she agrees. The DJ is now playing one fast rhythmic song after another in his personalized mix. The floor becomes crowded as more guests start to dance.

While Jason and Lori are dancing, a waiter interrupts them and speaks to Jason. Jason nods, then asks Lori to wait a moment. He'll be back in a minute. Jason walks over to the DJ, says something in his ear, then returns to Lori.

At an appropriate break in the music, the DJ makes an announcement, "Ladies and gentlemen we have a special treat. Jason Henry has arranged for a special preview of the TV episode featuring the police academy. Please, follow the attendants to the lower level theater room. You may take your drinks and food."

Most of the people applaud, and all follow the direction of the attendants. Ellis escorts Jill down the steps and into what can only be described as a makeshift mini movie theatre. Rows of comfortable chairs have been placed in an arc. All are facing a large white screen. Sound absorbing panels have been placed in front of the walls of the room to improve the acoustic quality of the show.

When all the guests are seated, the attendants ask each guest if they would like anything to drink or eat before the show starts. Several guests give orders. The attendants then go off to fill the requests.

Jason Henry walks in front of the screen, "Thank you for coming to this party and the viewing of this episode of 'Torrence for Hire.' A special thanks goes to the guests of honor, Brenda Cervetti, Ellis Taramelli and Lori Daniels, all recent graduates of the real police academy." Jason pauses for the applause. "Let me add kudos to Brenda, who finished top in her class." More applause and some whistles. "As a matter of fact, my sources say she finished with the top grades ever at the academy." More applause. "Their help and assistance were invaluable making this episode. Now on with the show." More applause.

Jason walks from in front of the screen and goes to the back of the room.

"That was very sweet of you to mention us and recognizing Brenda's achievement is very classy," Lori whispers to Jason, as he meets her near the rear of the room.

The door opens and bumps Jason on the arm as one of the guest steps into the room. "What did I miss?" he asks Jason.

"The show has not started yet. Take a seat," Jason directs.

The lights are dimmed, and the projection starts. The opening theme song and credits are followed by, what is familiar to Ellis, the façade of the academy entrance. The next scene has Jason Henry talking with a cadet in front of a classroom door. Twenty minutes into the episode, Ellis feels the need to relieve himself. He is starting to feel the effects of the shots and beers.

"Excuse me for a minute," he says to Jill.

"Sure"

Ellis walks around in back of all the seating, then goes through the main door.

Out in the corridor, he asks one of the attendants where a bathroom is.

"That door there is a bathroom, but it is in use now. You can use one on the second floor or wait for this one," The attendant tells him.

"I'll go upstairs." Ellis asks, "How do I get there?"

"Take the stairs. When you reach the top, go straight ahead…third door on the right."

"Thanks."

Ellis takes the two flights to the second floor and heads down the corridor. A waiter stops Ellis and asks, "Do you want to use a restroom?"

Ellis nods.

"Sorry sir, that one is occupied right now. You can wait or use one of the bathrooms on the third floor."

"Third floor, how do I get there?"

The waiter directs, "See that opening on the right. It leads to a stairway. At the top of the stairs, take the third door on the left."

"Thanks."

At the top of the stairs, Ellis feels a bit light headed. He walks down the corridor and mistakenly opens the third door on the right.

Through a short hallway, Ellis sees a large bedroom. On top of the bed, he sees what could be some odd sculpture of two naked people. After a second, he realizes the two people are a man and woman naked in bed. Then Ellis recognizes the people as Lori Daniels straddling atop Jason Henry. His pumping motion is raising and lowering Lori rapidly while his hands are holding her breasts.

Sensing the bedroom door open, Lori turns and sees Ellis.

Stunned, Ellis blinks wide-eyed then turns away and slowly heads back out the door.

CHAPTER FOUR
Missing Squad Member

The phone on the desk of Lori Daniels buzzes. "Daniels," she answers.

"Have you heard from Regina Boris today," Captain Tony Petracelli asks. Regina did not report for work yesterday. Calls to her cell phone went directly into voice mail.

Lori is very protective of her team and very loyal. Her first reaction is to defend a squad member from criticism. She responds, "No, I have not. Yesterday, after work I stopped by her apartment, but no one answered the door. I called her cell again this morning, but nothing there again. This is not like her, cap."

Tony Petracelli says, "I know Regina has really stepped up lately since we have been hitting the gangs hard. She spends a lot of time helping with the logistics of raids. I am not criticizing her. I am genuinely concerned."

"I know you are, cap. I will go over to her place again today after my shift," Lori says.

"You have some major work to do with the new task force. I'll have one of the other detectives stop at her place and also call her parents," Petracelli tells her. Changing the subject, he asks, "How is the orientation of Officer Gail Scott coming?"

"She will be complete with orientation tomorrow. She seems to be a very quick learner, cap," Lori praises.

"Well, you'd better get her involved with the task force work. Once we get a tip, we have to act fast. I got a bad feeling about Regina being incognito," Petracelli says.

Lori and Brenda at JDs

Lori walks down Pugh Street into JD's Whiskey Buffet[2], a crusty old bar which has accommodated the influx of police officers from the local precincts since 1933. Small tables cover the immediate left and the center of the floor space. A long bar stretches the remainder of the left side. Booths are along the entire right wall. At the end of the bar, a small hallway leads to the backroom, where two pool tables sit. There is a small kitchen in the back of the bar. The restroom entrances are located at the far wall.

Brenda is not at a table, so Lori immediately walks down the line of booths looking for her. It's 4:00 in the afternoon, but the place is busy. The sharp clack of pool balls can be heard coming from the back followed by loud talk and laughter after an apparently easy shot is missed.

Brenda smiles as Lori comes into view and waves her over. Sliding into the other side of the booth, Lori asks, "How ya feelin'."

"Still a little sore, but the vest did its job," Brenda replies. "Is there any word about Regina?" she adds.

"Nothing yet. It is not like her to not show up without a word," Loris says.

"Well, maybe she ran off with her secret boyfriend," Brenda suggests.

"If she did, Petracelli will crucifier her for not letting us know where she's at," Lori responds.

Grinning slyly Brenda continues, "Speaking of secret boyfriends, where'd you go last night? I saw you discussing the raid with Costner then you were gone!"

Lori lets out a deep breath of air, looks down at the table, then at Brenda and confesses, "I left with Mike," another sigh, "we have been seeing each other, a lot."

Eyes wide, Brenda loudly whispers, "What!??! You just met the guy!"

"I know, jumping into another relationship so quickly is probably one of the stupidest things I've done in a while, but something about him gets to me."

"You just dumped Tom Exeter because you thought he was getting obsessed with you. Now, you hop into bed with Costner!" Brenda chides. After a few seconds of silence, Brenda asks, "How long have you been seeing him?"

"About two weeks."

Brenda with mock indignation says, "Girl, the worst thing about this is that you have not told me sooner. What's up with that?"

Lori with false humility pleads, "Forgive me, oh wise one, I knew not what I did."

More seriously Brenda adds, "You're still holding back something. What is it you are not telling me?"

Pleadingly, Lori explains, "He says that he is seeing another woman right now, but has not been intimate with her yet."

"And you believe him."

Putting her head down and hesitantly meeting Brenda's eyes, Lori continues, "I really like the guy. Okay!"

"So you'll swallow what he gives you," Brenda scolds shaking her head.

Reflectively Lori answers, "I'm really crazy about the guy, Brenda. Not since high school, have I felt this strongly about someone."

Just then Ramirez, Taylor, and Morgan arrive at the table. Taylor grabs one of the floor tables and abuts the end to the booth table. "I saw Stetzler and Scott pulling into the parking lot. We'll need the extra room," he explains. Right on cue in walks the two.

"Alice, Gail, over here," calls Ramirez. The way his face lights up is a dead giveaway about how he feels for Gail. He arranges the seating so he can sit next to her.

The waiter arrives to take their order. Taylor tells the waiter, "Rick, is it my imagination? How do you get to be our waiter no matter where we sit? And more importantly, we'd like two pitchers of beer and two baskets of popcorn."

"You mean the usual…," replies the waiter smiling, "I'll be right back with the beers."

Immediately, Alice looks at Jason Taylor and smiles, "Have you got any more dating stories, Jason."

A chorus picks up from the table, "Yeah, let's hear about your exploits!"

"Ugh, don't you young people have any other form of entertainment when we get together?" complains Jason.

"No!" another chorus from everyone at the table laughing.

"Okay, okay, I'll amuse you with my latest. This happened two weekends ago. My date belongs to a hiking club, and she invited me on an eight-mile trail walk for Saturday morning."

Gail interrupts, "Eight miles?!!?"

Jason continues, "Yeah, eight miles, this woman is really hot so I'm trying to impress her. Backing out is not gonna happen. I keep in pretty good shape, so I thought keeping up wouldn't be so bad.

Saturday morning we arrive at the starting point, and there are ten others there. The hike leader goes over some basic common sense rules to follow; then she asks everyone to introduce themselves and tell about one of their latest hikes.

Well, gods truth, this is what came out, two hiked to the base camp of Mount Everest, four just came back from a week-long hike along the Andes in Peru, two just returned from traversing the entire Appalachian trail last month and one guy just got back from a hiking expedition on some Pacific island. My date and the leader were regular trekkers and hiked all over the country.

For the past few years my only hiking experience is walking around my housing development a couple times when the weather was nice, so when it was my turn, I lied, telling them I had hiked the rim of the Grand Canyon a month ago."

A snicker arises from the table.

Jason goes on, "It was the best I could do on the spot like that. Well, we start out, and the group is moving fast. All these experienced hikers kept up a pretty good pace, going up and down mountain trails. I'm dying and sucking air, but doing a good job of hiding it.

During the hike, we take a couple of short breaks, which I really needed. At the third break, the leader announces that we have completed about seven miles of the eight-mile course. Then she said, because our pace was so fast, we would finish one hour ahead of the estimated time. She continued by saying that, if no one minds, let's do another three miles to fill out the time slot.

'FUUUUCKKKKK!' is the first thing that came into my mind.

'Yeah, let's do it,' is what everyone else says aloud, including me when it's apparent we're going to do it."

"Why not back out?" Lori asks.

Jason sighs, "Not with four women in the group and one is my date. Not a chance! We eventually get to the end of the hike and then my date suggests we go to her place to shower and have dinner. I was so tired and sore I made up some bullshit about being on duty that night. Went home and slept for ten hours."

•   •   •   •   •

While Jason is telling his story, Donald Ramirez and Gail Scott are talking between themselves. "You've been with the squad for three weeks, how do you like it so far?" Ramirez asks.

With a genuine smile, Scott answers, "I feel lucky getting to join this squad. Everyone has been helpful and free with their time showing me the ropes, especially you, thank you so much."

Ramirez can't help smiling back at her.

Scott continues, "Don, who did I replace on the squad."

Ramirez pauses, then answers, "Regina, … Corporal Regina Boris."

"Did she transfer or move?" Scott asks.

"She has been missing for about three weeks. No one knows where she is or why she is gone. Routine inquiries by the precinct HR department have turned up nothing," Ramirez answers.

"Shouldn't an investigation be launched?" Scott says incredulously.

"We had her parents file a missing person report, but that does not carry the weight of a full criminal investigation, which takes precedence for precinct manpower," Ramirez says.

After a pause Scott changes the subject, "Lori seems young to be a squad leader, shouldn't Jason be in charge? He is the oldest."

"Jason is the oldest. He served in the military 25 years before becoming a cop. Three years ago he became the oldest graduate the academy ever had. He is steel in a fight. Great instincts. Quick reactions. Bad luck for any bad guy in his sights. Stetzler and Riccini come close to his prowess in a firefight. Both have risked their lives for a squad member. Going into a raid with these three is reassuring, to say the least."

Scott looks directly at Ramirez and says, "You handle yourself very well, second to nobody if you ask me."

Smiling proudly because of Gail's compliment, Ramirez continues, "Lori is squad leader because she deserves it and the entire squad trusts her. She is uncanny at reading a situation and getting positive results, whether in an investigation, arrest, interrogation or firefight. She has everyone's six. Several times she has placed herself in the line of fire to get one of us out of trouble. She's the reason this squad is so tight."

"Brenda and Lori seem very close," Scott comments.

"They went to the academy together. Brenda finished at the top of her class...really, smart. She is headed for a top brass position, no doubt about it. As a matter of fact, she has taken the exam for internal affairs. That is a major step to advancement in the precinct."

Scott frowns stating, "You'd think she would be the squad leader then."

Ramirez explains, "Brenda is very smart for sure. Although Lori finished more towards the middle of her class mainly due to her test scores, apparently, she does not do well on written tests. Lori's strength is the ability to quickly assess real-life situations and make decisions. Those skills are what matters most out in the field. In tactical training, Lori got the highest score ever recorded at the academy. I'd rather have Lori as my leader than anyone else."

Ramirez stops and shakes his head. Scott looks puzzled and asks, "What? Is there something you left out?"

Hesitantly, Ramirez responds in a lower voice, "Although it is none of our business, there is one thing that puzzles anyone who knows her. Lori seems to pick the worst guys to date."

Scott reddens getting a bit angry at this last remark, and accusingly says, "Why because she won't go out with you?"

Ramirez jerks back a bit. Wide-eyed he says apologetically, "No Gail, I'm not interested in Lori. You can ask anyone. Please, don't think that." He pauses, then in a softer voice says, "I especially don't want you to think that." He almost reaches out to hold Scott's hand, but stops himself halfway.

This time Scott's face reddens for a different reason. She looks into his eyes with a gentle smile then apologizes for interrupting and asks Ramirez to go on.

Reluctantly, he says, "Lori is the first to admit it after she breaks up with the guy, but while she is involved, she won't listen to anything negative said about a boyfriend. Maybe it's something to do with loyalty, like always backing her squad members. That is one of her strengths…and maybe one of her weaknesses."

CHAPTER FIVE
Fruit Stand

Lori pulls her old SUV into a fruit stand along route 30. The car has over 150,000 miles on it, but, being a bit of a tightwad, Lori keeps putting money into keeping it running, instead of buying a new one. The wheels crunch on the gravel lot.

Six tables under canopy covers line the front of the fruit stand. All kinds of vegetables and fruits are neatly arranged in wicker baskets ranging in size from a pint to a half bushel. Handwritten signs display the pricing for each fruit or vegetable. This stand has been here for years. It is apparent from the fresh paint look, neatness and symmetry of the displays that the owner takes pride in its appearance.

Picking up the folder she has taken from the precinct, Lori gets out of the car. The dust kicked up by pulling the car into the lot has not settled. Lori coughs and fans the folder in front of her face. She approaches a Caucasian woman, medium height and weight, with short blonde hair wearing an orange tank top and powder blue shorts. She is setting out ears of corn at one of the tables.

The woman says to Lori, "Sorry about the dust. Jimma will hose down the lot a little bit later. You're here pretty early. We're just opening the stand."

"Not a problem Lynn," Lori replies.

"Haven't seen you in a couple weeks, Lori. We've got some fresh tomatoes today. The corn is fresh, too." the woman says smiling back.

"Thanks, where is Jimma?" Lori asks.

"He's out back sorting tomatoes. Make sure you take some and also the corn. We have some Silver Queen and White Magic."

Lori walks through the tables then moves past a small shed. Jimma, a short, stocky man with long black hair, is wearing a white tee and blue jeans. Jimma is second generation Greek descendent. He is putting tomatoes in pint size baskets.

"Jimma, good looking tomatoes." Lori greets him.

"Jimma Koustafus, a former police detective and instructor at the police academy, is now running his own fruit stand. He turns and bellows a laugh. "Good to see you, Lori!" He moves from the work table and gives her a hug. Reaching back he says, "Here take a basket. I picked up these Heirlooms this morning. Less than 24 hours off the vine, delicious." Handing Lori the basket he had just filled, they trade. She takes the tomatoes, and he takes the file folder.

"What's this?" he asks.

"It's an updated file on the Fifth Street Gang from the state police. Petracelli gave it to me today. I need it back pretty quickly," she replies.

Jimma opens the file and scans some pages. "Turgeson is still running the gang, isn't he?"

"Yep, but no one has been able to get enough evidence to arrest him," Lori replies.

"Man, if you can take them down, it would be a big blow to the drug trade in the city," Jimma comments.

"That's the plan."

"I can make a recording for you tonight," Jimma says.

"Great." Lori then asks, "I need to get the file back to my office before it is noticed missing. Are you going to the produce wholesaler's markets tomorrow? I can come early, before you leave."

"I've got to go all the way down to Fremont to pick up peaches, so it'll be earlier than usual when I leave, 4:00 AM. I won't be back until 10:00." Jimma says sympathetically.

Lori sighs, "Okay, I'll see you before 4:00."

Heading back to her car with the tomatoes, she exchanges some small talk with Lynn who gives her a dozen ears of corn. Lori gets back into her car and drives away.

A parked car about 100 feet up the road pulls into traffic and continues to follow Lori. The car is driven by Police Captain Tom Exeter.

Back to Fruit Stand

Lori walks along a quiet suburban street. It's her hometown, but nothing looks really familiar. She thinks she sees her mother's dog, Winnie, running across the road. Then she thinks that can't be right, Winnie died years ago and so did her mother. She does not recognize any of the houses she passes.

Looking down at herself, she is wearing her dress blue police uniform. Now she notices she even has the cap on too.

Finally, she sees a house that she recognizes. It's Ellis Taramelli's parents' house. That's it, now she remembers. Ellis is dictating a police file on to a memory stick for her.

Lori walks on the front porch and goes to the door. She presses the doorbell. It starts to make a loud buzzing sound and won't stop. She tries pushing on the button, but the buzzing continues. She realizes Ellis' parents will be sleeping at this late hour. He told her not to use the doorbell, but she must have forgotten.

Lori is beating on the button and then frantically tries to use her fingernails to pull it out. She starts to sweat. She promised Ellis she would be quiet and now, no matter how hard she pounds or pulls, the buzzer keeps going.

To Lori's surprise, the front door opens. It's Jimma Koustafus from the fruit stand. Ellis is standing behind him. He is also wearing his service blues. "What is Jimma doing at Ellis'," she thinks. Jimma starts to hand her a carton of tomatoes. Lori is confused, then she screams, "Jimma, I'm not here for tomatoes. Help me quiet the doorbell before Ellis' parents wake up!"

To her surprise, Winnie also appears at the door and jumps into her arms. She falls to the porch floor as she tries to wrestle him off her. "Help me, please, help me, Ellis. I'm so sorry for ringing the doorbell!" Lori pleads.

Suddenly, Lori wakes up on the floor next to her bed. She is clutching her pillow in her arms. She can feel sweat over her neck and chest, and her hair feels damp. The alarm clock she set for 2:30 AM is buzzing.

Lori remembered she put the alarm on the loudest setting, so she would get up in time to meet Jimma at the fruit stand by 4:00 AM.

Turning on the lamp beside her bed, she sits back down on the floor still holding the pillow. A full minute goes by before she pulls herself off the floor using the edge of the bed. Throwing the pillow back on the bed, she goes into the bathroom and turns on the light.

Holding her hand over her face to shade her eyes, she takes a peek into the mirror. "Ugh!" Her eyes have bags under them, and her hair is sticking up in at least three places. She leans over the vanity, bracing herself with both arms. She turns on the water. Lets it get lukewarm, then starts to splash water on her face. "Shit, why does Jimma have to leave for the fruit markets so goddamn early?" she grumbles.

Lori braves another look into the mirror. "Not much improvement," she sighs.

Convinced that she has no time to make things better, she wanders into the bedroom then over to her closet. She finds a pair of jeans that fit. Doesn't bother putting on a bra and throws a sweatshirt on. She digs out an old pair of sneakers from the back of the closet and starts to root around for something else.

"Ah ha…" she exclaims triumphantly, "…found you." Holding up an old red baseball cap with a stylized white "P" on the front, she punches the inside of the cap to get it into something close to its original form. Pulling the cap over her frazzled hair, "Time to go," she painfully concedes.

Thankfully, on the way a fast food restaurant's drive-thru is open. After just narrowly missing knocking over the menu board with the left fender of her car, she orders a large coffee, black.

Lori is happy about one conciliation, the traffic is very light. Like almost no cars.

As she pulls into the gravel parking lot of Jimma's fruit stand, she sees Jimma folding a tarp and putting it into the back of his ¾ ton pickup. The pickup is well worn and has to be at least fifteen years old.

Lori parks her car, gets out, and walks over to Jimma.

He nods, goes back to the shed behind the fruit stands and retrieves the file. Reaching into his pocket, he gets the memory stick and offers both to Lori, then comments, "Whoa, you look a bit rough!"

Lori smiles, "Thanks,…hey, a girls gotta do what a girls gotta do."

With a serious expression, Jimma says, "Did you know Tom Exeter was tailing you after you left here yesterday?"

Lori with a stunned look says, "No."

Lori breaks up with Tom Exeter

… weeks earlier

Tom Exeter is sensing a change in Lori Daniels. A change he does not like. He pulls into the parking spot in front of her small suburban home. The lawn is neatly trimmed. A sloped concrete sidewalk leads up to the front steps. A new wreath Lori made graces the front door. He is just about to ring the doorbell when the door opens.

Lori, wearing blue jeans and a lime green button down blouse, waves him in. She is not smiling, which tells Tom his perception was correct, this is not going to be a pleasant encounter.

"Thanks for coming over so quickly," Lori says almost business-like.

Exeter replies, "Well, you said it was important, though, I have to tell you I was working late at my office. This better be good. I hope it's not the same garbage about me being too possessive. I told you before; I expect you to tell me what you do when you're not with me. Because of my high ranking in the police force and my aspirations of an eventual political position, your loyalty is essential. I chose you to be by my side…"

"Stop right there, Tom" Lori Interrupts. She looks down and takes a deep breath as her hand goes to her forehead.

Exeter looks at Lori in shock; he does not tolerate being interrupted. Before he can say anything, she continues, "I don't want to see you anymore."

"What! You can't break up with me. Who do you think you are?" he screams indignantly. "I'm doing you the favor by choosing you. The relationship does not end unless I say it does!"

Lori sighs, "This is why I'm breaking off our relationship. You think you own me."

Tom turns red with anger, "Don't you speak to me that way. I'm Captain Tom Exeter. I'll make sure you never get promoted in the force. I'll make sure you never get hired by any other police force…"

Again Lori interrupts, "Get out Tom," she says as she reopens the door.

"You are going to regret this!" is the last thing he says as he walks out and heads to his car.

Lori can hear the screeching of car tires as Tom drives away.

Jimma and Exeter

With a puzzled expression, Lori says, "I broke up with Tom a couple weeks ago. Now he is following me! This is bullshit!"

"Taking confidential files out of the office and letting me read them. You can be thrown off the force for what we're doing here. Exeter could make it nasty for you," Jimma says sympathetically.

Lori is looking off at the horizon. A faint light is just starting to show itself. She turns to Jimma saying, "I don't want anyone in the force to know I have trouble reading and comprehending files. That will end my chance of advancement for sure. Not only that, your comments are insightful and have helped me solve quite a few cases. No, I'm not going to stop what we are doing. As long as you are okay with it?"

"I'm okay with it." Jimma looks down at his shoes then raises his face to look Lori in the eyes. "I never told you this… then, when you starting dating Exeter, I definitely knew that was not the time to tell you." Looking down at his shoes again then back to Lori, Jimma adds, "You get so wrapped up in a guy; he can do no wrong…"

Lori gets a bit annoyed at what Jimma is saying and asks, "Jeez, Jimma, we've known each other for a long time. What the hell? What did you not tell me?"

Jimma gives a very skeptical look at Lori. Then she adds, "Okay, okay, you're right. I get very defensive about criticism of the guys I am dating. Please, be straight with me, what is it you have not told me about Tom?"

"Tom Exeter is the reason I got out of field duty and started teaching at the academy."

Lori, in shock, says, "What!"

Jimma explained, "When I was a detective, Exeter and I were on a raid. He was just a rookie on the force then. We got a tip about drugs being sold from a row home in the Northeast. This was very unusual back then. The Northeast section of the city was all residential, strictly families and corner stores. No major crime to speak of."

Jimma and Exeter on a Raid (Ten years ago)

Four police cruisers and a van park a block away from the home from which a pusher is suspected of selling drugs. The neighbors noticed the unusual amount of people going in and out of the house at all hours of the day and night. With permission of the owners living in a house across the street a surveillance crew set up a camera to spy on the house.

With the video footage and testimony by the neighbors, a search warrant was issued. Now the police are deploying to conduct the 3:00 AM raid.

One street away Lieutenant Brock Horsham deploys the team conducting the raid. "As per the plan, Gleason, Tate, O'Reilly, and Petri will come with me and enter the house through the front door. Sergeant Koustafus and the rest of the team will circle around to the alley and enter through the rear door and basement garage door. Jimma let me know when your team is in position." Lt. Horsham commands.

"Will do," Jimma confirms.

As silently and quickly as possible Jimma leads the other six officers down the alleyway that runs behind the homes. The alley is one story below the first floor which allows for basement garages in the homes at one side of the block.

Jimma stops his team at the rear for last-second instructions. "Corporal Zenda take Exeter and Pellis. Go through the basement door. The rest of the team will come with me to the back deck and enter through the patio door."

Once the team is in position, Jimma radios Lt. Horsham, "We're all set, Brock."

Horsham radios back, "Okay, we enter on three... one, two, three, go, go, go!"

•   •   •   •   •

Meanwhile, five minutes before the raid starts:

Raymond Polartis wakes up. His mouth is parched, and he has to take a wicked piss. Pushing Tina's arm off his chest, he sits on the edge of the bed. Fumbling around looking for his pants, he finally finds them and then puts them on. As he gets up, his head feels like a basketball, and he stumbles, then he goes into the adjoining bathroom and relieves himself. Because he is so thirsty, he decides to get a beer from the fridge. He walks down to the kitchen, but there is no beer in the fridge.

"Shit," he grumbles while scratching his ass.

He now heads down the basement. In a blind corner, formed by an offset in the basement wall and a small wall supporting the basement stairs, is a second fridge. Extra beer is stored here along with the dope stash. The freezer section of this fridge also serves as a hiding place for his money. Raymond thinks he is clever keeping his cash in a plastic bag in the freezer. He doesn't know that every cop now routinely checks freezers for contraband.

Just as Raymond is about to open the door of the fridge, he hears several loud cracks then a lot of shouting. He hides in between the fridge and the basement wall.

The tramping of footsteps can be heard on the upper floors and then the rasping of boots on the dirt floor of the basement. Suddenly, Raymond hears, "Exeter, you stay down here and keep watch. Pellis and I will head upstairs to see if we can be of help."

Raymond is just about to take a peek around the edge of the fridge when he hears footsteps approach. He quickly ducks back. Abruptly, a light scares some of the darkness away. He hears a plastic bag being removed from the open refrigerator. Raymond tries to make himself as skinny as possible, but in doing so bumps the fridge and causes it to rock.

A second later an automatic rifle is pointed at his nose. In the dim light of the refrigerator, he can see a cop dressed in body armor and helmet holding his plastic bag of money and pointing the gun. Two seconds go by which seem like an eternity to Raymond. Then he experiences what to him is a miracle.

"Get the fuck outta here and don't come back," the cop whispers as he moves aside and waves the rifle in a "shooing" motion.

Raymond does not hesitate, he runs.

•   •   •   •   •

"This is the police! This is the police!" is shouted as the doors are pried open, and police enter the house from the front and rear. Using night vision goggles, the police methodically search each room thoroughly.

Upstairs can be heard, "Hands where I can see em," and "Don't move," as Jimma leads his team through the rooms of the first floor. Within a few minutes, all the first floor rooms are cleared.

Corporal Zenda and Officer Ellis come out of the stairway leading to the basement. Zenda reports to Jimma, "The basement is clear. No one has been found. I left Exeter down there to keep watch."

"Okay," Jimma replies.

Walking to the patio door, Jimma notices a man wearing pants, but no shoes or shirt running down the alley. Jimma goes out to the rear deck then down the deck stairs. As he turns, through the open garage door he sees a light. Stepping out to get a better look into the garage, Jimma sees Tom Exeter taking money out of a plastic bag and putting it in his pocket.

Suddenly a large commotion can be heard on the first floor. Jimma runs back up the deck's stairs. At the same time, Exeter turns to see a police officer moving away from the garage door. On the officer's arm is the chevron of a sergeant. He suspects Koustafus has seen him taking the money.

After biting the hand of Officer Petri, Tina uses her shoulder to push Officer O'Reilly aside. Running out the patio door, she is tackled by

Jimma at the patio deck. Petri and O'Reilly quickly follow, and both help get Tina under control.

"Take her to the van and don't lose her this time," Jimma tells the two officers.

Jimma goes back into the basement. Because Exeter is only a rookie, Jimma intends to give him a chance to return the money and not ruin his career. When he gets to the basement, Exeter is gone. Jimma decides to confront Exeter back at the precinct.

Corporal Zenda is left in charge, and with Officers Tate and Pellis, will photograph, gather up, catalog, and bag the contraband.

Jimma drives back to the station alone. He pulls into the parking lot, and as he finds a stall, Lieutenant Horsham and Corporal Gleason are waiting for him. As he gets out of the cruiser, he asks, "What's up Brock?"

"I don't like doing this Jimma, but I have to check under the driver's seat," Horsham says. He then waves to Gleason and says, "Corporal."

Gleason hesitates for a moment, looks Jimma in the eyes saying, "Sorry."

He opens the car door. Bending down and with his left hand, he starts to reach under the seat. A couple of seconds later he comes up with a packet of money held together with a rubber band.

•　　•　　•　　•　　•

Lori asks, "Tom framed you?"

"Yep. When I tried to explain to the precinct commander what happened, he took Exeter's side. I was not charged with anything, but my record was stained. Knowing that my career in the field was practically over, I looked for other alternatives. I was good friends with the captain at the academy, so he gave me a position as an instructor."

CHAPTER SIX
Lori's Car Breaks Down

After taking a shower, Lori spends an hour fixing her hair and makeup. She slips on her new red blouse. Mike likes her in red. She then struggles into a pair of skin-tight jeans. Mike commented about how he likes women in tight jeans. He said he is an "ass man." Often he will squeeze her ass when she walks past.

Because rush hour in the city lasts until almost 7:00 PM, she knows it might take over an hour to get to Mike's place. She takes a bottle of his favorite wine out of the refrigerator. Putting that bottle in a cooler along with a bottle of her zinfandel, she then takes some cool-packs out of the freezer. Carefully, she places the packs around the wine to keep it cold. Lori takes one last look in the mirror. Spritzes some perfume under each ear, then with an index finger on the top button pulls her blouse away for her chest and spritzes between her breasts. Pleased with what she sees, she grabs the cooler and heads for her car.

In the car she makes a call, "Hi Mike, I'm on my way."

"Great baby. You're bringing wine, right?" he says.

"Yes, your pinot and my Zinfandel, it might take a while getting there. The radio said traffic is still heavy," Lori says.

Mike replies, "Well, hurry. I need some attention, quickly."

"I will sweetheart. Love you."

"Hurry up," is all Mike says before hanging up.

Lori starts the car. Backs our out of her drive and travels down her lane. At the stop sign, she makes a right on to the main street that loops around her development. She is soon out on County Line Road heading for the Schuylkill Expressway. As expected, traffic is heavy, and there is a line of cars in the on-ramp for the Schuylkill. She frowns thinking about the delay in getting to Mike.

Finally merging into the right lane, she is not surprised that the traffic is creeping along. Lori has grown to hate the Schuylkill.

She is anxious to get to his place so she can please him. In her passenger's side mirror, she notices blinking lights. A state police cruiser is traveling up the shoulder. "An accident must be the problem this time with the traffic," she thinks. The traffic now stops. Lori begins nervously tapping her fingers on the steering wheel.

After about a minute, traffic starts to slowly move again. Lori puts a little pressure on the accelerator pedal when a sputtering sound comes from under the hood and the car jerks forward twice, then stops completely. The engine stalls. Red lights appear on the dash. One is the check engine symbol.

Car horns start blaring behind her. Getting louder and greater in number as each second passes.

"No, no, no," Lori mumbles under her breath. She turns the ignition key to the off position and then tries to restart the engine. "Please, please, please, start," Lori prays. The electric starter valiantly tries to turn the engine over, but to no avail. Lori keeps repeating the off/on action with the key. The engine sputters a couple of times again, then shuts off completely. No life returns. Lori is stuck on the Schuylkill. She bangs her hands on the steering wheel a few times. Cars blare their horns as traffic starts to maneuver around her. She puts her forehead on the top of the steering wheel. "Shit!" is all she says.

A few minutes go by then Lori dials the number for PennDOT Roadside Assistance. After what seems like an eternity on hold, she explains her situation and location to the operator. Her next call is to Mike.

"Hey, babe, what's up?" Mike says flatly.

Lori sighs saying, "Nothing good Mike. My car stalled in the middle of the Schuylkill and won't restart. I call roadside assistance, but traffic is so heavy…," almost in tears now Lori pauses, then continues, "… god knows when they'll get here… Cars are beeping their horns at me."

"It's that fucking piece of junk you drive!" Mike complains.

Lori sniffling says, "I know it's my fault. I'll make it up to you."

"Well that's all fine and dandy, but I am ready for a hot date tonight," Mike sarcastically explains.

"Mike, please, understand," Lori pleads.

Mike very slowly and deliberately says, "Oh, I understand, now you understand. I'm making other plans."

"I know you are seeing someone else. I saw her text to you. Who is Elaine? You fucking bastard!" Lori screams.

"Oh, so now you're spying on me. You've got some nerve. I'm Mike Costner, baby, who do you think you are spying on me?" Mike yells.

Composing herself, Lori says in a softer voice, "Please, don't Mike. I love you. You know that, please, don't call her."

"I never told you we were exclusive, babe. Live with it." Mike says matter-of-factly.

Unable to control herself again, Lori yells, "Mike, how could you do this to me, you son of a bitch! You know how much this hurts me."

"Who do you think you are, yelling at me. You're the one who fucked up." Mike says as he hangs up.

"No Mike, I'm sorry, I'm sorry, please…" Lori says to the deadline. She frantically tries to call him back, but her call goes directly into voice mail. She leaves a pleading message begging Mike to call her.

Lori finds it hard to breathe, because she is crying so much waiting for Mike to call her back. The call never comes, and her calls to Mike are not answered. A half hour later the roadside assistant truck arrives to load up Lori's car and take it off the Schuylkill.

On the way to the maintenance shop, Lori calls Brenda for a ride home. Brenda arrives 30 minutes later. "Getting stuck on the Schuylkill is rough. You okay, Lori," Brenda asks with concern.

"It's not getting stuck that's bothering me so much. Mike and I had a fight." Lori confides.

Brenda with genuine concern asks, "Damn girl, what was it about this time?"

Lori answers, "It is my fault. I was headed to his place for a special night he planned. Then my car broke down. I called him to explain, but he got angry. I know he's going to call that Elaine. I just know it..."

Brenda interrupts, "Wait a minute. Let me get this straight. Mike knows you are broke down and he didn't say he would come to get you. Then he tells you he's gonna see someone else because you can't make it. That's bullshit, girl!"

Lori puts her head down. Then she looks at Brenda and says, "We live so far apart, I can see why he has a girlfriend close to where he lives..."

"What! Are you kidding me! You're putting up with this shit. Why?" Brenda interrupts again.

"I love the guy, Brenda."

Regina Boris

The black BMW[4] SUV makes a left turn off of Mansard Road into the driveway of the marina. The car takes a left at the fork, slows for the speed hump painted neon yellow and heads for the boat docks on the west side. A marina security patrol car is coming down the lane towards the BMW. When alongside, it stops, and the driver rolls down the window.

Ken Ubaldo stops his BMW and rolls down his window. The security officer smiles and says, "Hi Ken, you picked a beautiful day for going out on the river."

"Hey Tom, thanks, it is a nice day. Have you come across any troublemakers lately?" Ken jokes.

Smiling, Tom nods, then adds, "Just you and your boys."

They both laugh.

"My sons and I are going fishing. We're gonna head up the river this time. Hopefully, we'll have better luck than last week." Ken shakes his head as he says this.

"You have the worst luck, Ken. Getting your cabin cruiser fouled up in an abandoned fishing net is bad enough. For that net to have a world war two coastal mine entangled in it, is unbelievable. It's very fortunate no one was hurt," Tom consoles.

"We were out there ten hours until the coast guard got us untangled." Ken laments. "Get this, we're pulling away from the coast guard vessel when one of their other vessels fires at the mine to detonate it. When it explodes, a large chunk of shrapnel goes whizzing by and almost hits the upper cabin of my boat."

"Geez, that's crazy... Well anyway, good luck fishing up river. I saw Mark and Ken Jr. at your dock. They were loading a couple coolers on to your boat."

Ken nods, "Good, it's about time they brought the beer."

They both laugh again.

"Oh, here comes Craig. Now we can head out," Ken says as he looks in the rearview mirror and sees a white pick-up truck pull in behind him.

On cue, the pick-up blares the horn. Craig sticks his head out the window and yells jokingly, "Hey, move that piece of junk out of the way!"

"See ya later," Tom says smiling as he pulls away.

"Take it easy," Ken replies as he drives ahead. Ken's sons are all in their 30's. They try to get together at least once a month, but with everyone's schedule that is not always possible. This is a rare occasion to meet two weeks in-a-row. They hope to do some fishing. That morning a friend of Mark gave them a location where the fish were biting.

After parking their vehicles on the gravel lot, Ken and Craig carry bags of groceries across the wooden dock to Ken's cabin cruiser. "Glad you could all make it," Ken tells his sons.

Ken Jr. is transferring beer from the cardboard cases to the coolers. Mark grabs a bag of ice and drops it on the deck to loosen the cubes. He then dumps the cubes over the beer. Craig slides open the cabin door and starts loading some groceries into the refrigerator. Ken hands Craig another bag of groceries.

"Keep the salsa out and open a bag of corn chips," Ken instructs Craig. Walking back out of the cabin, he tells Mark, "Hand me one of those beers, please."

After all the beer and groceries are stowed, Ken starts giving instructions, "Mark, get the bowlines. Craig, unplug the power cord.

Ken, you have the stern lines." He then climbs the steps to the cockpit. Standing at the console and helm, he starts the engines then checks to see that all the lines and power cord are removed. He eases the boat forward out of its slip.

It is 10:00 AM on a beautiful sunny Saturday. The boat traffic is heavy. After clearing the channel leading to the river, Ken swings the cruiser to port heading north. All three boys join him in the cockpit. Each has a beer, Craig has put a bowl of salsa and a bag of chips on the console.

After cruising for about forty-five minutes, Ken slows the boat as they get near the location for fishing. He puts the engine on idle and yells to Mark, "Mark, go down and get set to drop the bow anchor." Craig and Ken Jr. are already on the stern deck prepping the poles and attaching bait. As Mark is about to walk back to the stern deck, he sees what looks like a log has got caught in the anchor chain.

"Dad, something just got caught in the chain," Mark calls to Ken.

"Jesus Christ, well, we better free it. It could start catching other debris floating down the river," Ken says. As he gets down from the cockpit and walks around the cabin to get to the bow, he sees Mark just standing and staring. A sense of foreboding comes over Ken. He walks up next to Mark and looks where Mark is staring. Not a log, but a human corpse is caught on the anchor chain.

It takes less than twenty minutes for the river police craft to reach them after Ken radioed. One police officer is taking pictures as the second is getting statements from Ken and his sons. Another river police vessel arrives an hour and a half later with a forensic team and two detectives. The body was found in the area of Precinct 3. The precinct captain, Lila Brown, assigns the murder investigation to Detective Sergeants Carol O'Reilly and George Tate. The detectives question Ken and his boys again, this time individually on the river police vessel.

After three more hours of investigation and interrogation, the forensic team and the detectives leave with the body. All the testimony by Ken and his sons is consistent and rings true. None of them have criminal records. The detectives file no charges.

The first police craft and two officers then leave, but not before confiscating all the beer on board Ken's cabin cruiser and issuing a citation for open alcoholic containers found at the helm of the boat.

When the river police leave, Ken tells Ken Jr. to hoist the bow anchor and the other boys to stow the fishing gear. He then turns to port heading south. They arrive back at the slip by 7:00 PM. "Well, maybe we'll have better luck the next time," Ken says optimistically.

• • • • •

Two weeks later, through DNA analysis, the body is identified as Corporal Regina Boris of Police Precinct 11. The autopsy determined that death was from blunt force trauma. The victim was tortured and beaten to death. Now that it was revealed that the victim is a cop, the case is given top priority by Precinct 3. All the local news agencies lead off with the story as a follow up to the floating corpse story.

"How the hell did the story get on the news so quick?" Tate complains as he and O'Reilly drive to Precinct 11.

Captain Anthony Petracelli of Precinct 11 is notified of the death of one of his officers and of the investigation being assigned to Precinct 3, where the body was found. Detectives O'Reilly and Tate arrive at Precinct 11 and conduct routine interrogations of Petracelli, Lori Daniels and all the squad members who worked with Corporal Regina Boris. The testimony of all the members of Precinct 11 is consistent and rings true. No further interrogations are scheduled.

Some of what the detectives find is that in the month prior to her disappearance, Regina seemed troubled. She did not confide to any member of the squad why. They all thought it might have something to do with either the guy she was seeing or her brother, Tito. She was always bragging about how Tito is so smart and a wiz with computers, but he had not been able to keep a job for very long. Everyone on the squad liked Regina. Her death shocked all the squad members.

No officer likes to lose a team member, but especially when off duty and under suspicious circumstances. As is common practice in a situation as this, Detective Carol O'Reilly promises "cop to cop" to keep the squad leader, Lori Daniels, in the loop with the investigation.

Before leaving the precinct Tate and O'Reilly talk to Lori confidentially. O'Reilly says, "Both George and I learned the ropes on the squad under Jimma Koustafus. We know you are close to him too. We respect him a lot and think he was railroaded by Tom Exeter. Just wanted you to know that."

Lori nods saying, "Thanks for telling me. Jimma mentioned he had contact with some of the members of his old squad. Thanks again for keeping me informed of any developments with Regina's case."

●　　　●　　　●　　　●　　　●

The next day Detectives O'Reilly and Tate go to Regina's apartment. The forensic team has already dusted the apartment for fingerprints and sealed off the place when the detectives arrive. Tate loosens the red tape attached to the apartment door and the two enter. They are immediately met by Officer Cheryl Brown.

"Hi Carol, George," Brown nods to them, then she calls into the bedroom, "Edna, they're here."

Sergeant Edna Rierson, leader of this forensic team steps into the living room. "Hi, Carol. Your puttin' on some weight there George," she says.

"See, I told ya," O'Reilly adds as she smirks at Tate.

"We waited til you got here and have not looked into closets or drawers or under mattresses yet," Rierson tells them.

"Thanks, Edna," O'Reilly says.

Tate and O'Reilly start to search through her closets and dresser drawers finding nothing unusual. Tate starts to strip the bed and lift the mattress and box spring. Next, he starts to look under and behind the furniture. O'Reilly searches through the kitchen, opening cabinets, drawers, microwave, freezer, and refrigerator. Nothing unusual is found.

In the small living room, O'Reilly opens a drawer in a small end table next to a love seat. Two remote controls are found, also a small chalkboard and box of chalk. These last two items O'Reilly tell Rierson to put in an evidence bag. "George, come here. What do you make of this?" O'Reilly asks holding up the evidence bag.

"Damned if I know, Carol," Tate answers.

●　　　●　　　●　　　●　　　●

The detective's visit with Regina's parents, Sally and Allen Boris.

They drive to a suburb of the city known for working-class families. The streets are lined with small two-story homes, all on lots no bigger than a quarter acre with small front yards and larger backyards. The address for Mr. and Mrs. Boris brings them to a small Cape Cod style home painted white. The lawn is neatly mowed. Rows of flowers are planted in narrow swaths of mulch on each side of the walk leading to the small front stoop. Rhododendrons are growing on either side of the stoop. A large bow of black ribbon hanging on the front door can be seen through the screen door.

Tate rings the doorbell. A small man in his early seventies with a full head of gray hair answers the door. He is wearing gray slacks that are well worn and a blue flannel shirt.

"Mr. Allen Boris?" Tate asks. The man nods. Tate and O'Reilly show their badges. Tate continues, "This is Detective Carol O'Reilly, and I am Detective George Tate. We are investigating the death of Regina." The man nods again. Tate, asks, "May we come in and ask you and your wife some questions?"

"Oh, of course, of course. Please, excuse my manners. Here come into the living room. Make yourself at home. Sit anywhere…" He points to a small room to the right of the stairs. "Sally, come down, two police detectives are here about Regina," Mr. Boris calls up the stairs to the second floor.

"I'll be right down. See if they want some coffee, I just bought some TastyKake[3] coffee cakes. See if they want some, too," Mrs. Sally Boris calls back.

Tate sits on a love seat, and O'Reilly sits on a matching Queen Anne wingback chair. Into the living room enters a small slightly overweight woman with gray hair cut in a pageboy. She is wearing a one piece house dress in a floral pattern with buttons down the entire front. She smiles at the two detectives and, as she is walking towards the kitchen, asks, "How do you like your coffee?"

O'Reilly answers, "None for us, we don't want to impose. Especially, at a time like this. We are sorry for your loss."

With her back to the detectives, Sally stops, seems to sway a bit. She then turns to the sofa where her husband is sitting. He notices her momentary swoon and gets up to help his wife to the sofa.

Tate begins the interview, "I know this is difficult, but we are trying to find out what happened to Regina. When was the last time you saw her?"

"Last month. I remember because it was exactly 17 days ago. It was Tito's birthday. I made a cake, and we had some with coffee. Afterward, they both left in her car," Allen Boris answers.

"How long was she here that day?" Tate follows up.

Allen Boris pauses thinking, "Not more than an hour." Sally Boris nods in agreement.

"Do you know of anyone who would want to hurt Regina?" Tate asks.

Both Sally and Allen shake their heads "no." Allen added, "Regina was a good girl. We are proud of her. We thought it was something to do with police business. You mean you don't have any idea?" They both start to cry.

"She was off duty and not on a specific case when this happened," O'Reilly tells them.

"Then it has something to do with Tito, I know it. Growing up she always protected him," Sally adds sobbing.

"What do you think she was doing with Tito?" O'Reilly follows up.

Sally shakes her head, "I don't know, but Tito was acting very worried that day." She then starts crying again.

"Where does Tito work?" O'Reilly asks.

Allen answers, "He works on computers. Regina got him the job. Tito has a knack with those things. It comes naturally to him. He never got good grades in school, but with computers, he has a way with them. We thought he would turn his life around with this new job."

O'Reilly asks again, "Could you give us the name of the company Tito works for?"

Allen puts his hand to his brow saying, "Something pen, I don't remember exactly." He turns to his wife, "Do you Sally?"

Holding a tissue at her nose, she shakes her head "no."

"Do you know what type of business it is?" O'Reilly presses.

Allen pauses to think, then says, "All I remember is that the company uses trucks."

Sally adds, "That's right. Tito mentioned trucks."

After a pause, Detective Carol O'Reilly says sympathetically, "We won't be much longer. Can you give us the names of Regina's friends or someone she would associate with after work?"

"She has…had a couple friends." Sally pauses before going on, "Allen please, get me our address book and a pen and paper." Looking at O'Reilly she continues, "I'll write down their names and phone numbers for you. Carmine Dinatto is…was her best friend."

"We appreciate that, Mrs. Boris," O'Reilly says.

Sally adds, "She also was seeing some guy, but she would never admit it to me. No matter how many times I asked, but a mother can tell. I don't know who he is or where he lives."

Tate takes the sheet with the names and phone numbers from Sally. "Carmine is the only address I have of Regina's friends. The rest are phone numbers. We called them all when Regina went missing," Sally says, then takes a deep breath to help control her emotions.

After looking at the paper, O'Reilly asks, "Do you have an address and phone number for Tito?"

Allen speaks out, "No address. He never told us where he lives. Regina mentioned it is near Springfield, but that is all I know. Here, I'll add the number to the list." Allen writes down Tito's phone number and hands the paper back to O'Reilly.

O'Reilly and Tate stand up and are about to leave, when Tate asks, "Did Regina have any young nieces or nephews or small children she would take care of?"

Sally replies, "Tito is her only brother, and he is not married and has no kids. Regina never mentioned taking care of any children."

"Do you take care of any small children?" Tate asks.

Both Allen and Sally shake their heads with Allen saying, "We have not had young kids in the house in a long time. We were kind of hoping for grandkids…" Then Allen starts crying. Sally puts her arms around him.

O'Reilly waits a while before saying, "One last question. Do either of you know why Regina would have a small chalkboard and chalk?"

Both Sally and Allen shake their heads no. "Do you think it is significant?" Allen asks.

"Thanks for all your help," O'Reilly finishes without answering the question.

A half a block away sitting in a small hybrid car with dark tinted windows, a woman takes pictures of the officers leaving the Boris home.

In the squad car, Tate says sardonically, "Great a company with "pen" in the name and they use trucks. That narrows it down to a few thousand."

O'Reilly adds, "Let's go see this Carmine Dinatto next. From the address she only lives twenty minutes from here, maybe she's home."

The woman in the small hybrid does not follow the squad car, but stays parked. The woman makes a phone call.

• • • • •

O'Reilly and Tate take I-95 south to I-476 north. Getting off at exit 3, O'Reilly drives past a strip mall. Then on the left is a three-story brick veneered apartment building with large address numbers on the front. A parking spot is found in the lot next to the building.

Tate and O'Reilly walk through the double aluminum and glass entrance door into a small lobby. One wall has rows of mailboxes. On the opposite wall is a bronze colored metal panel with handwritten names on paper slats next to the apartment numbers and a small speaker. A button is next to each number. Pressing number 24, O'Reilly identifies herself and Tate. The click of the lock opening on the inner door is heard, and the two go into a smaller inner lobby with a single elevator. Getting off on the second floor, they turn left and find the door labeled 24. Carmine Dinatto lets the officers in.

Carmine is a tall Caucasian woman, slim build with bleached blonde hair. She is wearing a waitress uniform that is tight across the bust showing cleavage. Tate has a hard time not focusing on the cleavage as he walks past her into the small living room. O'Reilly discretely gives Tate an elbow in the ribs and a chastising look when Carmine has turned to close the door.

"I just got back from my shift and have not had the time to straighten the place up. Oh, wait a second," Carmine says as she gathers up blouses, panties, and bras draped over the backs of the sofa and two chairs in the living room. "Once in a while, I use the furniture to dry some of the things. Mostly the more personal delicate stuff. Now you can have a seat."

O'Reilly says, "No a problem Ms. Dinatto. I do the same myself." This elicits a sly smile from Tate which O'Reilly sees, but ignores. Tate sits on one end of the sofa and O'Reilly on one of the chairs

Carmine asks, "You're here about Regina, right?"

"Thank you for seeing us. We do have some questions about Regina Boris. We were told that you were friends with her." O'Reilly states.

Carmine sits down on the opposite side of the sofa from Tate. Her short skirt rises high above her knees. Tate again has a hard time looking away. "Poor Regina, who could have done this to her? I was always worried about her being a cop. I am probably Regina's best friend. We shared everything with each other," she pauses then quickly adds, "… about dating and family, I mean. She never discussed police business."

Both Tate and O'Reilly are skeptical, but O'Reilly continues, "We're sorry for your loss Ms. Dinatto…"

"Call me Carmine. "Ms. Dinatto" makes it seem like I'm real old or something."

"Thank you, Carmine, when was the last time you saw Regina?" O'Reilly asks.

"It was last month. The fifth I think, it was a Friday. She met me after my shift ended and we came back here. I got dressed, then we went to a couple clubs. At around one o'clock we decided to call it a night, so she drove me back here. That was the last time I saw her," Carmine starts to cry. "Why would anyone do this to her?"

"Do you know of anyone who would want to hurt Regina or had threatened her?" O'Reilly asks.

Calming down a bit, Carmine shakes her head and says with a sniffle, "I'm not sure. She was seeing this guy and the way Regina talked about him, he could be violent. She was just seeing him off and on,"

Carmine blushes a bit saying, "…no pun intended."

"Do you have a name for this guy?"

"No, she would not tell me his name. She said it was for my own good. He was somebody important in the police department is all she would tell me."

With a note of concern O'Reilly presses, "A cop? Did she say what department or precinct?"

"No, just that he had a big ego and thought himself to be mister wonderful. She would fake orgasms to boost his ego. That is what I did not understand. It's not like she was crazy about the guy. It was like it was part of some business deal. I'm not saying that Regina was a whore, she was far from that. This was not like any other relationship she ever had. Tito was involved in the deal, too, somehow."

"You mean her brother Tito. She was mixed up with him in this deal?" O'Reilly asks.

"I really think so, but Regina would never say anything bad about Tito. I put two and two together is all," Carmine says.

O'Reilly asks, "What do you mean? What about Tito?"

Carmine answers, "I've known Regina and Tito all my life. We grew up living a block away from each other. Tito is a very intelligent guy, but as stupid as they come. He'd spend most his time on his computer. Never wanted to get a job. He got a scholarship to Penn, but dropped out after a year. He didn't want to spend time studying. It was the party life he liked. After Regina became a cop, she got Tito out of several scrapes. She adored her older brother."

"Do you know where I can find Tito?"

Carmine shakes her head, "No, when he moved out of his parents… I should say got kicked out of his parent's house, Regina helped him find an apartment. I never asked Regina where he moved to. One thing though, lately Tito must have come into some money because I saw him driving around a new Mustang."

O'Reilly interrupts, "What color?"

"Blue… One more thing, Regina made me promise to keep it a secret, well, now that she's gone, I guess I can tell you. She came into money, too. She said she bought some stock, and it paid off, but I didn't buy that. She was into something. Heck, she started paying for most of the drinks and would pick up the tab for dinners when we went out. So I did not press her about it. Let sleeping dogs lie; you know what I mean?" Carmine adds.

"Did Regina ever do any babysitting or have kids at her place?" O'Reilly is doing all the questioning.

Carmine pauses to think, "No, she don't have any kids. She never mentioned about any babysitting. That just doesn't seem like Regina to babysit."

After about ten more minutes of questioning. Nothing significant is revealed. O'Reilly and Tate leave their cards with instructions for Carmine to call if she remembers anything else.

• • • • •

Back in the squad car, O'Reilly pulls out of the parking spot and heads to Precinct 3. She asks Tate, "What do you think?"

"Um…ah, nothing right now." He says.

O'Reilly looks over at Tate, shakes her head and scolds, "Well, when the blood rushes back up to your brain talk to me. You should have been paying attention, instead of staring at her legs."

A bit annoyed, Tate replies hotly, "I was just trying to think, is all. Who could have Regina been seeing that was a cop, an 'important' cop?"

O'Reilly skeptically deadpans, "Uh huh."

"Geez Carol, you really piss me off sometimes."

With a satisfied smile on her face, O'Reilly drives back to the precinct without saying another word.

• • • • •

Back at the precinct O'Reilly and Tate have desks facing each other. O'Reilly dials the phone number for Tito, but no one answers. Then she says to Tate, "I'll check with PennDOT about Tito's driver's license and car registration. Maybe we can get an address. I'll also follow up getting information from Regina's cell phone carrier. You check on Regina's financials."

Both detectives place their requests for the information. Now they have to wait. Some of the information could take days to get. They put out a BOLO for Tito, as a person of interest in the death of Regina Boris, and for his Blue Mustang, but until they get the license plate number, it is unlikely he will be found. They would like to look into Tito's financial record, but a search warrant is needed, which they cannot get because Tito is not charged with anything. At 6:00 PM they both call it a day, and head home.

Tito Boris

Tito Boris is hurriedly pulling clothes out of his closet and placing them on the bed. Next, he picks out a pair of cross-training shoes and a pair of black loafers and puts them on the bed. He stops, gets the phone from the top of the dresser and speed dials the burner phone of his sister Regina. After five rings it goes into voice mail, he had already left two frantic messages, so this time he simply hangs up.

He takes a small carry-on bag into the bathroom. Electric toothbrush, toothpaste, mouthwash, electric shaver, shampoo, conditioner, and body wash all get shoved into the bag. Next, he heads to the dresser again. This time he opens the top drawer and takes out underwear, which he holds in one arm while he closes the top drawer and opens the next one down. He grabs a hand full of socks. He dumps all on the bed. Opening the bottom drawer of the dresser, he looks then closes it. He decided not to take pajamas.

He dashes into the spare bedroom and gets a large suitcase from the closet. Back in the bedroom, his suitcase is placed on the bed and opened. All of the items collected are crammed into the suitcase and closed. He quickly looks around to see if he missed anything. Deciding he got everything; he grabs the suitcase and bag.

In the living room, he stops to unplug his laptop which he puts into its carrying case along with a wireless mouse. He slips the strap from the case over his shoulder. Looking around the living room for anything he might have missed, goes to the end table to get framed photos of his sister, mother, and father. Kneeling on the floor, he opens the suitcase, drops the photos on top of the clothes and shuts it.

He feels his left jacket pocket to reassure himself that the money he had withdrawn from his bank account is still there. He picks up the suitcase and bag and heads out the door. He does not take the elevator, but walks down the three stories to the back door of the apartment building that leads to the rear parking lot, where his blue Mustang is parked. He glances left and right to see if anyone is watching, then quickly walks to his car, throws all he is carrying into the back seat, hops in the driver's seat and pulls out.

•   •   •   •   •

A little over a year ago, Tito was able to join the Fifth Street Gang. They were looking for someone who could help them with IT. Even crime organizations recognize the need for talent in the use of high tech devices.

Working for the Fifth Avenue Gang, Tito saw huge amounts of money being transferred digitally. Over the course of the year working for them, he developed a plan to make some extra money for himself. It was such a brilliantly simple plan.

One of Tito's duties is to transfer payments to the drug cartel that supplies the gang. These payments would be in the millions of dollars done over a computer in an office at a warehouse owned by the gang. At that warehouse, the Fifth Street Gang has its operation center. Bernie Tontas also has an office there. At this office, Tontas keeps the only computer used to make money transfers.

Tito had heard about "crypto-currencies" and how they are used by all sorts of organizations in lieu of US Dollars or any other country's currency. The crypto-currencies are not controlled by any government. It is merely digital codes tracked on "block-chain" type of software cloud. Every unit of digital currency could be tracked by anyone at any time. No one can introduce "counterfeit" currency into the system because everyone can see the total amount of units in the block-chain at all times. The only thing that is not seen by anyone is who owns the units. These units can be bought and sold over the block-chain cloud.

Over the past year, the unit value of some crypto-currencies skyrocketed. In the previous three trading days, the currency has increased over 5% per day. All the "talking heads" on the business shows were predicting even further rises.

On this particular day, once the delivery of the drugs is confirmed, Tito's job is to transfer ten million dollars to the cartel. Tito has made several such routine transfers over the past year without any problems. Bernie likes not having any problems. When Tito enters his office, Tontas smiles and greets him warmly.

This time, however, Tito plans something different. Bernie Tontas, Mark Turgeson's right-hand man, who watches Tito during the money transfers doesn't know computers. Tito figures that Tontas will not be able to follow what Tito is doing on the computer.

As is the usual routine, one hour before the transfer is to be made, funds from an offshore bank in the Caribbean is deposited in an account. This account is used to wire money to the cartel. Ten million dollars is now sitting in this account waiting for confirmation that the drugs have been delivered. In anticipation, Tito starts to sweat a bit and his stomach is now in knots.

As before, Tontas is not paying much attention to what Tito is doing. When Tontas gets occupied with a call, with three mouse clicks, Tito purchases 10 million dollars of the crypto-currency using the money in the account. Now Tito will wait until the value goes up. Even if the currency value rose only one-tenth of one percent, he would pocket ten thousand dollars. He will then sell the crypto, then convert it to US Dollars and put it back into the account. All this should take less than thirty minutes. He would then send the ten million to the cartel and rest he would transfer to his own bank. No one will be the wiser.

What Tito does not know is that minutes after he purchased the crypto, South Korea announces restrictions on the trading of crypto-currencies and the European Union announces that it is considering restrictions on the use of crypto-currencies. These two announcements cause the value of the crypto to drop almost 30% in fifteen minutes. Everyone holding crypto is trying to sell it.

Tito is monitoring the crypto and is in shock at how quickly the value is falling. He starts to fidget and sweat.

Tontas tells Tito that the gang has received the drug shipment and he gives the okay for Tito to transfer the ten million dollars to the cartel.

"Okay, will do," is all Tito says. He wipes his brow with the sleeve of his shirt. His armpits are now wet.

After a few minutes, Tontas start to get suspicious and asks, "By now we should have gotten the bank confirmation that the transfer is complete, shouldn't we?"

"The computer is a bit slow today. It should come through any second. Keep an eye out for it while I take a leak," Tito instructs Tontas.

Tontas nods saying, "Okay."

Tito, as casually as he can manage, gets up and walks slowly down the corridor leading to the restroom. Once he is around the corner, he runs to the rear exit. Bypassing the steps that lead to the parking lot, he jumps from the loading dock and makes a bee-line to his Mustang[5]. Reaching his apartment building, he quickly takes the rear door and stairs to his apartment.

•   •   •   •   •

After leaving his apartment, Tito is driving fast, but not so fast as to get pulled over by the cops. He heads north. Because of traffic problems, he avoids the Schuylkill Expressway and takes Gulph Mill Road, eventually getting on US 422 heading west. After an hour he stops just outside of Reading at a motel that offers free WiFi. He plans on logging on to the crypto-currency website. He will then convert the remaining crypto to US Dollars and transfer the money into his own bank account. Even with the crypto-currency falling, he should still be able to pocket a few million dollars. First, he makes a phone call.

He speed-dials Regina's burner phone again, but once more it immediately goes into voice mail. He has to tell his sister, what has happened. She is the one, through the guy she is seeing, who got him the introduction to the Fifth Street Gang. In desperation, he breaks with protocol and, instead of calling Regina's burner phone, he calls her personal phone. Tito is relieved when the phone does not go to voicemail and is answered.

"Regina, I have been trying to reach you on the burner all afternoon, so I called you direct…"

"It's good to know you care about your sister so much, Tito. She and I are having a party. Why don't you join us," Bernie Tontas announces ominously.

"Bernie, listen to me, Regina had nothing to do with this. It was all me. Please, don't hurt her," Tito pleads.

Tito hears a tortured scream from his sister over the phone then the voice of Tontas again, "Your sister don't like pliers too much, Tito." Another horrifying scream pierces Tito's ears. "Better come back here quick, Tito. You might be able to keep her in one piece."

"Bernie listen, only about 3 million is lost. There is about seven million dollars that is still available. I can get that back to you, just let Regina go." Tito bargains.

Tontas sighs, then says, "Tito, Tito… you are not the only whiz kid on computers in this place. Keystrokes, Tito, we were able to recreate what you did by tracking the keystrokes. By the way, only about one million was lost. The value of the crypto came back up. We got nine million of our money back. It's just you we want now."

Tito hangs up. Gets back into his car and keeps heading west. He tosses his cell phone out the car window into a creek as he drives over a bridge.

•   •   •   •   •

Back at the warehouse, Tontas puts down the phone. "Well, it seems your brother doesn't want to talk anymore. Guess it is up to you to start talking. Where is Tito going?"

Breathing heavy from the pain and tied to a wooden chair completely naked, Regina sobs, "I don't know what he did. I don't know where he's going. Please, believe me." She looks up at the man holding the pliers and pleads, "Why are you doing this to me? I've always given you everything you asked for."

"I know babe. We had fun in the sack. But business is business," the man answers unsympathetically.

"Please, don't hurt me anymore. I don't know where Tito is. You've got to believe me."

Tontas sighs saying, "I will eventually believe you, but not until your boyfriend here is done using up the tools in his bag. Show her what a ball peen hammer can do."

The man Tontas is talking to applies duct tape over Regina's mouth to muffle the screams. He then grabs the handle of the hammer and brings it down on her bare foot.

CHAPTER SEVEN
Turgeson talks to Bernie about Regina

Bernie Tontas is a bit nervous. Although he has worked with Mark Turgeson over 20 years and helped him start the Fifth Street Gang, he is still apprehensive. This type of thing only pops up once every few years, and the two of them work it out, but Tontas is still anxious. Telling Turgeson bad news is not pleasant and telling Turgeson that he, Bernie, could have prevented the bad news can be downright painful. He stands on the sidewalk in front of his suburban home waiting. Mark Turgeson is always punctual, so Tontas knows he will not be waiting too long. As expected, a dark green sedan pulls up to the curb. Tontas gets in.

Mark Turgeson does not smile or start small talk. This is a "tell" to Tontas that this will not be an easy discussion. Losing a million dollars is troublesome. Tontas likes the word "troublesome." It can be used to describe all sorts of situations.

Turgeson asks, "Bernie, please explain to me what happened."

Tontas in a low voice starts to explain, "Not to worry boss. We eventually made the payment to the cartel, although it was late and we did lose a million..."

"Not that," Turgeson quickly interrupts, "Fuck the million, that's peanuts. Fuck the cartel; we will be bypassing them soon. What about my insurance policy, Regina! Why was she killed?"

Tontas is a bit surprised at Turgeson's disregard for the payment and the loss of a million dollars. He takes a moment to respond. Clearing his throat he starts, "When Tito ran out, I figured Regina knew about it or at least knew where Tito would be going…"

"Did she?" Turgeson interrupts again.

"Ahhhh, now I don't think so boss," Tontas says apologetically.

"So you and that arrogant prick kill her for no good reason. You know it took me years to recruit someone in the 11th precinct." Turgeson screams.

Tontas in a low voice answers, "I screwed up boss, I know. But I did not know the guy loved inflicting pain so much. I never saw anything like him. I left him alone with her for ten minutes, and when I came back, she was a bloody pulp. He kept ripping at her with pliers…"

"Okay, okay Bernie. I get the picture. I'm going to call that cocksucker and straighten him out. If he doesn't give me some good answers, he'll be the one who's a bloody pulp."

Mark Turgeson Call

Mark Turgeson doesn't understand the intricacies of the new digital communication age, which makes him all the more cautious and suspicious using smartphones and computers. The assurances by his younger gang members regarding encryption security means nothing to Turgeson. His version of cyber-security is very low tech, but very effective.

While sitting on the sofa watching television, he changes the channel to one of the financial networks and on a piece of paper he writes down the seven-digit number for the previous day's closing of the Dow Jones Industrial Average[6]. He then puts the paper in his pocket. Turning off the television set, he gets up off the sofa.

"I'm going out to buy some cigars," he yells to his wife, who is in the kitchen.

"Get some onions, I'm making stew for dinner," his wife replies.

"Do you have carrots? You know I like carrots in the stew."

"Well, then get carrots, too. Buy the little ones in the bag," she tells him.

Before going to the market, Turgeson drives a half mile to a small office center. He parks his car on the street then, wearing a baseball cap and sunglasses, he walks a block to a four-story office building. On the second floor is a small office with two rooms. The rent is paid by the Fraternal Institute for Public Safety. A not-for-profit organization which is a front Turgeson uses to pay for "safe" locations throughout the city. A similar type of front organization pays for the buildings and storage areas the gang uses in the city.

On paper, the charter members of these fronts have names and social security numbers gleaned from local cemeteries. Another layer of protection Turgeson uses.

He opens the office door and immediately punches in the security code before 5 seconds elapses to prevent a false signal that a break-in is occurring being sent to the security company.

The front room is furnished with fake plants, reception desk, copier, bookshelf and all the other paraphernalia of a fully functioning business, although none of the equipment is ever used, nor does anyone ever work there. The back room is similarly furnished befitting a typical mid-level manager. However, Turgeson is the only one who ever uses it.

Turgeson almost never talks to anyone about business except a few close associates. These discussions are always in locations completely free from any chance of being recorded or videoed. Almost never over a phone. Today is one of the exceptions. The risk of being seen talking to this person is too much of a gamble for Turgeson, so he will use a phone.

Turgeson sits at the desk. On top of the desk is a small reading lamp that leans over a large green felt desk pad. To the right of the pad, is a business style phone, stapler, and notepad. None of which has ever been used. To the left is a large ashtray with dust remnants of previous use. On the side of the desk is a dark green waste paper basket.

He opens the middle drawer then takes out a phone charger cord, a small chalkboard and a box of chalk. From the bottom drawer on the right, he removes one of the several pre-paid disposable phones which are still in their plastic sealed containers. The phones were purchased with cash by Bernie Tontas, his close associate. Impossible to trace back to Turgeson.

Using scissors, he cuts the plastic and unwraps the phone. After turning it on, he checks the phone charge and sees that it at 50%. He replaces the unneeded charger cord in the center drawer. He then uses the phone to download an app for sending pictures. This particular app has the feature that, when the photo is viewed by the recipient, it will disappear in fifteen seconds without any chance of recovering the image.

He takes the paper with the Dow Jones number from his pocket. On the packaging for the disposable phone, he finds the phone number. He then adds the Dow Jones number and the burner phone number to get the sum of both. Now he writes this sum on the chalkboard. Using the phone, he takes a picture of the number on the chalkboard with the newly downloaded app. He erases the chalkboard then puts the burner phone in his pocket. The piece of paper is also placed back in his pocket.

Carrying the discarded phone wrapping, he leaves the office and locks the door. The wrapping is put into the garbage chute, and he returns to his car. Pulling away from the curb, he sends the photo via the picture app.

The time of day that Turgeson sends this photo is previously arranged. The recipient gets an alert on their phone that a photo is received. They have fifteen seconds to write down the number on the chalkboard shown on the photo before it digitally vanishes. The recipient writes down the number from the photo on a piece of paper. He then subtracts the previous days Dow Jones closing number. The remainder is the phone number for Turgeson's burner phone.

The recipient is the guy who mutilated Regina Boris with pliers causing her to die. Turgeson does not like the guy, but he still wants his services for now. Turgeson always follows the dogma, "Keeps your friends close, but your enemies closer." He will be complimentary at first and then show a little anger, as a father would be to a son who misbehaved, not giving his true intentions away to the guy.

Turgeson is driving around the city when his phone rings. He immediately answers it and says, "I saw on the TV about the raid on the Irish Boys. At this rate, before the year is out, I should be the only major player in the city. Good work." After a pause, Turgeson controls his anger saying, "Yeah, you got the extra three grand. The payment is being made to your account today."

Turgeson takes the on-ramp to I-76 and heads north. He then continues with sarcasm, "Now what are you going to do about replacing my informant at the 11th? Since you so conveniently ripped her to shreds." Another pause, "...That sounds simple enough for a short-term solution. Well, make sure you have it in place soon and it better work. I'm paying you lots of money, don't let me down. It is not a healthy thing to do. One more thing, I don't care about your personal problems with women, but don't let it interfere with our business. Don't screw this up."

Turgeson listens again then says, "Okay, but don't you go high-and-mighty to me. I expect to get the services I pay for. Another thing, do something about that police investigation. That is another thing you are being paid for. I know you are not in that precinct. Send them off on a wild goose chase for a while. The other gangs are close to going under. I am getting more of their men joining my gang now that they see I will be the only organization left in the city."

There is another pause by Turgeson as he listens. Signing off, he says, "You better be right... We'll talk again next week unless something important comes up before then."

Still, in the right-hand lane of the highway, Turgeson slows a bit to let a tractor-trailer pass him on the left. As the rig is going by, he lowers his window and tosses the disposable phone into wheels of the rig.

At the next exit, he gets off the highway and drives to the grocery store. He thinks, "That arrogant bastard pisses me off." After a sigh, he says aloud to no one, "Eh, maybe I'll also pick up a chocolate cake while I'm here."

Crimson Blade Raid

In the emotional lull prior to each raid before the adrenaline starts pumping Lori begins to feel protective of her team. Especially this mission, a few weeks ago Corporal Regina Boris, a member of the squad, was brutally beaten to death. Her body was found floating in the Delaware River, below the Navy Yard. On this mission is a rookie, Officer

Gail Scott, Regina's replacement on the squad. Even with the extensive training a recruit goes through, there is the inevitable unpredictability of an individual in a high-risk situation. Self-preservation is a powerful instinct. It is natural for a person to want to run and hide in the face of danger. It takes a special person to move towards jeopardy, instead of away from it.

This is the first combined raid for the newly formed task force. The suspected warehouse and lab of the Crimson Blade gang is the target. Outside, what looks like an abandoned factory, squads from Precincts 7, 9, 11 and 13 position themselves at all the exits and at strategic points to prevent anyone from escaping from the building.

A block away in an unmarked brown van Lt. Barbara Maylars sits at a console with several video screens. Images from the police officers' body cams appear on the screens with the name of the officer who is wearing the camera. All participants entering the building have video and audio equipment attached to their helmets. At the moment the images Maylars selected to show on her video screens are of the squad leaders from each precinct, Sgt. Umile, Lt. Brown, Sgt. Daniels and Lt. Costner.

Earlier at the embarkation point, which is the police garage of Precinct 13, Maylars sensed the tension of the squads. Now that they are assembled outside the target, Maylars makes an effort to ease the stress. Through her headset, she announces, "This is a team-wide systems check of audio and visual. Just to recap, Precincts 11 and 13 are entering through the double doors at Rainer Street. Precinct 9 is covering the 10th Avenue exits; Precinct 7 is covering the Lindon Street and 11th Avenue exits. Umm...Lieutenant Costner, whose butt are you staring at?"

Laughs and chuckles can be heard throughout the squads.

In a mock radio voice Costner replies, "My helmet cam must be outta alignment. However, the butt belongs to Sergeant Daniels, sir."

Again laughter is heard from the squads.

Maylars continues, "All kidding aside, be careful and safe. Watch your buddies back. Is everyone in position?"

All four squad leaders reply in the affirmative.

"This is a go. I repeat this is a go!" Maylars commands.

Corporal Jason Taylor inserts the pry bar between the two doors and yanks it open. Corporal Alice Stetzler and Officer Carlos Riccini are the first through the doors, immediately followed by Lori Daniels. She feels a push on her back as Costner and Corporal Nina Tabrini of Precinct 13 rush in behind her. "Geez, Costner is anxious, he almost knocked me down," she thinks.

Stetzler and Riccini have positioned themselves in defensive positions on each side of the doorway as Lori moves to the left with her squad following and Costner leads his squad to the right fanning out across the factory floor.

Rusted equipment is scattered throughout the large area, which squad members use as cover in their methodical movement to the two-level super-structure in the center of the building. Light can be seen coming from the windows that were once the offices for the previous owner of the building.

Stopping the squad, Lori looks over to Officer Scott, the youngest and newest member of the team. Scott is breathing hard and looks nervous. Going over to her side, Lori whispers to Scott, "Gail, are you all right?"

Gail nods yes.

Lori continues, "We are all nervous and scared. That's just natural. Use it to stay alert. You have trained extensively for this. You can do it. I would not have assigned you to this team, if I did not have absolute confidence in you. Listen, I'm going to split us up. You will be going with Jason Taylor. Follow his lead; you'll do fine."

Lori's squad is about 25 feet from the first office door when a short fat guy wearing a gray hoodie and blue jeans walks out while lighting up a cigarette. Looking up, he sees the squad and reflexively moves back to the door.

"Freeze," Lori commands, "kneel down, hands behind your head!"

The guy stops dead in his tracks and doesn't move. The cigarette drops from between his fingers. Riccini approaches the guy, commanding, "Kneel down. Hands behind your head." Riccini then clamps on handcuff on the guy's right wrist. Swings the wrist down, then swings the left wrist down and clamps the cuffs. He tells the guy to stay and don't move.

When all the squad members have taken defensive positions around all sides of the central office area, through a bullhorn Costner calls out, "This is the police. The building is surrounded. Come out one at a time with your hands behind your head. No one has to get hurt."

In less than a minute the Crimson Gang members start walking out of the office doors with hands behind their heads. Seeing the first guy on his knees, the rest do the same as they emerge. A total of seven are kneeling when officers approach them and start handcuffing each.

Lori walks up to the first man caught and asks, "Are there any more inside?"

Looking wide-eyed he turns to one of the other gang members, hesitates a second, before shaking his head "no."

"This guy is lying. Be careful searching the offices," Lori tells her squad.

Officer Gail Scott, Officer Joe Morgan and Corporal Jason Taylor of Precinct 11 approach the metal exterior steps leading to a door on the second floor while three members of Precinct 13 enter the doors on the first floor.

Taylor is the oldest of the squad and the most experienced with searching urban structures. Having served four tours with Special Forces in Iraq and Afghanistan, he usually takes point in close quarters situations. Lori has admonished him several times for not letting someone else take the lead, but Taylor, feeling like a father figure to the squad, always goes in first.

Using hand signals, Jason tells Scott and Morgan to position themselves at the base of the metal stairway with a clear view of the door at the top landing. Both officers shoulder their automatic rifles in the firing position to cover Taylor as he ascends the stairs.

He takes each step carefully to avoid making a sound. The old stair edifice wobbles slightly with each step obliging Taylor to halt so as not to make a noise. Although he has years of experience, sweat begins to form on his brow. No matter how many times it is done, approaching a closed door raises fear and increases adrenaline. Senses become heightened. Anything, from an armed assailant to a booby trap, can await the opening of the door.

Scott and Morgan raise their weapons and take aim at the door with fingers on triggers. The squad has become very close over the past weeks of training, including Gail Scott, the rookie. The insight and acumen of Jason Taylor in close quarter combat has helped all of them. His patience with each officer has touched them all. Their respect and admiration for Taylor create a personal responsibility to do whatever has to be done to protect him, even with their own life if necessary. A feeling akin to love.

•　　•　　•　　•　　•

Nervously holding his Glock[9] Jamal Harrison, head of the Crimson Blade gang, eyes the door of his inner office on the second story. His hope is that, by ordering his men to easily give themselves up, the police would not do a completely thorough search; and his hiding place will not be discovered. He knows it is a long shot.

He takes a silencer out of his pocket and screws it into the barrel of the Glock[9]. He thinks that he may have to kill a couple of cops in order to make his escape. Keeping his shots quiet will help him sneak out.

He can make out the light metallic sounds of footsteps climbing the stairs. Next Harrison hears the squeak of the outer office door by the stairway opening. Then silence. His hand becomes moist, so he momentarily switches the gun to his left hand while he dries his right hand on the knee of his pants.

Through a crack in his hiding place, he sees the door to his office slowly open. A tall black cop wearing helmet and body armor quickly enters then abruptly stops, scanning the room. Harrison switches the gun to his right hand and brings it up ready to fire. The gun accidentally touches the metal side to his hiding place, Harrison silently curses himself for the blunder.

Taylor hears the dull clink and immediately pauses his scanning of the room to try to detect the direction of the noise. Unsure of the exact location, he sees a row of metal lockers against the wall on his right, pointing his automatic rifle, he slowly approaches and methodically starts opening each locker.

Harrison, now realizing that his spot will eventually be found, quietly brings the barrel of the Glock automatic up and takes aim. He will shoot when the cop is most vulnerable, a wide gap in the body armor will be exposed on the left side when reaching for a locker door.

Slowly moving to the next locker, Taylor pauses a second then starts to reach for the locker door.

Harrison sees his chance. Needing to fully raise the lid of the storage bin he is hiding in, he braces himself and starts to push.

Suddenly, another cop appears at the door pointing an automatic rifle at Harrison. "Drop it," a woman's voice commands, "or I'll blow your fucking head off!"

Harrison immediately drops his gun and raises his hands. Taylor, who has already turned towards Harrison, aims his weapon at the head of Harrison, while Gail Scott, still pointing her rifle, moves in to get Harrison out of the storage bin and cuff him.

Joe Morgan appears at the door saying, "All the other rooms are clear," then looking at Harrison he adds, "... what have we got here? Why if it isn't Jamal Harrison himself. Nice catch Jason."

Taylor smiles and nods. "This room still has to be thoroughly searched," Taylor commands.

While Scott escorts Harrison out of the room at gunpoint, Morgan and Taylor finish the sweep.

Down on the main factory floor, the gang members are assembled and led off to the awaiting police vans for transport to Precinct 13 for processing and interrogation. Lieutenant Costner takes one of the cruisers back to the precinct to initiate the interrogation of the prisoners.

State Police Lieutenant Maylars enters and walks over to the Lori, Sergeant Umile and Lieutenant Brown, who are giving instructions to their squads. Maylars notices a piece of fabric dangling from Lori's bulletproof vest. "Hey, good work on the raid. That is great that no one had to fire a shot," she praises. Then she adds, "Daniels, your vest has a tear."

Lori turns her head to take a look, but cannot see it, so she removes the vest.

Maylars takes hold of the dangling piece of fabric and comments, "It looks like a slice from a sharp object. What did you back into?"

"It must have been cut by a sharp edge on one of the pieces of rusted equipment. Funny, I don't remember having my back against anything," Lori ponders.

"Nevertheless, this can't be worn anymore. You need a new one, Daniels," Maylars tells her.

Lori frowns, "It takes weeks to get a new vest."

"Bad luck."

As Corporal Jason Taylor, Officer Joe Morgan and Officer Gail Scott walk by, Lori calls out, "Nice collar Corporal. Nabbing Jamal Harrison will get you a commendation."

Taylor smiles and says, "Thanks Lori, but it's not my collar. Gail Scott is the one who had him in her gun sight. She nailed him. It's officially her collar."

Gail is taken aback by what Taylor says. She doesn't know what to say.

Lori walks over to Scott and shakes her hand. "Your first collar and it's Jamal Harrison, head of the Crimson Blade. Congratulations!"

Immediately, all of the officers crowd around Scott and start to applaud. Many come up to shake her hand or pat her on the back. All give their praise and congratulations. Gail Scott is blushing and mumbles "thank you" many times.

When Corporal Donald Ramirez approaches her to shake her hand, Scott is so happy that she instinctively gives him a big hug. Realizing what she just did, she quickly releases him and starts to blush.

Ramirez is equally as surprised, because for weeks he has been trying to build up enough nerve to ask Scott for a date, but kept putting it off.

All the officers start to laugh and begin applauding again.

Exeter instructions to Brenda

"Your 4 o'clock is here sir," Sergeant Faschnaght says into his phone.

Looking up at Brenda Cervetti, he nods, "Go right in."

Brenda smiles, "Thanks." As she turns to the office door, a man who Brenda thinks looks just like Mister Potato Head walks out of Exeter's office carrying commemorative sports plaques. He nods to her, while obviously checking out her boobs. Brenda does not nod back. She opens the office door and goes in.

Tom Exeter, sitting at his desk, says "Take a seat, Brenda."

•   •   •   •   •

Brenda immediately notices that Exeter is not in a good mood, then with a determined tone he begins, "Brenda, what I am about to tell you is top secret. It has been cleared by Captain Petracelli, State Police Captain Celia Bouton and State Police Lieutenant Barbara Maylars. Maylars is the head of Section 3, the special task force operating in the city," he raises his head a bit, touches his fingertips in an inverted 'V' then continues with a smug tone, "…I am now a special advisor to the task force. Sort of a mentor to the State Police because of my experience and insight to our city."

Brenda says nothing, but just nods. Thinking, "Working for this guy is going to be a pain."

"The plan I have devised is this. You are being reassigned back to your old squad and placed in the task force," Exeter explains. "Your cover story is that you did not like it in internal affairs and decided to return to Precinct 11."

Looking very skeptical, Brenda asks, "Okay…then, what is my purpose for going back?"

Exeter, changing to a very stern tone, looks Brenda in the eyes and says, "I have some very disturbing information to give you. Sergeant Lorraine Daniels is an informant for the Fifth Street Gang. Your assignment is to observe every move of Sergeant Daniels. Listen to her phone conversations, watch who she sees and try to follow her where ever she goes. Most importantly, let me know in advance of any raids on the Fifth Street Gang she will be leading. Daniels and her accomplice, Lieutenant Michael Costner, work for the Gang."

It takes all of her willpower to not immediately burst into laughter, and tell Exeter he's a fool, but instead, Brenda very calmly and with a professional demeanor asks, "Can I see what evidence you have accumulated so far on Daniels and Costner?"

Taken aback a bit, Exeter hesitates then says, "Um… well, the file is incomplete, but let's just say that they both have been under some surveillance and their actions are very suspicious."

"When do I start?"

Glad that Brenda does not ask anymore follow up questions about Daniels, Exeter regains his composure stating, "In two days. It will give you time to clear your desk and get prepared for moving to the 11th. I expect weekly reports about her movements. You are to report to me personally. No one else is to see or know what you are doing."

"Yes sir, understood," Brenda replies. "Is there anything else?"

"No, that is all. You may go."

As she walks out of his office, Brenda thinks, "How did that jackass ever get to be a captain."

Lori & Costner Make Up

As is the routine, Lori drives to Mike Costner's apartment to hook up; Mike never wants to go to her place. The drive takes about 45 minutes in favorable traffic. Rush hour can add 30 minutes. Lori has bought a new all-wheel-drive sedan, and she is excited about showing it to Mike. She hopes the new car will show him that she is committed to continuing their relationship and she can come to his place in any weather even though they live so far apart. It bothers her that he might still be seeing other women. She knows of at least one woman because she caught Mike in a lie. The other woman texted Mike and Lori saw it on his phone.

It is four days after the raid on the Crimson Blade Gang and the capture of Jamal Harrison. The night after the raid Lori called Mike about the other woman. She was horribly upset and used language she did not think was in her. Mike was patient with her and did not yell back.

She was so happy to get a call from Mike today. All during the call Mike was calm and kept telling Lori that he would stop seeing the other woman. "Trust me," is what he said several times.

Now Lori wants to patch things up and tell him that, even if he is seeing someone else, she really loves him. Loves him much more than any other woman could. She would show Mike that she is the only one for him. She can't stand the thought of losing Mike.

Lori is able to find a parking spot in front of his apartment building. It is after six PM, so no money is needed for the parking meters.

Undetected by Lori, about a hundred feet away, a sedan pulls to the curb. Tom Exeter watches Lori go to the door of the apartment building.

As she reaches the door of the building and presses the button for his apartment, Lori smiles in anticipation of showing Mike the new car. "It's me," she says into the speaker.

"Great, I'm glad you are early. Come on up," Mike replies.

Before the "buzz" ends, Lori has opened the door and is hurrying up the stairs. The lobby she passes through has an ultra-modern design. No wood anywhere. The floor is white tile with a stylized Liberty bell logo in the center. Silver gray painted walls have faux chrome accents in the corners and across the ceiling. There is one elevator, and it is in use. Lori did not want to wait for it. She quickly climbs the three stories and almost jogs to the door marked 334. She knows it will be unlocked and rushes in.

Mikes apartment is also ultra-modern. "Sparse" is best to describe the décor. No curtains, no flowers or plants. The large main room has two sofas and two chairs. One in an off-white and the other a dark gray. At one wall is an ultramodern gas fireplace which consists of a chrome mantle with a pane of glass under it. Behind the glass is a tube with holes across the top from which flames emanate. Minimalist framed paintings are on the walls. A hall leads to a guest bath, spare bedroom and then to the master bedroom and bath.

At the other end of the large room is a kitchenette with a center island. The island has a white marble top. A "swan neck" faucet spout rises from a deep set chrome sink. The cabinets have a black enamel finish. The appliances are also chrome. The kitchenette is so pristine that it looks like a meal was never prepared in it.

Just off the kitchenette area is a small alcove with a built-in desk, a chrome metal chair with a black seat pad sits at the desk. A file folder and small box are on the desk. The first time she saw the apartment, Lori wondered how Mike could afford such a place.

Mike rushes to meet her. They embrace while passionately kissing. He is the first to speak, "I am so sorry we fought. I have been a wreck the past two days. I love you so much."

Hearing this Lori can't contain her tears of joy. "Oh, Mike I feel the same way. I don't ever want us to fight again."

Once again they kiss. Their tongues almost dancing in the passion. Lori breaks off the embrace and says, "I know you are seeing someone else, but I want you to know that I am committed to a long relationship with you. I'll show you that I'm the one you should be with. Come downstairs with me. I want to show you my surprise."

"What surprise?" Mike says with a puzzled look.

Lori smiles, "Just get a jacket on and come with me."

Down on the street, Lori waves her arm triumphantly at the car. "See it is brand new and all-wheel drive. I will be able to see you in any kind of weather. No more piece of junk car."

Smiling slyly, Mike turns from the car to Lori. He kisses her and says, "I have a surprise for you, too, well two surprises actually. Let's go back upstairs."

Back at the apartment, Mike says, "I have a big surprise and a smaller surprise for you. Which do you want first?"

With her finger tapping the side of her head, Lori feigns struggling to make a decision, "Hmmm, which one first?" She can't help beaming; she is so happy. "The smaller surprise first."

Mike goes into his bedroom. Lori can hear a dresser drawer opening then closing. Now she is very curious. While waiting for Mike to return, she idly walks through the kitchenette admiring the quality. She lets her hand run along the countertops and then to the desk.

Walking out into the living room, Mike is carrying a package wrapped in silver paper that looks like a small pillow. "Am I not just the best boyfriend ever? You have my permission to open the present," he says.

Lori, walking back into the room, smiles and takes the package from

Mike. She hefts it a bit and then, wearing a puzzled expression, proceeds to unwrap the gift.

Lori immediately sees it is something that is dark blue in color. Dropping the wrapping paper to the floor, she holds the gift up by its shoulders. "A body armor vest!??!" Lori happily cries. "How did you know mine got torn?"

Oddly, Mike hesitates a bit, "I have my sources," he says slyly. "I want you to be safe. This vest is the best vest money can buy."

Lori hugs Mike, "This is so sweet of you. How'd you get it so quick? These things take at least a month to order."

"I pulled some strings and twisted some arms. Nothing is too good for one of my girlfriends! Now for the bigger surprise." Mike pauses then says, "I am not seeing Elaine anymore. I know how much it bothered you, so I broke it off today. I love you, baby."

Lori looks at Mike skeptically. "Don't tell me that if it is not true, Mike. Please, don't," she pleads.

Taking out his phone, Mike shows Lori a series of texts to and from Elaine. They show Mike telling Elaine it's over between them and that he is in love with Lori. Elaine writes some nasty things about Lori. Reading the text messages, Lori hopes Mike is sincere.

Almost in tears from happiness, Lori caresses Mike whispering, "Oh, Mike is this true. Are you really done with her?"

Mike kisses Lori and says, "Its true baby. I've chosen you and you alone." Then he gives her a passionate kiss. Pulling himself away from her a bit, he unzips his pants saying, "Now you can give me a present."

Lori gives Mike a quick kiss then kneels. Pulling down his pants then underwear, she takes his dick in her right hand. After kissing it, she gives it a few licks and starts to feel it gorging to an erection. She then begins to suck on his hard dick in a slow rhythmic motion moving her head back and forth.

Mikes breathing begins to speed up as he starts to pump slowly, then gradually increases the speed of his motion. Lori quickens her movement to match his. She braces herself by grabbing his butt with her left hand as she strokes with her right. She knows this excites him and she wants to show Mike how much she wants to pleasure him.

He starts to make a low groan while firmly holding her head which will prevent her from pulling away when he starts to ejaculate.

Lori doesn't mind because she is willing to continue until Mike is completely finished. She wants to please him.

His groans become higher pitched as his pumping becomes almost frantic. Lori continues to match his movements.

Although he slows his thrusts, he makes them more forceful. An uncontrollable shiver travels through Mike as he slows the pace of his motions even more. Warm fluid starts to fill Lori's mouth, but she continues.

Lori can feel the firmness of his dick begin to weaken but she does not stop. Lori wants to please Mike so much. Mike moans with satisfaction and continues pumping more slowly with smaller steady strokes. Lori massages his ass cheek with her left hand. After all the firmness is gone, Lori breaks away. She stands and gives Mike a passionate kiss, then says, "I love you so much."

Mike pulls up his pants, and they both go to the kitchen island. Lori sits down on a stool, while Mike gets two glasses from a cupboard. He takes out a box of Zinfandel wine from the refrigerator and fills her glass. He then takes out a bottle of pinot grigio and fills his glass. Sitting beside Lori at the island, he smiles. They toast each other and take a sip.

"So Lori, I've not asked about your past before. Do you have any brothers or sisters?" Mike asks.

Lori replies, "You are right about that, you are so full of yourself that our conversations are always about you and your career,"

"That's not true!" Mike snaps back and grabs Lori's arm. She can see his face turn red.

"Mike, you're hurting me," Lori complains.

Mike pulls his arm away and puts both elbows on the island countertop. He then covers his face with his hands. "Sorry, I have a bad temper," he says as an explanation.

He turns to Lori and with a conciliatory tone says, "Go ahead tell me about you."

Lori looks at Mike with a worried expression and says, "Oh, Mike I was not trying to make you angry. I'm the one who should be sorry for saying that."

"Thank you," Mike replies, "Now go ahead and tell me about you."

Lori starts, "Well, I have three brothers, Ted, Rick and Bobby. Ted is older than me. Bobby is five years younger. Rick is dead. He was caught in a crossfire between a couple gangs during a shootout."

"Sorry to hear that," Mike consoles.

"Rick is the reason I became a cop. I don't want anyone else to have someone they love killed because of gang violence. My mother is alive and lives in Missouri. She moved there to be near her sister after my father died."

"How did your father die?" Mike asks.

"He died from his own pigheadedness, the son-of-a-bitch. He had a pain in his leg, but did not go to see a doctor because my mother told him to. He wouldn't listen to anyone, especially my mother or any other woman. It turned out to be a blood clot that eventually traveled to his brain, serves the bastard right. He treated my mother like shit and me like his serving girl. I'm glad he's dead," Lori says coldly.

"He must have been a real piece of work for you to hate him so much," Mike consoles.

"When I was seventeen, I was seeing a guy for over two months. We were pretty intimate. On one night, after a dance, he drove me home. He then walked me to the front porch, and we kissed pretty passionately. I said goodnight and went into the house. My father was waiting by a front window and apparently saw me. You know what he said to me, 'You never kissed me like that.' That is the type of creep my father was."

Then in a softer tone, Lori says, "This is the first time I have talked about my father with anyone since his died."

Mike smiles slyly, "You must really be hooked on me."

Lori playfully pushes Mike with her right hand and looks into his eyes saying softly, "Maybe."

Mike gently holds Lori's shoulders in his hands and warmly tells her, "You can trust me with anything, babe. You know that, right?"

"I know that, Mike. I love you."

Mike smiles, "I love you too, babe."

They passionately kiss. Their tongues dance between their mouths.

He reaches down and puts his hand between her legs. "Let's hop into bed and see what you can do to make me happy."

Lori smiles and nods.

• • • • •

Later while lying in bed and looking a bit more serious, Mike says, "I want to share something with you. It is highly confidential, but I would like your help, so please, do not repeat our conversation to anyone."

Lori also puts on a serious demeanor and says, "Of course, Mike. You can confide in me. I would never break your trust."

While collecting his thoughts, Mike turns on his pillow to face Lori. Then he starts, "There is a high up informant in the police force supplying one or more of the crime gangs in the city. I would like you to help me find out who it is."

"Do you have anyone in mind?" Lori asks.

"I don't have anything concrete yet, but I think it may be Tom Exeter," Costner says.

Lori with a gasp of surprise asks, "What makes you think it could be him?"

Costner looks Lori in the eyes and says, "I have been told that he is nosing into the business of Precinct 11. Especially, regarding the raids of the Fifth Street Gang."

"Jesus, that may be why he is following me. I thought it was because he was overly possessive, but…" Lori ponders.

"Tell me everything you know about Exeter," Mike commands.

"Well, we dated for a couple months. He is very secretive. He is very ambitious. He has an enormous ego. His next goal is to be commissioner of the entire city police department. Not that this will help, but he collects sports memorabilia. He buys a lot from a dealer in Lemoyne."

Costner interrupts, "Lemoyne, PA?"

"Yes"

"Do you know the dealer's name?" Costner asks.

Lori tries to think, but after a few seconds says, "No, I don't. I do remember the guy looks like Mr. Potato Head."

Costner with a disappointed look says, "That's not much. If you think of something, let me know. You mentioned to me that your friend, Brenda, is now working for Exeter. Maybe she can keep tabs on him for us?"

A bit surprised and perturbed at his suggestion, Lori replies, "Brenda is in a highly sensitive position. If she starts talking to anyone about what Tom Exeter is doing, she could be charged with divulging classified information. You know that!"

"Okay, okay. It was just an idea. Don't get your panties in a twist!" Costner recants.

After an uncomfortable pause, Costner asks, "So, who is better in the sack. Exeter or me?"

"Jesus, men," Lori says sardonically, as she gets out of bed without answering his question.

CHAPTER EIGHT
Regina Investigation Continues

It takes two days for PADOT to supply the information about Tito's driver's license and car. Sergeant George Tate adds the license plate number to the BOLO first put out earlier in the week. The address on Tito's license is his parent's house. The address on his car registration is an apartment building in King of Prussia. O'Reilly and Tate request a car from the motor pool and drive to the apartment. On the way, they call the apartment building owner to make arrangements to be let into the apartment if Tito does not answer the door. The owner, who lives in Florida, gives Tate the phone number of the realtor that is managing the building.

When they arrive at the apartment building, the realtor is not there yet. Taking the elevator to the third floor, they find the apartment and knock. After several knocks and "open, this is the police," O'Reilly stays at the apartment while Tate goes down to the first floor to wait for the realtor.

When the realtor arrives, she refuses to let the detectives into the apartment without a search warrant. O'Reilly apologizes to the realtor for taking up her time. They leave the building.

Subsequently, over the next few days, the detectives interview the rest of the names on the list they got from Sally Boris, but nothing new is discovered.

Two more days go by before the financial information of Regina is received. It shows she deposited $5,000 cash into her checking account from time to time. The deposits started about eighteen months ago. A follow-up conversation with her parents reveals no explanation of where the cash could have come.

The search of Regina's apartment and interviews develops no new leads. The large periodic deposits into Regina's account is significant, but the source of the money is not clear yet. O'Reilly decides it's time to talk to Lori Daniels. Maybe she can shed some light on the case.

Because all members of the police squad that worked with Regina Boris are potential suspects in her death, O'Reilly has to get an okay from Captain Lila Brown of Precinct 3 to share some of the case file with Lori Daniels. Brown gives her permission.

O'Reilly calls Sergeant Lori Daniels desk phone.

"Daniels," is heard after the click of a phone receiver being picked up.

"Hi, Lori. This is Carol O'Reilly of the third."

"Hi Carol, what can I do for you?"

"George and I would like to review some items of the Regina Boris case with you. Lila... our captain, Lila Brown, gave us the okay. When would you be available?"

"The sooner, the better, any time today is good."

"Great, we'll be by later this morning.

O'Reilly hangs up.

"I'll sign out the case file. Call the carpool and get us a ride, will ya George?" O'Reilly asks.

Across the desk, Sergeant George Tate looks directly at O'Reilly; he puts down his sandwich; and answers with food in his mouth, "Okay, Carol."

"Eeww, that's disgusting. Next time wait until you're done chewing," O'Reilly complains.

Tate swallows his mouthful of sandwich and calls for a car.

After getting a cup of coffee from the breakroom, Lori Daniels sits at her desk at Precinct 11. From the top of the small stack of file folders on her desk, she grabs the top one and starts finishing the paperwork needed to close it out of the system. The desk phone rings.

Picking up the receiver, "Daniels," is all she says.

The desk sergeant says, "Sergeants O'Reilly and Tate of the third are coming up to see you."

"Thanks." Lori answers.

A few minutes later O'Reilly and Tate are standing at Lori's desk. Lori rises and says, "Good to see you guys. I reserved us a small conference room." Waving her hand, Lori continues, "Right this way. Would either of you like a cup of the worst coffee in the city?"

"I'll have one," Carol says.

"Me too," George adds.

"Okay, we'll go to the coffee station first," Lori says as she leads them over.

"By the way," O'Reilly complains, "I resent the statement about the worst cup of coffee in the city. Precinct 3 holds that honor, at least fifteen years running. Ever since I joined the precinct, anyway."

They all laugh as they pour coffee from the large chrome urn.

O'Reilly gives Lori the low down on all the information uncovered about Regina Boris.

"It's hard to believe that Regina was dirty, but what else would explain the deposits of cash," Lori says solemnly.

"Any cop that turns bad hurts, but one that you worked with for years, really stings," O'Reilly consoles.

"Anything with the chalkboards and chalk. I guess it could just be a red herring," Lori adds.

"Nothing so far," Tate responds.

"Let me make note of the dates of the cash deposits into Regina's bank account. I'll go through my files and see if anything pops," Lori says.

Empty Raid on Fifth Street Gang

The gate opens at the rear of Precinct 11. Out through the gates a police cruiser, two police vans, and then two more cruisers hurry down Whittaker Avenue. This convoy is in a top secret operation. A raid on the suspected main distribution center for the Fifth Street Gang.

The location is a building in the heart of the area covered by Precinct 11. Because of this, only Precinct 11 personnel and the State Police are aware of the raid. Secrecy is the utmost importance to their success. Prior to leaving the Precinct headquarters, the exact location is only known by squad leaders, police Sergeant Lori Daniels, police Sergeant Clyde Macturner, State Police Lieutenant Barbara Maylars, and police Sergeant Raoul Menendez, driver of the lead cruiser. The other vehicles in the convoy are instructed to follow Menendez.

Once within a block of the target, each squad leader tells the van drivers where to deploy. Each of the two following cruisers is assigned to a van.

These are the security measures dictated by State Police Captain Celia Bouton. Some of the local police resent the implication that a police officer may tip off a gang, but the State Police are in charge of the raids, and they make the rules. In response to the complaints by several police precinct captains, State Police Captain Celia Bouton said, "Ruffling egos is not a concern of mine. Getting the bad guys is."

In the first van, Lori is just about to give instructions to her squad. Not having Brenda at her side feels odd. Lori takes a breath and starts.

"Listen up Red Team, this is the first solo raid by Precinct 11 in conjunction with the State Police Task Force. The target is a drug facility being operated by the Fifth Street Gang at a supposedly abandoned building in our district.

Ramirez will be point on the entry. Stetzler and Riccini will hold the door and follow the remainder of the squad guarding our backs. Taylor, Hayden, Morgan, Scott and myself will follow Ramirez. Once the point of entry is secured, Ramirez and Hayden will start the sweep through the rooms, followed by Taylor, Morgan, Scott and I.

As you will recall from the floor plan, we will be entering through double doors into a long corridor with multiple rooms on each side. Each room must be cleared. One officer will search a room while another covers from the doorway. We work in pairs systematically clearing each room along the corridor. Stetzler and Riccini will watch the corridor.

In the other van is the Blue Team. They will be entering from the west entrance and will clear the rooms off the corridor that is perpendicular to our corridor. On the outside patrol officers will be watching all windows and exits.

Stay alert and stay safe."

•　　•　　•　　•　　•

A distinctive alert signal beeps, and the phone vibrates. Bernie Tontas, a tall, overweight man with dyed black hair, narrow eyes and thin pointed nose, swipes the screen of his smartphone. It shows an alert. This alert must be acted on immediately. This alert is also sent to the phones of each of the gang lieutenants that run the drug distribution for the Fifth Street Gang. Bernie Tontas is the righthand man of Mark Turgeson. Turgeson is the boss of the Fifth Street gang. Bernie immediately goes back to his desk. He opens a laptop computer and single clicks an icon. The icon opens a program that shows a map of a simulated diagram of the city streets. All the lieutenants have the same program on their laptops and phones. Bernie likes to use his laptop, because, at 60 years old, the screen on his phone is too small for him to see it properly. The program has a grid of blues lines with the names of each street and avenue. A pulsating red dot travels along the blue lines of the grid. The dot represents a transmitter traveling through the city. This is not any ordinary transmitter. It is a transmitter secretly positioned to let the Fifth Street gang know when a raid is taking place. How this transmitter was put in place is known only to Mark Turgeson and one other person. As the dot starts to head towards one of the gang hideouts, Bernie immediately picks up his phone and places a call.

Richie O'Shea, an Irishman, who immigrated with his parents to the United States when he was 12 years old, is at the other end. He picks up his ringing phone. O'Shea, who also got the alert and is tracking the signal, has already told his men, in his Irish brogue, to quickly evacuate the building. Two of O'Shea's crew are out with deliveries. The remaining four men start taking the boxes of drugs to the loading dock in the rear of the building. A white, unmarked van sits at the loading dock, whenever drugs are at the warehouse. This van is ready to quickly carry the drugs to another location in case of a raid.

Bernie asks O'Shea, "You get the alert?"

O'Shea answers, "Yes, Bernie, for sure. The lads are packin' up the goods as we speak. It'll be gone in a flash. I'll be bringing you the tally sheet and cash straight away."

"Good, bring it to my office and make sure you don't fuck up." Bernie then hangs up.

O'Shea mutters to the quiet phone in his hands, "Ah, foock you too, ya fat ole baustard!"

In O'Shea's office is a steel safe bolted to the floor. The safe has an electronic lock that can only be opened by using his username and an encrypted password. The password has been installed on O'Shea's smartphone. He opens the app on his phone. Types in his username. The encrypted password appears under his username with a log-in button underneath. When he presses "Log-In," the safe opens. He removes all the cash that was collected from that day, and stuffs it in a satchel. At the same time, Bernie gets a notification on his phone that the safe was opened.

This hideout is one of the main distribution centers for the Fifth Street Gang. When given the command, the men know that they are to be packed out and driving away in fifteen minutes or less. Gang Boss Mark Turgeson personally selected them to run such an important center. They are all family men with no drug habits of their own. Their job is to distribute the drugs to the pushers and collect the payments. Turgeson is reasonably confident that they will stay loyal. Not in small part, due to the fact that he knows where their families live, and the men are aware that he knows, too.

Laptops are unplugged, the safe with the money is emptied, and the entire building is now vacant. O'Shea and two of the men drive away in the van while the other two follow in a sedan. The entire process takes 11 minutes.

•   •   •   •   •

No sirens or lights are used by the caravan as they travel through city traffic. Less than 20 minutes after leaving the Precinct, the squads are starting to deploy at the building in preparation for the assault. Lori, commanding Red Team, hurries out of the rear of their van leading her squad. They immediately set up in a defensive position outside the main door at the south side of the building. Through her helmet mike, Lori asks Blue Team leader Sergeant Clyde Macturner if his team is in place.

The helmet mike and cameras are from the state police. All raids conducted under the auspices of the State Police task force must use them. All the audio and video that is recorded can be used as evidence in a court of law. Under a grant by the Federal Government, a pilot program was started in the state. The audio and video footage has proved helpful in obtaining convictions.

After a few seconds, Macturner answers, "We are in position. I repeat. We are in position."

"Then let's do this, go go go!" Lori gives the command.

Officer Bill Hayden, using a pry bar, yanks open one of the double doors. The other door is then swung open freely. Ramirez is the first to enter shouting, "This is the police. Come out with your hands in the air!" This is repeated several times. No one appears in the corridor. Faintly at another end of the building, a similar command is heard being repeated.

The corridor is dimly lit by overhead lights in a shabby looking metal ceiling grid that at one time was painted white. Dingy water has apparently damaged most of the acoustical ceiling tiles. Half of the tiles are missing, and most of the others are cracked, and have rust stains. The walls are made of cheap wood paneling. The floor is vinyl tiles that are all covered with grime. Most of them are cracked.

Stetzler and Riccini position themselves on either side of the entrance doorway. Ramirez and Scott go to the nearest office door adjoining the corridor. The squad quickly goes from room to room following the length of the corridor systematically clearing each. Because they have encountered no gang member yet, they continue yelling the warning to come out with hands in the air as they enter each room.

Most of the rooms are completely empty except for discarded plastic soda bottles, remnants of food wrappers, and assorted garbage. There is an eerie silence as the team progresses. The footfalls of their movements echo down the corridor. Their pace increases as each empty room is cleared.

Towards the back of the building near a loading dock Ramirez suddenly pauses at the door of the last room. He smells the aroma of fresh made coffee wafting through the doorway. He immediately stops and signals Hayden. The other squad members also see his signal and focus their attention on this room.

Moving next to Ramirez at the doorway, Hayden shoulders his automatic rifle in the ready. Ramirez takes a peek and scans the room. He sees that the only place for someone to hide is behind a six-foot-long metal desk at the center. He silently signals Hayden to take a look into the room. After Hayden peers in, Ramirez signals that Hayden is to go around the desk from the left side while he circles to the right. Hayden nods. Taking a deep breath, Ramirez rushes in followed by Hayden. With their rifles pointed, cocked and ready they encircle the desk. No one is there. Then check the leg space underneath the desk. No one is there.

On the desk is an ashtray with several cigarette butts and a laptop power adapter plugged into an extension cord leading to a wall socket. Out of the same socket, a coffee pot is connected. It sits on a shabby bookshelf. The pot is half full and still warm.

Within a few minutes after checking all the rooms, the squad members walk into the corridor with puzzled looks on their faces. Corporal Jason Taylor is the first to speak. "This place was cleared out right before we arrived. It's like someone tipped them off."

With a very concerned look, Lori commands, "Maybe so Jason. You, Ramirez, Scott and Hayden start a sweep of the upper floors. I'll get Blue Team to join you. Remember there still might be perps in the building. Stay alert!"

After talking with Precinct 11 Captain Tony Petracelli, Lori calls in a forensic team to search for clues.

Sergeant Clyde Macturner of the Blue Team walks up to Lori. "What the hell happened?"

Lori shakes her head, "Damned if I know. This was planned with the tightest security."

"Have your team assist Red Team to clear the upper floors," Lori commands.

Macturner sends four officers to join Red Team.

Then Lori notices a couple of pair of parallel lines made in the dust and dirt on the floor. The lines lead from one of the rooms down through the corridor. Staying alert with their weapons ready, Lori and Macturner follow the lines, being careful not to muss them up. Lori and Macturner are led to the loading dock area. The tracks then stop at one of the overhead doors.

An electric garage door opener switch is located to the left of the door. Lori presses the green "UP" button, and the overhead door starts to rise. Macturner is positioned at the right of the door in a crouched position with his rifle ready. The door opens to reveal no people or vehicles in sight. Lori sees a fresh set of tire tracks which was caused by a tire splashing through a small puddle of water near the building. She instructs Macturner to take a picture of the tire track in case it evaporates before the forensic team arrives.

$$\bullet \quad \bullet \quad \bullet \quad \bullet \quad \bullet$$

By the time the forensic team arrives, the search of the upper floors is completed. No contraband or people are found. Lori orders most of the squad members back to the precinct. She tells Sergeant Menendez to get a ride back to the precinct in the van and leave the cruiser for her. Lori plans on staying with the forensic team.

To the forensic team, she says, "Take careful examination of that room, especially the coffee pot. There are also cigarette butts in an ashtray. Maybe a DNA match can be found. Most of the other rooms look like they have not been used in years, but check them out. Don't waste time on the upper floors. The only footprints found up there in the dust are from rats. The rodent kind, not human."

Putting on a pair of latex gloves, Lori first goes into the room with the desk. Officer Cheryl Brown, a forensic tech, is dusting the desk and contents for prints.

"Hi Cheryl, how is married life treating you?" Lori asks.

Brown looks up and smiles, "Hey Lori. Married life is just fine. When are you going to try it?"

Lori stops and ponders, "Ya know, now that you mentioned it. I might be close."

"Well, that's just great. I hope it works out for you. Anybody I know?"

Brown asks.

Lori slyly smiles, "I think you do, but let's leave it at that for now… Have you found anything interesting yet?"

Brown starts opening the drawers of the desk. The first two are empty. Then she opens the bottom drawer on the left. "Huh, look at this!" she says. With her gloved hands, she holds up a small chalkboard and box of chalk and shows them to Lori.

"Look at that. A chalkboard and chalk are odd enough that it could turn out to be significant. " Lori says.

Brown says, "I will keep it near the top."

"Thanks, and if you could make it a priority to get me the results of prints, I'd appreciate it too," Lori adds.

"Ya know, I've found much weirder things over the years. Some of the stuff is totally disgusting," Brown grimaces. "Once, these guys screwed up trying to rob a hotel. They couldn't make a getaway fast enough and ended up holding hostages in a kitchen for ten hours with no bathroom…"

"Enough said, Cheryl, I get the picture," Lori interrupts.

They both laugh.

"I'm going to check around. Let me know if you find anything else out of the ordinary," Lori asks as she moves to the other rooms.

Back at the precinct, State Police Lieutenant Barbara Maylars gets the bad news about the raid from Captain Petracelli.

"Damn, Tony, this proves our suspicions are correct. Corporal Regina Boris was not the only mole being used by the Fifth Street Gang," Maylars says solemnly.

O'Reilly & Tate to Lori

Police Sergeant Carol O'Reilly calls the desk phone of Sergeant Lori Daniels. After two rings it is answered.

"Daniels," is heard in a matter-of-fact tone.

"Hi Lori, this is Carol O'Reilly again."

"Hi Carol, glad you called. I have a little info for you. Hold on, let me get it. I made some notes. Okay, here it is. It took some digging, but

I think I got a lead for you. The large cash deposits you pointed out, well, the dates of the deposits are always a day or two after we conducted a raid on the Fifth Street Gang. A raid, I must point out, that never turns up anything significant. No drugs, no money, and no perps. It's obvious she was tipping them off. If you don't mind, I'm going to share this with Lieutenant Barbara Maylars of the State Police. She's heading the drug enforcement task force here in the city."

O'Reilly says, "I know Barbara. Go right ahead. Hope it helps. Just don't get too far ahead of my investigation."

Daniels answers, "I know what you mean. This was the only bit of info I am sharing with her. One other thing, the chalkboard and chalk you found at Regina's place, well, another chalkboard and box of chalk were found at the raid we made on the Fifth Street Gang. I have no idea what that is about, but I thought you should know."

"That makes two of us. Why would they be writing on chalkboards? Maybe, it's nothing," O'Reilly responds.

Lori hesitates, then says, "My gut feeling says different. That board and chalk lead somewhere. My advice is not to let go of that string."

"I'll keep it near the top of the list, thanks for your help. The tie-in of the raids with the cash deposits Regina made is huge," O'Reilly says.

"Thanks, but in my opinion, the key to the entire case is finding Tito Boris. Alive. He certainly did not torture and kill his sister, which means he's not hiding from the police. I think he's hiding from one of the gangs, probably the Fifth Street Gang. Remember the chalkboard and chalk were found at Regina's apartment and the gang raid. Also the correlation between the money deposits and the raids on Fifth Street. Tito is being hunted by the Fifth Street Gang. Finding him before they do is critical."

O'Reilly pauses, then answers, "That makes sense. Of course, Tito <u>is</u> the key. You've been a great help, Lori. I'll mention your help to my captain."

"Just doin' my job," Lori replies.

"Let me know if anything else pops," O'Reilly asks.

"Will do, and you do the same," Lori then hangs up.

• • • • •

After the phone call, Sergeant Lori Daniels is at her desk doing paperwork and following up on unfinished business. She picks up her coffee cup and takes a sip. Cold.

She heads into the breakroom to get a fresh cup. At the sink, she dumps the cold coffee and rinses the cup. Captain Tony Petracelli walks in and waits for Lori to finish at the sink. She turns then sees Petracelli and says, "Hi cap, how is Veronica doing after the operation?"

"Veronica is doing well. They put her leg in a cast. Now she hobbles around on crutches barking orders to the kids. They now know how good they had it before she broke her leg. She makes them do their own laundry, dust their rooms, vacuum the carpets… Heh, heh, it's like they have been put in boot camp. I love it," Petracelli relates.

Lori smiles and moves aside so Petracelli can rinse his cup out.

She pours a cup from the chrome urn.

Petracelli does the same.

While standing there, Lori asks, "Did you ever get a report on the cause of the explosion at the warehouse during the raid on the Irish Boys? Nothing has come to me."

"Come to think of it, no. Follow up on that and let me know what happens. We should have had that report a week ago. If you are still being stonewalled, I will rattle some cages." Petracelli says.

"Will do, cap."

Lori heads back to her desk and starts making calls. She is told on the phone by the tech, who is writing the report that the explosion was not caused by an accident in the lab. It was an explosive device that was detonated. The tech also tells Lori that it seems the gangs are very worried about the advances in forensic science and detection. With this latest evidence and similar findings from other raids, it is now evident that the gangs are deliberately setting off explosives in an attempt to make evidence gathering that much more difficult.

She reports back to Petracelli. He says, "I'll get this latest information to the Commissioner and the other precinct captains. Having bombs being set off during a raid puts our people in more danger."

CHAPTER NINE
Lori and Brenda Reunite

Lori Daniels and Brenda Cervetti hug each other outside the entrance to JD's Whiskey Buffet. They have not seen each other in a couple of weeks, but to them, it seems like a lot longer.

"I'll buy the first round," Lori says with a smile.

Brenda brings her right hand up pointing the thumb at herself saying, "I'm good with that."

They find a booth near the front door and sit across the table from each other. A waiter comes over and says, "Hi Brenda, Lori, haven't seen you two together in quite a while."

"We were working in different areas," Lori tells him.

"And now we are back together," Brenda adds.

"Hey Rick, you seem to always be our waiter," Lori says smiling. Then with mock seriousness she adds, "You're not spying on us, are you?"

Looking grave, Rick hesitates for a second, and seems to gather his thoughts before saying, "I was hoping I could ask you out, Ms. Daniels."

Lori puts on a sympathetic grin and explains, "Thank you so much, Rick. I am seeing someone right now."

Recovering quickly from the rejection, Rick says, "Oh, well I figured I'd give it a try. What can I get you? A pitcher of lite."

"You know us well, Rick, a pitcher it is," Brenda tells him.

Rick leaves to get their order.

"Aw, you broke his heart," Brenda teases.

"Stop it, Brenda. He probably asks a lot of women out. After all, he sees quite a few in here," Lori says.

Brenda continues her teasing, "Hmmm… I don't know. He did take the time to find out your last name. He must have a pretty good crush on you."

"He's only about 21 years old," Lori then smiles slyly and in a sing-song voice says, "Anyway, I don't need another guy!"

Brenda sits up and looks directly at Lori, "Mike?"

Lori can't help smiling broadly, "He dumped that Elaine. I really think he loves me."

"Well, good for you girl, but please, be very careful. You know your track record," Brenda says cautiously.

"He's the one, Brenda. I realize now, that in the past, I would always settle. Going out with a guy because there might not be anything better coming along. This time I'm not settling. I love Mike, and I am fighting to get him. I think now he feels the same. He showed me the text messages from Elaine and his response. She said some nasty things about me, but I don't care." Lori confides.

Brenda with a confused look says, "You told me that he didn't tell Elaine about you. That you were meeting on the sly. Isn't he lying to you?"

"Maybe he did lie back then, but it's over with Elaine. That's all that matters. Can't you be happy for me?" Lori asks.

"Of course I am happy for you. Here comes the beer. Let's have a toast to real love and no more settling," Brenda proclaims.

Rick put a tray on the table. Takes two glasses one at a time and fills them from the pitcher. Lori and Brenda clink their glasses together and drink.

After emptying a third of the glass, Lori asks, "So, why'd you leave Internal Affairs?"

A bit unsure about how to answer, Brenda says, "I got fed up with your old boyfriend."

"Tom, that son-of-a-bitch. I never told you this, because I didn't think much of it at the time, but when I broke up with him, he threatened to get even by ruining my career. I then find out he has been following me." Lori confesses.

Brenda looks at Lori with a shocked expression, "That bastard! Well, honey, I have a confession I have to make to you. I did not leave Internal Affairs. Exeter put me on an undercover assignment, and get this. My assignment is to watch you and Mike then report back to Exeter. He especially wanted to learn about anything to do with the Fifth Street Gang."

Lori is now the one with the shocked expression, "What!??! He is such a rotten sonofabitch. How did I ever go out with him? ... Ya know, Mike said he suspected Exeter of being the informant for one of the gangs. And another thing, I still see Jimma Koustafus once in a while. You remember Jimma."

Brenda interrupts, "Yeah, I see him too, at his fruit stand."

Lori continues, "Right. Well after I broke up with Tom, Jimma told me about having Tom on his squad years ago and that his career was ruined when Tom planted a wad of money in Jimma's cruiser. Then Tom tells his captain that Jimma took it from a drug suspect." Lori relates to Brenda the entire story that Jimma told her.

"So Exeter is up to his old tricks. He is trying to frame you and Mike," Brenda says. "It will be hard right now proving that Exeter did something years ago, but I do know what we can do."

Lori eagerly asks, "What?"

"Last year the police commissioner set up a workplace harassment counsel to handle complaints. Lila Brown of the 3rd is the chairman. I met her when they were touting this counsel in the news. She came to the 11th on a sort of promotional awareness tour," Brenda explains.

"I remember. I was out of town on a case, so I missed it," Lori says.

"Well, we should see her about Exeter," Brenda encourages.

"I'm in. Let's do it," Lori volunteers.

•   •   •   •   •

Brenda makes a phone call to Captain Lila Brown. After a brief explanation from Brenda about the threat that Tom Exeter made to Lori and about how he then started to follow her, Lila says they should first meet privately away from the office.

Lila suggests an Irish pub near Precinct 3. "The place is a dump, but we can talk without interruptions," she adds.

That evening Lori and Brenda walk into the pub. The place is packed. Lively conversations can be heard coming from the tables and the barroom. They see Lila Brown sitting at a booth waiting for them.

The place is divided in two by a wall of mahogany with etched windows across the upper half. The windows have depictions of the Irish flag and coats-of-arms for Irish clans long forgotten.

On one side of the wall is a bar made of the same wood as the wall. Padded bar stools cover the length of the bar. The stools are old, and most of the seats have tears and cracks. Behind the bar is a large mirror etched with the Irish flag and a motto in the Irish Gaelic language. Liquor bottles line the shelves on each side of the large mirror.

The other side has booths along three walls. Small tables fill the remainder of the room. A corridor at the far end of the bar leads to the restrooms and employee room.

Lila smiles when Lori and Brenda take a seat across the table in the booth. "I didn't order yet. Is beer okay?" Lila asks.

Both Brenda and Lori nod consent.

"Hi, Captain Brown, we never met. My name is Lori Daniels. I'm the one Brenda told you about."

"Call me Lila, please. Sergeant Daniels of the 11th, I have heard of you. All good things, I might add," Lila compliments.

"Thank you, it is nice of you to say," Lori answers.

A young man in his early twenties walks over to the table. He is tall with brown hair and eyes and a slim but muscular body. The women notice immediately that he is wearing tight blue jeans …and eventually, notice his Kelly green shirt. They also observe that the two other waiters are young men in tight jeans.

They order a pitcher of beer. And before they continue the conversation, their eyes follow the waiter back to the bar with a focus on his butt. "Cheap beer is not the only attraction here, Lila," Brenda comments.

They all laugh.

"So, Lori, tell me the story again. I heard Brenda's version, but I want to hear it from you," Lila says. Captain Lila Brown is a smart cop who rose through the ranks 20 years in a male-dominated profession. She knows to how to run an investigation and the tendencies of people to exaggerate, misinterpret and also lie. She wants Lori to re-tell her complaint about Tom Exeter. This way she can look for inconsistencies from the version Brenda told her over the phone.

Lori relates the story about her break-up with Exeter. Exeter following her to the fruit market. Mike Costner suspecting Exeter of being the informant. Jimma Koustafus accusing Exeter of planting money in the cruiser. "Then Brenda tells me, she has been assigned back to the 11th to spy on me with the probable intent to frame me as being an informant to a gang," Lori concludes.

Lila thinks for a few seconds, then tells them, "You have very little to go on. Koustafus told you Exeter followed you, but you did not see him yourself, Lori. Costner suspects Exeter, but offers no proof. Just suspicions. Koustafus says Exeter planted the money, but again no proof. Brenda is assigned an undercover role to watch Lori for suspicious activity, but maybe Exeter has a legitimate reason for doing it. I'm not saying you are an informant, but maybe Exeter is acting on info he received.

Having said that, I will open a confidential file on Exeter under the auspices of the workplace harassment counsel. Lori, make note of any and all contact you have with Exeter. Whether it is in the line of duty or casual, it does not matter. I will get an affidavit from Koustafus about witnessing Exeter at the fruit stand. Brenda to help Lori, let me know of any directives you get from Exeter. I know you are working undercover, but this official counsel investigation will protect you from being accused of divulging confidential information. That is the best I can do right now. I will assign a couple detectives from Precinct 3 to follow up on this complaint. You will be hearing from them soon.

Lori replies, "You're right Lila. Most of what we got is considered hearsay and circumstantial. We need more solid evidence."

"You are as smart as I've been told, Lori. Yes, this is equivalent to a criminal case, hard evidence carries the day," Lila compliments.

For the next half hour, they don't talk about the complaint, but have small talk and finish the pitcher of beer, while watching the waiters walk back and forth serving other tables.

•   •   •   •   •

The next day Captain Brown assigns Detective Sergeant Morgan Indigo and Sergeant Louis McCrew to investigate the complaint against Captain Tom Exeter. Their first task is to interview Lori Daniels and Brenda Cervetti. Next, they interview Jimma Koustafus and get him to sign an affidavit stating that he saw Captain Tom Exeter following Lori Daniels to his fruit stand.

Investigation of Regina Boris Continues

Detective Sergeant Carol O'Reilly takes the third box of evidence gathered from the apartment of slain Police Corporal Regina Boris and plops it down next to her desk.

Sitting across from her at his desk, Sergeant Detective George Tate is opening a pack of chocolate cupcakes with white icing and is about to bite down on one.

O'Reilly and Tate are frustrated because Regina's brother, Tito Boris, has not been found yet and the case seems to be going very cold.

"Are those the cream filled ones?" O'Reilly asks.

"Yep," is all Tate answers.

"Care to share, Sergeant," O'Reilly presses, as she begins examining the contents of the box.

"Nope," is all Tate answers again, as he takes the second bite, which consumes the remainder of the first cupcake. Then he smiles a "Cheshire Cat" smile.

O'Reilly frowns, "You're getting too fat, ya know that."

"Flattery will get you nowhere," Tate quotes as he starts on the second cupcake.

Still frowning, O'Reilly complains, "Well, use up some of those excess calories and help me look through this stuff."

Tate gets off his chair and walks around to O'Reilly's desk. He reaches down and grabs two armfuls of items then returns to his desk. He immediately picks up the last cupcake and takes a bite.

"Disgusting," O'Reilly says under her breath, but loud enough for Tate to hear.

Tate smiles again and looks through the pile of stuff he just got out of the box.

A little while later Tate finds a travel mug and holds it up to O'Reilly. "Look at this," he says to O'Reilly.

"A mug from Starbucks[13]. Hmmm… you're thinking maybe she went to Starbucks a lot so she bought a mug. And maybe she frequented a particular Starbucks. And maybe she met the guy she faked orgasms with there," O'Reilly conjectures.

Tate shrugs his shoulders and says, "Maybe."

After running a search online, they find out that there are 17 Starbucks within a quarter mile of Precinct 11 and 5 within a half mile of the apartment. They then call the motor pull for a car and get started.

They spend five days showing her picture to all the work shifts for all the Starbucks in the vicinity of her apartment and Precinct 11. Some employees only work one or two days a week and at different times of the day. They eventually talk to 134 employees including managers and assistant managers. Finally, they find the place Regina visited almost every day. Two employees recognize her photo, Lamar Alderman and Latisha Hendricks.

At a small table in the coffee shop, they speak to Latisha Hendricks first. A medium height Caucasian girl in her late teens with a dragon tattoo at her neck and a nose ring. "Well, she is a very nice cop. Always courteous and always puts her change in the tip cup. Is she in trouble for somethin'?" Latisha asks.

"She's dead. It was in the news. She was tortured and beaten to death. Then her body was thrown into the river," Tate responds matter-of-factly.

The bluntness of his statement had the effect on Latisha that Tate wanted. Wide-eyed, she says, "Oh my god! That's horrible! Who could have done that!"

"That is what we are hoping you can help us with," O'Reilly answers.

Starting to tear up, because of the shock, Latisha says, "Me? What can I do?"

O'Reilly continues, "Tell us, did she ever meet anyone here."

Latisha calms a bit, "Well, let me think. It was only once that I saw. This guy comes up to the counter and asks about Regina by name. It was after we had just opened at 6:00 AM. I told him that she usually shows up about 7:30. He said he'd be back."

"Did the guy leave a name?" O'Reilly asks.

"Nope"

"What did this guy look like?"

"Well, let's see, blond guy, tall, business type. Ya know the guy who looks like he has spent a lot of time at a desk. Starting to get soft. We get them in here all the time. ," Latisha says.

"Any personal identifying characteristics," Tate asks.

Latisha looks at Tate and mutters, "Huh?"

"Any tats, scars, maybe a lisp, anything we could use to identify him," O'Reilly says as she secretly smirks at Tate. Tate, just a secretly, flips a middle finger at O'Reilly.

Latisha thinks for a few seconds then says, "Well, he had a coat and tie, he didn't look at my boobs when he talked to me, most guys do, ya know," she points at Tate, "like him, and he talked like his shit was ice cream."

Trying not to laugh, O'Reilly leans towards Latisha asking, "How so? Like what did he do?"

"Well, using big words." Latisha changes her voice to sound deeper and continues, "*It is the utmost importance, Grave consequences*, stuff like that."

"What happened next?" O'Reilly asks.

"Well, a little later Regina comes in as usual. I tell her about mister softy. She seemed worried after that. Having coffee at the table she would keep looking up from her phone then back down to her phone then look up again..."

Tate interrupts and says impatiently, "Okay, okay she's nervous. Then what?"

Latisha stops talking and gives Tate the "you talkin' to me" look.

"George, get us some coffee, will ya please?" O'Reilly pleads.

Tate gets up from the table saying, "Yeah, Yeah," and goes to the counter.

"Sorry about that, Latisha. Please, continue," O'Reilly apologizes.

"You should find yourself a new partner. That man is rude."

"Maybe so, but we've been partners so long he's kind of like an old pet dog. He has accidents once in a while, but he listens well," O'Reilly muses.

Latisha laughs, "I like you."

"Thanks, now what about Regina?"

"Well, this guy shows up and sits down at Regina's table without askin'. He shows her his badge..."

"He has a badge!??!" O'Reilly interrupts.

Latisha looks surprised, "Oh, yeah, I almost forgot. He had a badge."

"Was it a city police badge?" O'Reilly asks.

"I guess so. He kept askin' one question after another. Gettin' up in my face. So I gave him some 'tude" and told him to look it up on Wikipedia! That's when he yanks it out. It was in one of those small wallet things. He flips it open to show me. One side has a badge. The other side has a license or something with his picture and big letters IAD on it," Latisha replies.

"Would you recognize the man, if you saw him again?"

"Yep," Latisha answers.

"So what happened next?" O'Reilly urges.

"Well, Regina looks scared. They talk a bit. Next thing I know the two of them are leavin' together."

"Together, you're sure," O'Reilly pushes.

"Yep, he held the door for her and they walked out and passed the window together," Latisha explains.

"Is your manager here?" O'Reilly asks.

"What the heck! What'd I do!" Latisha says defensively.

"Oh, sorry, you did nothing wrong. In fact, you have been very helpful. Thank you. I notice the store has several surveillance cameras. I want to ask your manager if there is video of the day you saw the guy,"

O'Reilly explains.

Latisha becomes more relaxed, "Am I really that helpful, wow!"

"Yes, you are. Is a manager here?"

Latisha smiling proudly says, "Yep, she's here. I'll get her for you." She jumps up from the chair and hurries to the coffee counter. After speaking with a girl about her own age, Latisha returns. "She'll be right over."

Less than a minute later a woman in her early twenties sits at the table. She is African American, average height, dark hair with tight braids, "Hi, Latisha says you are a cop and you want to view videos from the surveillance."

"That's right. What's your name?" O'Reilly says.

"Nancy, Nancy Cavanaugh, I'm sure it will be okay. We've done it before for the police. Come on back to the office, I'll call the general manager,"

Tate comes back with the coffees. Sits at the table. Looks at Latisha and Nancy then at O'Reilly, "So, what'd I miss?" he asks.

•   •   •   •   •

The manager gives her okay and allows them to view the video at the store. Nancy Cavanaugh sets up the video for viewing in the small coffee shop office. She shows O'Reilly how to run the video. She then tells Latisha to stay with the officers and she will cover Latisha's work at the coffee bar.

O'Reilly is sitting at the small counter that has the video equipment. Standing behind her is Tate and Latisha. The video speedily goes through the hours of the day until it reaches the timeline described by Latisha, then O'Reilly slows it down. Once the video shows Regina, O'Reilly lets it run at normal speed.

It shows Regina getting her coffee and sitting at a table. A little later a man sits at the table but his back is to the camera. After a brief discussion during which Regina looks visibly upset, the two get up to leave. The image of the man appears on the screen. O'Reilly stops the video on his image. Both she and Tate recognize him.

"Latisha, please, get your manager in here. I want to ask her for a copy of the video," O'Reilly asks.

"Sure," Latisha leaves and returns with Nancy.

"Not a problem. We do it all the time. I will call our tech people and have a copy made. It will be at our main office. Do you want it mailed or will you pick it up?" Nancy asks.

"Pick it up. Thanks for all your help," O'Reilly says.

Back in their car, O'Reilly calls Captain Lila Brown to tell her of the video.

"Can you get a copy today?" Brown asks.

"Yes, we are headed to the main office now." O'Reilly answers.

"Good, bring it back to my office," Brown says.

•   •   •   •   •

A few hours later, back at the precinct, Captain Brown, O'Reilly, and Tate are standing behind a technician, Officer Merion Timberlake, in a small conference room at Precinct 3. The tech speeds through the timeline as O'Reilly did at the coffee shop. Eventually, the image of Regina and the man getting up from the table appears.

"Stop it there," Brown commands. "Well, well, well. That is none other than Captain Thomas Exeter, department head of Internal Affairs. I will have to call the Police Commissioner on this. For now, this information is classified. Do not divulge to anyone what we just saw. Do I make myself clear!"

All answer in the affirmative.

•   •   •   •   •

With a copy of the video in hand Captain Lila Brown meets with Police Commissioner, Marylin Rhodes, at the downtown central offices.

"That is definitely Exeter on the video," Rhodes says as they view it in the executive conference room.

Before Brown can say anything, a knock is heard at the conference room door and an assistant to the commissioner sticks his head into the room. "Commissioner, something has just broke on the news that you should see."

"I'm tied up right now, Jordon. I'll handle it later," Rhodes says a bit testily.

"My apologies commissioner, but it is about Captain Tom Exeter," the assistant insists.

The assistant goes to the podium. Presses a few buttons and the video they were viewing of the coffee shop disappears. In its place is an identical video playing on a local news television station. The voice of a reporter is heard,"… this is an exclusive from City 4 News. This reporter has uncovered a break in the death of Police Corporal Regina Boris. This video is from a local coffee shop on the day before Regina is reported missing from duty. In the video, a man is seen talking to Officer Regina Boris and then leaving with her. Sources close to the situation identify the man, you see here, as Police Captain Thomas Exeter. The official records list Exeter as the head of Internal Affairs for the city police department…"

"This has now turned into an official shit storm," Rhodes moans. No one in the room says anything for a few seconds while Rhodes gathers her thoughts. "The press is going to be all over this. We've got to handle it strictly by the book. Lila because the death of Regina Boris is being handled by your Precinct, have a couple of your detectives go to Exeter's office and bring him in for questioning. Jordon gets the DA on the phone for me. I'll have him get a search warrant for Exeter's office and home."

CHAPTER TEN
Capture of Tito Boris

Hearing Regina's screams is upsetting to Tito, but not upsetting enough to have him go back and see Bernie Tontas. He reasons, "They need Regina. Heck, the screams were probably fake anyway. Just a ruse to get him to come back. Regina is okay. And anyway she is the one who got him involved with the Fifth Street Gang. She knows what kind of people they are. She got herself into this mess. He was just trying to make a few dollars on the side, not steal money from them. So the plan went south, that's no reason for him to die. Regina is okay. She always takes care of me. She won't rat me out.

Tito decides to drop in on an old girlfriend, Melanie Bingham, who now lives near Harrisburg. He remembers she got a job working as a dealer in a casino north of the city. She gradually becomes annoyed with him because he never wants to go out, stays in the apartment all day, and keeps closing the window shades. She eventually kicks him out. "What the fuck, Tito! You've turned into some freakin' vampire. Get the hell out!"

That is when he remembers his uncles hunting cabin in Potter County. It is totally secluded in the middle of nowhere. Bernie Tontas will never find me there.

Driving north through State College, he stops at a convenience store to get gas. At the gas pump, he checks his wallet to take stock of his money, $170.00 in cash and a credit card. He tries to remember how much he has left of the $10,000 credit limit. Tito usually pays the minimum balance, but he figures that at least $1500 is still available. Tito is wrong. His cash is low so he decides to only use the credit card until the credit line is exhausted. That should get him enough gas and groceries to hold out at the cabin for a few weeks. By then he'll decide what to do. Right now hiding is all he wants to think about.

He slides the car into the gas pump. At the prompt, he acknowledges the card is credit not debit. He then types in his zip code. The monitor tells him to pick up the pump handle and press a button for the grade of gas. The car tank fills with gas.

•   •   •   •   •

Within fifteen seconds a text alert hits the cell phone of Sergeant Carol O'Reilly of the city police. Carol and Sergeant George Tate are leading the investigation of Tito's sister, Regina. Tito is a person of interest in the death of Regina. Because of this, a BOLO (Be On the Look Out) was issued for him, and a judge granted a search warrant on Tito which included his financials.

From the financial investigation, it was discovered that Tito had three credit cards. Two were maxed out, and payments had not been made in three months. A third credit card was still active with a credit limit of $213.48 remaining. Minimum payments have been made on this card for the past four months.

The text alert O'Reilly received is from the security department of the credit card company that Tito's card is being used. O'Reilly calls the credit card security department. It takes fifteen minutes waiting on the line for her to get the information she wanted. The department tells her that the card was used in State College, PA.

O'Reilly then calls the State College Police Department. It takes 10 minutes for her to get through to a desk sergeant for help. O'Reilly explains the situation to the desk sergeant and gives him the BOLO identification number. To speed up the process, she also faxes a copy of the description of Tito and his car to the number given to her by the desk sergeant.

O'Reilly receives a call 30 minutes later from the desk sergeant that the State College Police would investigate and look for Tito and the car.

Tito replaces the gas pump handle. He then closes the gas tank lid of his car and gets into his car and takes a right turn out of the convenience store parking lot. He immediately comes to a traffic signal and turns right on Atherton Street. After about a quarter mile he turns left into the parking lot of a grocery store.

Near the entrance to the store, he grabs a small shopping cart and makes his way through the store aisles. Tito by-passes the produce section. At frozen foods, he gets five frozen pizzas, five boxes of frozen jalapeno poppers, three half gallons of ice cream, and a bag of frozen corn.

His next stop if for beer and wine. In the bottom of the small shopping cart, he tries to fit five cases of Coors[7]. That is when he realizes he needs a bigger cart. Cursing under his breath, he leaves the small cart in an aisle and goes to the front of the store to get a larger cart. Back in the beer section, he loads the cases of Coors on the bottom of the cart. He then grabs five gallons of Carlo Rossi[8] Burgundy and places them on the beer. Next, he unloads the contents of the small cart into the big cart.

Tito starts to push the shopping cart and realizes it is very heavy. It takes all his effort to get the cart moving. As he heads to the checkout, he sees that the cash register with the fewest people is the "15 item or less" line. He cuts in front of an elderly woman carrying a loaf of bread. This allows Tito to be the second in line.

"That's very rude of you," the elderly woman complains to Tito.

"The early bird catches the worm, lady," Tito replies.

She frowns and says, "That makes no sense, and you have more than fifteen items, too."

"Live with it, grandma. I'm in a hurry," Tito tells her as he starts unloading the cart on to the conveyor belt. He leaves the beer in the cart.

When it is his turn to check out, he holds up the side of a case of beer for the cashier to scan the UPC code. "Four cases," he lies.

The cashier is a teenage girl with a stud in each cheek of her face and a silver circlet in the left nostril. One side of her head is shaved. The other side has her hair dyed with purple ends. A tattoo of a geometric repeating shape encompasses her neck. She has rings on all fingers and thumbs. Her name tag says, Marla.

With perfect diction and a slight Pittsburgh accent, Marla says, "Four cases, plus the one in your hand. Is that correct sir?"

Tito looks at her with disgust, "Yeah," is all he says.

"Is plastic okay, sir?" she asks.

"Yeah," he nods.

Holding up a gallon jug of wine, Marla asks, "Would you like these bottles in a bag?"

With a smirk, he says, "Yeah, I want everything in bags. And put them into my cart, too."

Marla gives Tito a fake smile and walks away from the register to his cart and loads all the items. When she returns to the register, Marla asks, "Do you have a bonus card?"

"No," Tito replies.

She presses one button then says, "That will be $247.89."

Tito takes out his wallet and puts the chip end of the card in the scanner.

"Debit or credit, sir."

"Credit"

A quick double beep is heard and on the small screen at the card reader in red lettering the words "NOT APPROVED" appears.

Marla hits a couple of buttons on the register then says, "There seems to be a problem. Please, try that again, sir."

Tito frowns as he pulls his card from the reader and re-inserts it.

Marla hits a couple of buttons again. The double beep is heard again, and the "NOT APPROVED" pops up on the screen. "Sorry sir, the card is still not working. Do you have another card?"

"No, I don't have another card," Tito snaps at her. "This card has plenty of money on it."

"Yes, sir. Please, try it again," she asks.

He does with the same results. The line behind Tito is now five people deep. Murmured complaints can be heard.

Turning red Tito realizes he does not have enough cash. He says, "Okay, how much is the beer and wine only."

Marla goes back to his cart and removes the bags of food. Placing them on the chrome counter at the end of the conveyor, she presses a couple more buttons on the register and starts to scan each item. The dollar total starts to come down. An assistant manager with the name tag "Bob" shows up and starts to help Marla unbag the items.

When the task is done, Marla says, "$152.36... , sirrr." The sir is said drawn out sarcastically.

Tito puts the card into the reader. It shows "Approved," and he signs the screen.

Handing Tito the receipt, Marla asks, "Do you still want the food?"

"Yeah, I'll pay for it in cash," Tito mumbles.

"For the love of mike!" a man's voice is heard from the line behind Tito. He ignores it.

"95.53," is all Marla says.

While he pays her and gets his change, Bob, the assistant manager, has already re-bagged the groceries and has them in his cart.

When Tito reaches his car and starts to unpack the groceries, he curses, "Fuck, fuck, fuck. I forgot to get a cooler and ice."

Twenty minutes later he is back at his car with a large Styrofoam cooler and two bags of ice. Loading the frozen items in the cooler, he then dumps the ice on top. On top of the layer of ice puts 12 cans of beer. As he gets back into his car and he sees a police cruiser pulling into the parking lot on the south side. The cruiser has two officers. It is slowly going down the lanes between lines of cars, and it looks like they are checking license plate numbers. Tito pulls out of his stall and heads out of the lot at the north end. The police cruiser continues its search and does not follow him.

About a quarter mile from the grocery store, Tito reaches into the cooler and gets out a beer. He pops open the tab and takes a swig. The cold liquid is refreshing, and he takes a couple more gulps. He smiles. For the first time today, he feels good.

Forty-five minutes later he is on PA Route 144 heading north. The route meanders through large portions of uninhabited forest and mountains in north-central Pennsylvania. Tito has been driving eight hours and has not seen an oncoming car in over an hour. Route 144 has dense forest on each side with no major towns and, because it is night, it is pitch black.

Sparsely populated villages line the route. Usually consisting of a handful of homes and maybe a gas station that also sells a few groceries. The customer base is not high enough to attract the convenient store chains. At this late hour, no lights shine from any windows.

Not ten miles past such a village, Tito turns left onto a dirt lane that has a small sign on a post. The sign reads, "Easy Street" and has a green painted mailbox on a four by four wooden post. Having finished his tenth beer, Tito stops the car at the entrance to the lane. He throws a beer can out the window into the woods, as he has done with every empty can on this trip. He gets out of the car. Unzipping his pants, he spreads his legs apart and takes a piss.

Back in his car, he drives up the dirt lane. Although the lane is wide enough for one vehicle, branches of trees still swipe the side of Tito's car from time to time. Small utility poles line the right side of the lane spaced at even intervals. After driving about 500 feet, he stops in front of a six hundred square foot cabin with a stone chimney at one end. As he gets out of the car, he leaves the headlights on to illuminate the front door of the cabin.

Tito has not been here in over a decade, but he remembers that his uncle Al kept a key behind a piece of loose porch board to the right of the entrance door. Prying up the board, Tito sees that the area under the loose board is pitch black. He sticks his hand down into the blackness to try and feel for the keys. Something tiny and sharp hits his finger. He immediately jerks his hand out and tumbles backward on his ass. He curses himself for not having a flashlight.

Getting back into his car, he turns off the car beams. Tito decides to sleep in the car until morning. Reclining his driver's seat, he passes out.

• • • • •

Tito is running down the street dodging in and out of the slow moving traffic. Then he realizes he is going back to save Regina. Stopping in the middle of the street, he wonders why he is doing this. Regina can take care of herself. He hears his name being called. As he turns, Bernie Tontas is aiming a pistol at him. Bernie fires and the pistol sounds like a rapid-fire machine gun. Tito starts to run, but his leg smashes into something hard.

Hitting his knee on the steering wheel and the tapping of a woodpecker wakes Tito from his dream. Looking out of the car window, he can see the sky starting to lighten. The woodpecker begins another volley of rapid tapping on a tree. Tito can't see which tree. Cursing the pain in his leg, he puts his driver's seat in the upright position. His mouth is dry, and then he remembers the beer he bought the day before.

He opens the cooler sitting on the passenger's seat. Looking inside, he sees the cooler is full of water. He reaches in and searches around for a beer. His hand pushes against a soggy object that collapses immediately coloring the water to a brown liquid cloud. Toto curses again. He realizes that the chocolate ice cream has thawed and he collapsed the box it was in. Now it has mixed into the water from the melted ice. Pulling his hand out, he gets the urge to take a piss, real bad. Drying his wet, cold hand on his pants, Tito gets out of the car. He unzips his pants and quickly reaches in to find his dick. He has to go very bad. When his cold hand grabs his dick, the shock startles Tito, and he involuntarily starts to pee in his pants. "Fucking Eh!" he cries. Although he stopped peeing quickly, his pants are soaked, so he lets them fall to his ankles.

Because he is not in his car which muffled the sound, the next foray of woodpecker tapping sounds much much louder. It scares Tito, and he falls on his back with the pants at his ankles. The jarring of the fall causes him to begin peeing again, this time soaking his shirt.

"Faaauck! Shut up," Tito screams at the woodpecker.

He gets up to finish peeing. Then he walks around to the passenger side of the car. Opening the door, he again reaches into the cooler. Swishing his hand around the light brown liquid, he comes in contact with a beer can. He pulls the can out and pops the tab, taking a big gulp of cold beer. "At least the beer is still cold," he thinks. After emptying the can, he starts to feel better.

Opening his trunk, he gets out dry clothes and socks from his bag. After changing clothes, Tito then walks to the front porch of the cabin and inspects the space under the loose floorboard. He sees the key for the cabin door hanging on the sharp end of a nail that was hammered through a floor joist. "That is what nicked me last night," he thinks.

The front door is flanked by two double hung windows. He uses the key in the door lock and goes inside. A wide room taking up about half the size of the cabin greets him. The place is very rustic. Overhead the roof beams and sheathing is visible. At the wall on the right is a cast iron wood-fired stove in front of a stone hearth and chimney. The flue pipe from the stove connects to the stone chimney. Three old time-worn sofas form a "U" around the stove. Several old standing lamps are on each end of the sofas. The floor is wooden planks. A thin layer of dust is over everything.

At the back wall is a wooden table with eight chairs. Only three of the chairs match. All the rest are a variety of old chrome with padded seats or dining room style chairs made of wood. To the left of the table is a small cabinet with a deep sink which has a gooseneck spout but no faucets. Two fluorescent light fixtures hang from a ceiling rafter over the table. Also on this wall are two doors, one at each end and a small gray electric panel. Tito walks to the panel and flicks on the main switch to turn on the electric power. Two of the standing lamps come on.

He then goes to the door on the left. This opens into the newest part of the cabin. A small addition with fiberglass insulated walls. The paper of the insulation is exposed. A small sink is attached to a wall at one end with a five-gallon water storage tank above it. A commode is at the other wall. An empty two-gallon plastic bucket sits next to the commode. The bucket gets filled with water and is used to flush the commode.

At the left wall is a pair of doors leading to two bedrooms. A large six-foot tall cabinet sits between the doors. Each bedroom has a pair of bunk beds. "Damn it," he mumbles as he notices the small refrigerator and microwave oven are missing. They used to be next to the tall cabinet.

Tito throws a switch at the left of the sink. The switch activates a pump down the hill along a stream. After a few seconds, a gurgling sound is heard then water starts flowing from the gooseneck spout at the sink. Tito fills the plastic bucket sitting next to the commode and pours some of it into the storage tank above the restroom sink. He then refills the bucket and leaves it at the commode.

He goes back outside to his car and removes the cooler. Dumping out all the brown water he curses because all the food he bought is soaking wet and ruined. He dumps the contents of the cooler on the ground and leaves it there. From the back seat, he gets the remainder of the beer and takes it into the cabin.

He then hops into the car and drives back down the dirt lane with the intention of going to the village just south on route 144. There is a gas station that also has a small store in the village.

Tito arrives fifteen minutes later and pulls into one of the four parking stalls in front of the store. No other cars are there. He walks through the single glass and wood door. A bell on a spring announces his entrance.

"Do you have a phone I can use?" Tito asks the store clerk, a tall, lanky boy in his late teens wearing jeans and a tee shirt resembling a Pittsburgh Steeler jersey. The teenager is standing near the cash register playing a game on his phone.

"Are you staying somewhere around here?" the teenage boy asks.

"At Al Cernobyl's cabin. Just up the highway," Tito tells him.

"Yeah, I know Al. Really a nice guy," the teenager replies.

"He's my uncle," Tito says. "Al should be coming up in a couple days," he lies.

The teenager reaches down under the counter. Tito jerks with fright and backs away a bit. When an old black phone appears in the clerk's hand, Tito relaxes. Gabbing the phone, Tito pulls the phone cord as far away from the counter as possible. "It's a very private call," he tells the teenager.

It takes three rings for the phone to be answered. "Hello," his father answers.

"Dad, I need your help."

"Tito, where the hell are you? Regina is dead. The police have been here asking about you. What have you been up to?" Mr. Boris starts to cry.

"Regina is dead!" Tito turns white. "Dad, dad, please, believe me, I had nothing to do with Regina being killed," Tito pleads.

"How did you know Regina was killed?" his father accuses. "I <u>knew</u> you were involved. Give yourself up to the police," Mr. Boris demands.

"I can't, dad. The same people who killed Regina are going to kill me. I need money," Tito tries to explain.

"No money, Tito. You've gone too far this time. No money. I'm hanging up and calling the police. Give yourself up," Mr. Boris says as he hangs up.

Tito is stunned. He slowly walks back to the counter with the phone in his hand. His mind starts to jump around thinking of ways to get some money. He begins to case the store. Looking around, he sees two surveillance cameras, one pointed at the entrance and one pointed at the cash register. A plan to rob the store starts to take seed.

However, for now, Tito is hungry, and he also wants a cold beer. He walks the aisles of the little convenience store. He grabs two bags of corn chips, a jar of salsa, five beef jerkies and three packages of cupcakes.

He puts all the items next to the cash register.

The clerk asks, "Will that be all sir."

"I'm going to get a bag of ice, too," Tito tells him.

After the items are totaled, the clerk says, "That'll be $22.49 plus $1.35 for the governor. Total $23.84."

While the clerk bags the food, Tito takes out his credit card and swipes it on the card reader.

"Debit or credit?" the clerk asks.

"Credit," Tito answers while staring anxiously at the small screen on the reader.

The clerk taps two buttons on the register. "APPROVED" appears. Tito gives a small sigh of relief.

"Would you like your receipt?"

Tito does not seem to hear the clerk as he grabs his bags and hurries out to his car. He then walks back to the large ice cooler with the two chrome doors that sits near the front entrance of the store. He opens one of the doors. Tito glances above the top of ice cooler and sees the clerk playing a game on his phone. Tito then grabs three bags of ice and scurries to his car.

Sitting at the precinct, Sergeant Carol O'Reilly is talking with her husband on her desk phone. "Yes, I will be home at a reasonable hour," ...a pause... "Spaghetti sounds great," ...a pause... "Yes, definitely, wine tonight and some very personal time for the two of us, too honey," ...a pause... "I love you too." O'Reilly's cell phone text alert sounds. She looks at it, then says, "Sorry babe gotta go. See you later."

The text is another alert from the security department of the credit card company with whom Tito Boris has an account. She immediately dials their number. This time it only takes 5 minutes to get a person on the line. O'Reilly is told that Tito's credit card was used at a small gas station on route 144 between Carter Camp and Galeton Pennsylvania.

By this time O'Reilly's partner, Sergeant George Tate, has returned to his desk. "Do you know where Camp Carter or Galeton is?" she asks Tate.

"Are they in Pennsylvania?" Tate questions.

"Never mind, hand me your map of PA," O'Reilly tells Tate.

Tate gets the map out of his drawer and hands it to O'Reilly. She unfolds it and checks the index of towns and municipalities. The grid number is P-5. She finds section P-5 is in Potter County.

"George do you know where Potter County is?" O'Reilly asks.

"Near Hogwarts?" Tate jokingly responds.

O'Reilly smiles, "May as well be."

After making a phone call to Regina's father and asking if he knows of anywhere in Potter County that Tito could be, she is told that his brother-in-law, Albert, has a hunting cabin. He also tells her about the call from Tito and that Tito knew about Regina being killed.

Back at her desk, she says to Tate, "Pack your bag, tomorrow we may be going on a road trip to Hogwarts. It might be an overnighter."

"Really, Potter County. Who the hell does Tito know up there?" Tate asks.

"Uncle's hunting cabin. I'll requisition us a couple rifles from the armory," O'Reilly says with all seriousness.

"Dorothy is not going to like this," Tate says.

O'Reilly says, "Yeah, Barry is always worried about me heading into harm's way, too."

Tate smirks, "Huh, harm's way, ah no. Dorothy is worried about me in an overnighter with you."

"Gag me with a spoon," is all O'Reilly answers.

Detective Carol O'Reilly walks over to Captain Lila Brown's office. The door is open, but O'Reilly knocks anyway as she enters.

Brown looks up from her desk and greets her, "Hi Carol. How is the Boris case coming?"

"We just got a hot lead on the whereabouts of Tito, Regina's brother," O'Reilly tells her.

Brown takes her hand off the computer mouse she is using and gives O'Reilly her full attention. Pointing to a wooden chair in front of her desk "Here, Carol, have a seat. What is the lead?"

O'Reilly takes a seat and says, "We got a hit that Tito's credit card was just used at a store on Route 144 in Potter County."

Brown frowns, "Is that in Pennsylvania?"

O'Reilly smiles, "Yes, cap. It's way north of State College. Tate referred to it as bum-fuck-egypt. Well, Tito's uncle has a hunting cabin near the place where we just got the hit on his credit card."

"And because of the time it took to have the local police respond to the hit in State College, you want to go there to get him yourself," Brown surmises.

"Yes, cap. George and I. Getting Tito alive before the mob gets him is vital to solving Regina's case. It is about a five and a half hour drive. We may have to stay overnight," O'Reilly explains.

"Dorothy is not going to like this," Brown says matter-of-factly.

"Geez!" is all O'Reilly says.

Brown grins and shakes her head, "I know. George has got to be one of the most unattractive men I ever met. But Dorothy is insanely jealous of all the women in the precinct." Brown continues, "That area seems pretty desolate. I'll give a call to Celia Bouton at the State Police. She owes me a couple favors. I'll get you two some back up if you need it."

"Thanks, cap."

•   •   •   •   •

The next day, Tate and O'Reilly meet at the precinct at 6:00 AM for the five and a half hour drive to Potter County. After drinking a 22-ounce cup of coffee, Tate has to make three "pit stops" before they get to Camp Carter on route 144.

They stop at a small diner to get some lunch before continuing north. The diner's name is "The Pine Needle." It is a small wood structure freshly painted light green. Three steps lead to a small front porch. A single glass door is the entrance off the porch. A sign on the door says "Handi-cap Accessible Entrance is in The Rear." Tate finds out later that the accessible entrance is through the kitchen.

The inside of the diner is one long room. A full-length counter is on the left and four tables with four chairs at each is on the right. The two sit at the counter. O'Reilly orders a turkey club, no fries or chips, and a seltzer water. Tate orders two burgers, an order of fries and a root beer.

While waiting for their food they identify themselves and show an enlarged driver's license photo of Tito Boris to the two waitresses, the cook, and four customers. No one recognizes the picture or remembers seeing Tito's car.

Back in their unmarked police cruiser, they travel north until they come upon the gas station where Tito used his credit card the day before. They pull into one of the two empty parking spots. As previously arranged by Police Captain Lila Brown, a State Police interceptor is parked in one of the other stalls. Tate waves to the two officers in the interceptor then he and O'Reilly get out.

They are met by State Police Sergeant John Dewars and Officer Rhianna Bailey. The four shake hands and introduce themselves. Dewars says, "Rhianna and I were sent from the Coudersport Barracks, Throop F. We're familiar with this area. In fact, I have met Al Cernobyl and been to his cabin. He had some vandalism a few years back. I investigated it."

"That is great. Since you are familiar with the layout, if you don't mind, we will let you set up the strategy for approaching the cabin," O'Reilly says.

"Not a problem, I was going to suggest that," Dewars replies. "What can you tell us about Tito Boris?' he adds.

O'Reilly shakes her head saying, "Not much. He has been in and out of jail a couple times for B & E and drug possession. Nothing violent. But I got a bad feeling about this guy. We should consider him armed and dangerous until proven otherwise."

"Agreed," Dewars nods. Then he continues, "I brought walkie-talkies for us all. There is spotty cell reception up here. We'll drive both vehicles to the driveway entrance. There is only one way out, so we'll park our cars to block any escape attempt. I suggest full body armor. I was told you have vests and rifles. That is good. Unfortunately, I do not have helmets for you."

"We'll make do," O'Reilly says.

"Okay, once we set up at the entrance we'll keep off the drive and walk through the trees to the cabin. It is about 500 feet. Once there, we can reconnoiter and approach the cabin," Dewars says.

"Let's do it," O'Reilly agrees.

• • • • •

After sleeping all night on a bare musty smelly mattress on one of the bunk beds, Tito gets up moaning. His back is sore and, having finished off a case of beer and one and a half bags of chips, his mouth is dry. The sun is up, but Tito has no idea what time it is. Checking his cell phone, he sees it has no signal.

He shivers from the dampness and decides to find some wood to start a fire in the stove. While still in his underwear, he goes outside to take a piss. Standing on the edge of the front porch of the cabin, he pulls out his dick. A line of ants about three feet away are making their way to the porch. He uses his piss as a hose washing the ants away from the porch. "Drown you suckers," he mumbles. Tito impresses himself with the intensity of his urine stream. "Still got it," he crows to himself.

A couple of pheasant fly out of the brush about two hundred feet in front of the cabin. Tito looks up towards the noise. Suddenly he is frozen with fear. He sees a heavy set man with a rifle making his way through the brush coming in Tito's direction. The man is having trouble maneuvering through the terrain. He is obviously not familiar walking through the woods.

Tito watches the man for a few seconds more; then he realizes that he is pissing on his bare foot. "Fuck," he cries and runs into the cabin. He puts his shoes on without socks and grabs his revolver. Going out the back door he heads left and makes a wide arch away from the cabin in the direction of the heavy set guy. "Mark Turgeson has found me," he thinks. He remembers the screams of his sister over the phone. He now realizes he'll have to fight. Being captured would mean the same torture for him.

The lessons about hunting he received as a kid from his uncle, Albert, is directing Tito. Because he knows the heavy set man is heading north towards the cabin, Tito will carefully walk in a wide sweep, first west then southeast. The plan is to come at a rear angle to the man and shoot him in the back. Tito moves quickly, but quietly, avoiding stepping on dry brush or twigs which will give away his position.

So far, he has traveled about one hundred and fifty feet in one direction now he starts to turn slightly left. After going about twenty-five feet, he turns slightly left again, repeating this pattern until he hears the man clumsily trudging through the brush.

Although he can't see him, Tito can tell that he is behind the heavy set man because the noises the man is making are slowly moving away. Tito carefully cocks his gun, so it makes no sound and moves directly towards the noises. Tito is so nervous he is sweating and impervious to the mosquitoes and flies chewing on him.

As Tito pushes forward silently through the brush, he can see the man from the side struggling to get his rifle untangled from a mountain laurel. Tito takes aim.

• • • • •

Police Sergeant George Tate has not been in the woods since he was nine years old. Many years ago, his father enrolled him in a summer camp near Lake Wallenpaupack in the Pocono Mountains of Pennsylvania. Little George hated it. The three weeks at the camp were one miserable day after another to him. An uncomfortable cot, bland food, endless activities that made him sweat, nearly drowning trying to learn how to swim, but the most traumatic event of that summer happened the last weekend.

One of the classes being given is to teach boys how to navigate through the woods. Boys were paired up with a partner and led out into the woods with a map, a compass and a canteen of water. The boys were then left to find their way back to the camp using only the map, the compass and the knowledge they gained from the weekly classes about hiking in the woods. The assignment started at nine in the morning right after breakfast. Most pairs of boys made it back to the camp in one and a half hours. Up to today, the longest it ever took was with a pair of boys from New York City. It took them 3 hours.

Unfortunately, little George and the boy who joined him, Johnny Steinmueller, have paid no attention in the classes about hiking.

After driving, then walking the boys to a remote spot, the counselors will head off on a path away from the cars and road. In this way the boys will not be given a clue on how to get back to the camp.

Although warned by the counselors not to follow them, when left alone, George and Johnny immediately followed the direction the counselors went.

After four hours the camp sent out search parties looking for little George and Johnny Steinmueller. By two in the afternoon the State Police were contacted, and a full force search was initiated, the same used to find escape convicts utilizing dogs and helicopters.

George and Johnny were eventually found at seven in the evening five miles from camp. They were hungry and thirsty with a few scratches and each with a light case of poison ivy.

George never went into the woods again until this day to find Tito Boris.

The instructions from State Police Sergeant John Dewars are simple. He and Officer Rhianna Bailey will walk up the right side of the lane. Sergeant Carol O'Reilly and Sergeant George Tate will walk up the left side. Dewars and O'Reilly will stay about 15 feet off the edge of the lane. Bailey and Tate will stay about fifty feet off the edge of the lane and keep within eyeshot of their partner. With this formation, they could approach the cabin without being seen.

Tate has veered off course and gotten lost, but is now encouraged because he sees the cabin in the distance and starts heading for it. As he walks through a green bush, the finger guard of his rifle gets caught in a branch. He hopes the bush is not poison ivy.

While struggling to free his gun from the bush, Tate feels a sharp pain in his left side. Simultaneously, Tate hears the blast from the gun that shot him. The force of the bullet spins Tate around. He immediately drops his rifle and falls into the mountain laurel bush.

•   •   •   •   •

Tito watches the heavy set man get jerked to one side by the force of the bullet from his gun. It is then that he notices the sizable white stenciling on the man's vest, "POLICE." He runs over to the man lying on the ground. Looking down, he mumbles, "Oh, fuck. Don't die, don't die."

The heavyset man is still breathing. Tito tries to think of what to do. He was hoping, as a last resort, if it came down to being captured by the Fifth Street Gang or the police, he'd choose the police. But now he shot a cop.

Suddenly, he hears multiple sounds of people running through the brush heading his way. He makes a beeline for the cabin.

•   •   •   •   •

Sergeant Dewars is the first to see Tate on the ground and a man in his underwear running away towards the cabin. As he runs to where Tate is lying, Dewars yells into the walkie-talkie, "Tate is down, repeat Tate is down. Suspect seen running towards the cabin."

Officer Bailey and Sergeant O'Reilly approach Dewars and Tate. Dewars signals Bailey to take a defensive position. O'Reilly runs to Tate. She unfastens his vest to assess the gunshot damage. The bullet entered under the left arm and exited through his chest. Lodging into the backside if the vest.

O'Reilly knows enough about anatomy to realize the bullet may have punctured a heart chamber or a major artery. She begins to well up as tears form in her eyes. "George! George! Stay with me!" she screams.

He lifts his head and looks at her and smiles. Then his eyes close and his head falls back. She grabs his shoulders crying, "George! George! Don't you die you son-of-a-bitch! Don't you die!"

Dewars reaches past O'Reilly and feels Tate's neck. "He still has a pulse, and it feels strong. I'll call for an air extraction," he tells O'Reilly.

Dewars switches his radio to a different frequency. His message carries to a buster transmitter in the interceptor car. He calls in an emergency medical evacuation for Tate. A minute later he receives confirmation of the evacuation and an ETA of twenty minutes for the medical helicopter.

Dewars tells O'Reilly and Bailey, "I gave them a rough position of our location. We'll need the flare gun and red smoke bombs from the car to help them find us. Another thing, the only clearing wide enough to land a chopper is in front of the cabin. Right now, we don't know if the suspect is working alone or has accomplices, also, what type of firepower they have. You two make your way as fast as you can to the car. Be alert and cautious. We don't need any more officers down. I'll stay here with Tate. When you get back, we'll all make our way to the cabin. Got that!"

O'Reilly and Bailey both nod and say yes.

Moving much more quickly than the first trip in, the two are back with Dewars is less than fifteen minutes. "This is the plan. The three of us carry Tate up to the edge of the clearing. O'Reilly, you stay here by Tate and keep us covered. Bailey and I will approach the cabin. Our first objective is to clear the cabin. Understood?" Dewars commands.

O'Reilly and Bailey nod in agreement.

"Let's move," Dewars orders.

•　　　•　　　•　　　•　　　•

Crouching down, Tito looks out one of the front windows of the cabin. He sees cops in full body armor assembling in the bushes just past the clearing. He is afraid to run out the back for fear that there are more police waiting for him there.

Then he sees two of the cops moving in a "leapfrog" formation coming towards the cabin. Panic starts building inside him. Then he remembers, in the movies, cops aren't allowed to shoot if the suspect throws his gun out and surrenders. That's what he'll do. Standing up, he opens the front door, walks out and throws out his gun. But before he can yell, "I give up." He hears the lead cop yell "grenade" and open fire.

• • • • •

After yelling "grenade," Officer Bailey dives to the ground in a prone position and fires wildly towards the open door of the cabin. Dewars drops to a kneeling position and fires, but misses the suspect because Tito is falling backwards into the cabin. O'Reilly starts firing at the cabin to give cover to Bailey and Dewars as they move and find cover behind Tito's car.

After waiting about thirty seconds, there is no explosion from a grenade. Dewars peeks over to take a look and the spots the object that Bailey thought was a grenade. He sees that it's a revolver and lets out a sigh. He now realizes the suspect wants to give himself up. "You in the house. I now see what you threw out is a revolver. Come out with your hands in the air, and we won't shoot. Do you have anyone with you?" Dewars calls.

"You're NOT going to shoot, right? I got my hands up, and I'm coming out. Don't shoot, right? No one else is here. Just me. You're not going to shoot, right?" Tito yells as loud as he can.

The sound of a helicopter can be heard in the distance. Dewars commands, "Come out with your hands in the air. No one will shoot!"

Tito walks out of the cabin, off the porch, and kneels to the ground without having to be asked. All the time holding his hands in the air. While Dewars holds his rifle pointing at Tito, Bailey puts him in handcuffs.

Dewars then gets the flare gun from O'Reilly and shoots two flares. He then sets off two red smoke bombs in the clearing next to the cabin.

Tate is picked up and flown to a nearby hospital.

Tito is read his rights and, although he says that he is alone, Dewars and O'Reilly search the cabin and the surrounding area for any signs of more suspects, while Bailey watches Tito. No signs of anyone is found. Dewars calls in a state police forensic team. O'Reilly places red police tape around the perimeter of the cabin and Tito's car.

Dewars says, "The forensic team will not be here for several hours. We'll take the suspect back to our barracks. You're welcome to come along Sergeant O'Reilly. The hospital is not that far away from the barracks."

"Call me Carol, please. I will go to your barracks. I want to interrogate Boris as soon as possible. I'll call my captain as soon as we get to a place that has a cell signal," O'Reilly answers.

• • • • •

At the state police barracks, Tito is sitting handcuffed to a table in a small interrogation room. Also seated at the table is Sergeant Carol O'Reilly. O'Reilly had contacted Captain Lila Brown who gave permission for her to stay overnight. Brown said she would contact Dorothy Tate about George and give her the name of the hospital.

"What were you doing at the cabin Tito?" O'Reilly asks.

"I want to make a deal. Before I say anything else, I want a deal," Tito demands.

O'Reilly sighs, then looks Tito directly in the eyes. "There's a police officer in the hospital because you put him there, Tito. That's attempted murder. I'll tell you the deal you're gonna get. If you cooperate, we won't fry your ass in the chair, and maybe we won't make you a bunkmate with some horny two hundred fifty pound lifer. "

Tito starts to whine, "I didn't know he wasn't no cop. I thought he was from the Fifth Street comin' to kill me. Ya gotta believe me. Listen I don't want much. It's just for my protection."

O'Reilly sits back in her chair. "Okay, Tito, what type of protection do you want?"

"I do not want to go back to the city. I'll talk all you want, but I do it from here. If I go back to the city, I'll get killed for sure. Turgeson has too many connections," Tito tells her.

O'Reilly shakes her head, "That's bullshit, we can better protect you in the city. We have more resources than this place. You want to stay here because you think you can escape easier."

"That's not true. Turgeson has one of your top guys on his payroll. I'm as good as dead if I go back to the city," Tito reveals.

A bit startled by this, O'Reilly takes a few seconds to gather herself, then she asks, "What's the top guy's name?"

"That I don't know…"

"Bullshit, you're handing me a bag of crap," O'Reilly gets up to leave, "I'm haulin' your ass back, today."

"No, no listen. Listen to me! Regina was seeing him. Regina was able to get me a job through this guy. No, bullshit, you gotta believe me!" Tito pleads. Tito starts to cry, "I tried to make some money on the side, and they found out. They thought Regina was in on it. So they tortured her. I heard her screams over the phone. I thought it was a put on, seein' they needed Regina so much. But they killed her."

O'Reilly sits down and in a calm, tender voice says, "Who are THEY, Tito? Help us get the guys who did this to your sister."

"Bernie, Bernie Tontas and this top guy. They were both in the room when Regina was being tortured. I heard both of them," Tito says.

Still, in a somber voice, O'Reilly presses, "Would you be able to recognize his voice, if you heard it again?"

"Yeah, maybe, yeah, I don't know."

"Why did Tontas need Regina so much?" O'Reilly asks.

"Listen, I want a deal. No more talking until I get to stay here. I want a deal!" Tito says with finality, as he sits back in his chair. Tears are running down his cheeks.

"I'll be back," O'Reilly says.

Tito is put back in a holding cell, while O'Reilly calls her Precinct. It is late when O'Reilly is done talking with Captain Lila Brown of Precinct

3. Brown agrees to keep Tito away from the city, all the arrangements won't be finalized until tomorrow.

O'Reilly books a room at a small local motel, she calls her husband, Barry. The two talk for forty-five minutes about everything, except the danger she had just been through that day. She never discusses being in harm's way. She can tell from his voice that Barry is worried.

Being the spouse of a cop may be one of the hardest jobs there is. Knowing, that any day, you might get a call that will turn your life upside down. They end the phone conversation saying "I love you" to each other.

Then O'Reilly gets word that Sergeant George Tate is awake and responsive. O'Reilly drives over to the hospital. It is a forty-five-minute drive, and she hopes Tate is still awake when she gets there.

The hospital is an ultra-modern facility, which shocks O'Reilly. She was expecting a two-story old brick building with faded vinyl floor tiles and sagging ceiling tiles. Instead, the hospital is a five-story building with a sleek silver and gray metal façade. A helipad lighted as bright as daylight is visible on one side of the hospital where the canopy for the emergency entrance is located.

At the main entrance, O'Reilly has to show herself and her credentials to a monitor in the foyer. A buzzing sound tells her the electric lock has been opened to allow her to pass through.

O'Reilly walks into a very large reception area with ceilings three stories high. Indirect lighting throughout gives the place a comfortable feel. Slim chrome columns reach the high ceiling. A glass and chrome rail lines a balcony area on the second floor.

At this late hour, instead of the usual attendant and volunteers manning the reception desk, an armed security guard presides.

The guard directs O'Reilly to the bank of elevators at the rear of the reception area. She takes one of the elevators to the third floor. At the nurse's station, she again shows her badge. It is past normal visiting hours when O'Reilly arrives, but the staff nurse lets her in to see Tate anyway.

As she enters, she sees that he is in a private room. Tate has the head of the bed in an upright position and he is watching television. An oxygen tube is attached to his nose and another tube is coming from an IV bag to his left arm.

Cops around the world have developed a "graveyard" sense of humor to help hide the pain of a comrade being hurt and to salve the basic fear of their own death, which can occur on any assignment. The affection and respect police officers have for each other is akin to the comradeship developed by troops in the armed services. "Pretty nice accommodations for a little scratch," O'Reilly jokes as she scans the room.

Without a blink, Tate replies, "Well, my bravery and heroism dazzled the locals. So, they put me in the presidential suite."

With the tone of his answer, O'Reilly knows that Tate had a rough go and, maybe, barely survived. O'Reilly has been in enough hospitals to know private rooms for cops are only for the very critical cases. Also an officer never even jokes about bravery and heroism unless he was scared. In this case, the doctors told him he almost did not make it. But now he is recovering nicely. The detective in O'Reilly knows that Tate must be doing well because he is allowed to sit up in bed and watch television. All of this only takes few seconds for O'Reilly to accurately surmise.

She is so relieved that Tate will live, she almost starts crying, but instead she says, "Bravery and heroism. You got lost and, as a result, got your fat ass shot. Then I had to lug it out of the woods."

"Did you get him?" Tate asks.

"Yep, and he is singing like a canary. It is a good catch. Bernie Tontas, the right-hand man of Mark Turgeson, killed Regina. Another guy was involved, too. He's a cop, but we don't know who." O'Reilly answers with a sense of pride for her and for Tate.

"What about Dewars and Bailey?" Tate asks with concern.

O'Reilly smiles, "They didn't fumble through the woods and get lost, like you did, so they didn't get shot." Police humor translation: the two troopers are safe and sound.

O'Reilly continued, "What got them cursing the most was hauling your carcass through the brush. When I told them I was coming to see you, they said to tell you to stay away from Potter County. They don't have the time to babysit." Translation: They did a professional job keeping Tate alive and safe. Also, they worry about his recovery.

In a more somber tone and with a break from the previous light banter Tate tells O'Reilly, "When you looked at the wound and started to cry, I got real worried, Carol. Thanks for saving my life."

Because she did not want to give Tate the satisfaction of revealing her true emotions, O'Reilly says, "Crying? I was not crying. And as for being worried, I was thinking of all the paperwork to be filled out if you croaked."

Before Tate can answer, Dorothy Tate, his wife, bursts into the room. "What is she doing here so late at night?" Dorothy demands to know.

"We were reviewing the case, Dorothy," Tate replies.

"Hello to you, too, Dorothy," O'Reilly says with a slight tone of sarcasm.

Dorothy looks at O'Reilly, "Humph," then she turns to Tate, "Did you to just have sex with her?"

"I'm outta here," O'Reilly says as she leaves the room. Halfway back to the elevator she bursts into tears because she is so happy that Tate is okay.

•　　•　　•　　•　　•

Arrangements were made by Precinct 3 Police Captain Lila Brown with the State Police and the city district attorney to allow Tito Boris to stay in custody in the medium security jail in Coudersport, Pennsylvania. Brown also agreed to pass on any relevant information gotten from Tito to the drug task force working in the city. Tito was assigned a public defender based in the city. They communicated via a secure phone line. If Tito cooperated fully, the charge of attempted murder of a policeman would be dropped. Tito will be charged with assault, carrying an unregistered weapon, and resisting arrest. The interrogation of Tito will be videoed.

"This is Police Sergeant Carol O'Reilly interrogating Tito Boris at the Potter County Jail. Mr. Boris has agreed to cooperate fully."

O'Reilly asks the first question, "Tito, in our previous interrogation you stated that you heard, over the phone, Bernie Tontas and an unknown man torturing Regina, your sister."

Tito responds, "Yes."

"How did this conversation arise?"

"I had come up with a scheme to make some money on the side. One of my jobs for the Fifth Street Gang is to transfer money to the drug suppliers after a delivery is made. The gang has an offshore account in a bank based in the Cayman Islands. It uses this account to deposit most of the money it makes.

When a payment has to be made, money is withdrawn from this account and transferred to another account based in Hong Kong. The money usually sits in the Hong Kong account for about an hour before the payment is made. I tried to make some money for me on the side by using the money in the Hong Kong account before a payment is made.

That plan went south, and I ran. Later I tried to call Regina's cell to warn her of what happened. That is when I talked to Bernie and heard him and the other guy torture Regina." Tito answers matter-of-factly.

"But at the time you thought it might be a set-up, that Regina was not really being tortured because they needed her. Why did the Fifth Street Gang need Regina?" O'Reilly asks.

"Regina would let Mark Turgeson and Bernie Tontas know when a raid was going to occur against the Fifth Street Gang," Tito explains.

"How do you know this?"

"Regina told me."

"Why did Regina agree to do this?" O'Reilly asks.

"For the money, I was in hock big time to a couple of bookies. Regina wanted to help me."

"How did Regina get recruited by the gang?"

"She wasn't recruited. She told me that during a raid she came across information at one of the Fifth Street Gang hideouts about a cop who was a gang member. She followed the guy to see where he hung out, then arranged a fake accidental meeting. One thing led to another, and within a couple weeks she was working for the gang."

"Did she ever tell you anything about this cop that can help us identify him?"

"Just that he was important and no one would suspect him to be an informant and he had a huge ego."

"Nothing else?"

"Nope."

"She then got you in the gang, right"

"Yeah."

"Did you ever meet Bernie Tontas or Mark Turgeson?"

"I worked with Bernie at the office about every day. Turgeson only showed up once. It was somethin'. Two of his goons show up and collect all the cell phones from everybody in the place, and we had to turn off all the computers. No one was allowed out of the building for two hours while Turgeson had a meeting."

"How did you know it was Mark Turgeson?"

"I didn't at first, but Bernie told me when I asked what the big deal was about. Then this guy comes in with two bodyguards. Bernie pointed him out to me."

"Who did he meet?' O'Reilly presses.

Tito shakes his head, "I don't know."

"Where is the office you worked at?"

"The NJDelPen Logistics warehouse on Myers Street. The place is used strictly for administrative work. It is set up to operate like a legitimate business."

"What else can you tell us about Mark Turgeson?"

"Not much. I know he is very cautious and does not trust computers, cell phones or any kind of electronic communications."

The interview continues for another half hour with Tito giving more details about the operation of the Fifth Street Gang. Afterward, O'Reilly heads back to the city, but not before visiting Sergeant George Tate in the hospital. Dorothy Tate is also there, so O'Reilly doesn't stay long.

• • • • •

As promised, Captain Lila Brown gives a transcribed copy of the interview with Tito to State Police Captain Celia Bouton. Bouton contacts Lieutenant Barbara Maylars to initiate a raid on the NJDelPen warehouse as soon as possible.

CHAPTER ELEVEN
Tom Exeter Investigation

Because Detectives O'Reilly and Tate are heading out of town on an assignment, Detective Sergeant Morgan Indigo and Detective Sergeant Louis McCrew are given the task to bring in Captain Tom Exeter. They both stand in front of Exeter's desk unmoved by his protestations.

"This is outrageous! How dare you come to my office unannounced without my permission," Captain Tom Exeter complains.

Indigo says, "If you come voluntarily, we will not have to put you in cuffs, sir. If you refuse," she holds up her cell phone, "I will call in for a warrant and have you forcibly removed."

Exeter turns to his assistant, Sergeant Lucas Faschnaght, who had followed the two detectives into the office, and says, "Get me Commissioner Rhodes on the line, right now. I'll put an end to this nonsense."

"Yes, sir," Faschnaght replies.

Suddenly, Exeter's phone rings. Faschnaght picks it up, "Captain Exeter's office," after a pause, "It's the commissioner, sir."

Visibly surprised by the call, Exeter takes the receiver from his assistant. "Commissioner, it is fortuitous that you called at this time. Two detectives from Precinct 3... what's that...you sent them." Exeter reddens with rage. "Now I see. You got wind of my campaign to replace you as commissioner, and now you have concocted this..., this farce to have me discredited. What's that, ... put you on the speaker phone with the detectives. Most certainly I will. I'll expect an apology. Now you can call off your dogs personally." He pushes a button on his phone. "They can hear you now commissioner. Have them remove themselves from my office," Exeter demands.

Over the speakerphone, Rhodes begins, "Tom, I have in my hand a warrant for your arrest for obstruction of justice. I will have the detectives serve this warrant if you don't voluntarily accompany them to Precinct 3. Do I make myself clear?"

Exeter is now purple with rage and replies, "You win this round, Marilyn, but I will get my pound of flesh in payment for this outrage! I will accompany your two detectives to the precinct." After hanging up the phone, he speaks to detective Morgan, "I want to talk to my aide in private for a few seconds before we leave."

"Okay, but we will be waiting just on the other side of that door," Morgan says.

When alone, Exeter tells Faschnaght, "I am going to stop at my apartment to pick up the report. I will use the clerical error excuse we talked about. I am counting on you. This could be the chance to discredit Rhodes."

"I won't let you down," Faschnaght replies.

•   •   •   •   •

Morgan and McCrew lead Tom Exeter out to the front door. But because of a large crowd of news reporters now gathering, they immediately retreat to the back exit, leaving the building and arriving at Precinct 3 unnoticed.

Once there, Exeter is taken to the largest of the interrogation rooms. As a courtesy, he is offered some refreshments.

Earlier that day Captain Lila Brown calls Lori Daniels. "Lori, this is Lila."

"Hi, Lila, what can I do for you," Lori greets her.

"Have you seen the news today?" Brown asks wryly.

"No, I have been at my desk all day prepping for … an "event" later," Lori says.

"It's okay, I spoke with Petracelli and Maylars today. Precinct 3 is lending resources for the raid," Brown tells her.

"I'm looking at my phone for the latest news. What should I be looking for?" Lori asks. Then she says, "Oh, I see the video now. What the heck is Exeter doing with Regina?"

"I am at Commissioner Rhodes office. She described it as a "real shit storm," and Exeter is in the middle of it. Detectives Morgan and McCrew, they're the ones that interviewed you ..."

Lori interrupts, "Yeah, I remember them. Seem like good cops. Asked all the right questions."

Brown continues, "They are good cops. Well, at the order of Commissioner Rhodes, Morgan and McCrew are on their way to Exeter's office to bring him into Precinct 3 for questioning."

"Wow, I would love to be at that meeting," Lori comments.

"That is why I am calling. Rhodes gets updates from me on the various Work Place Harassment investigations. She is familiar with your complaint. Because of that and the fact that Regina was one of your squad, Rhodes agrees to let you be present at the interview with Exeter. It will take place at our large interrogation room. You can watch and listen from behind the window," Brown explains.

"When is this taking place? I will be pressed for time," Lori says.

"Not a problem, there will be plenty of time. I told Maylars and Petracelli about this, and they are good with it," Brown says.

"I'm on my way, thanks," Lori says enthusiastically.

•   •   •   •   •

Commissioner Rhodes and Captain Brown are waiting in the interrogation room for Tom Exeter to arrive as Lori takes her place behind the observation window. Twenty minutes go by, when an officer walks into the interrogation room and asks Brown to step outside for a phone call.

Brown returns a few minutes later and says, "Commissioner, Detective Morgan just called. They are running late because Exeter insisted on retrieving a file from his apartment."

Rhodes sighs and questions, "What has he got up his sleeve?"

Another fifteen minutes pass, when Brown says to Lori, "I know you are cutting it close on time, Lori, but I'll make sure you get to the raid. Don't worry."

Captain Tom Exeter finally struts into the interrogation room with a file folder under his arm. He looks supremely confident as he fake smiles at Rhodes and Brown, before taking a seat across the table from both of them.

Not waiting for Rhodes to start, Exeter says, "This whole affair is an outrage to myself, personally, and to the office I represent. Both of you, and anyone watching from behind the window will pay dearly."

"We'll see," Rhodes says. Being a cop for thirty-five years, Marilyn Rhodes has been in hundreds of interrogations. She uses a classic tactic to get the upper hand. Ask questions the interviewee does not expect. "Why have you been following Sergeant Lorraine R. Daniels of Precinct 11?"

The smug look on Exeter's face is dropped. "What are you talking about?" he asks.

From a stack of file folders in front of Captain Brown, Rhodes asks for the top one. She opens it and takes out a document then hands it to Exeter. "This is a signed complaint form from Sergeant Daniels accusing you of threatening her when she told you she was not going to continue an affair."

Taking out another document and handing it to Exeter, Rhodes continues, "Here is a signed affidavit from retired Police Sergeant James Koustafus and his wife, Lynn, stating that while Daniels visited his fruit stand, you were observed pulling off to the side of Route 50. Waiting and then following Sergeant Daniels after she left the fruit stand. This takes place just two days after Daniels called off the affair."

Recovering his composure, Exeter begins to lie, "First of all, Daniels is a liar. I ended the affair with her. She did not end it. As a matter of fact, she threatened to discredit me because I dumped her. As for Koustafus, he is a disgruntled and disgraced cop who blames me for his misdeeds. This is just a baseless conspiracy to try to discredit my stellar reputation."

"So, you deny following Daniels to Koustafus' fruit stand?" Rhodes presses.

A small green light blinks at the left of the observation window. Captain Lila Brown rises saying to Rhodes, "Please, excuse me a moment."

Rhodes says to Lila Brown, "I understand completely. Tell her to be safe and good luck."

Brown leaves the room and goes into the observation room.

"I've got to go," Lori says.

Brown smiles, "I know. I wish I could accompany you. Arrangements have been made to get you to the site of the raid. You'll meet your squad there. Also, you can use my body armor. I had it brought up and put in my office. It's never been used. I even have the latest helmet from the State Police. It seems they gave all the precinct captains helmets. Probably as a goodwill gesture. Godspeed." Brown then re-enters the interrogation room.

When Brown sits down, she sees Exeter reading another document, and recognizes it as Sergeant Brenda Cervetti's statement about being recruited to spy on Lori Daniels.

"This is outrageous. I gave a confidential assignment to Cervetti. I'll have her brought up on charges for revealing Internal Affairs matters," Exeter shouts indignantly.

Rhodes responds, "These documents all point to a pattern of harassment towards Sergeant Daniels. You simply denying the claims, will not work. As for you bringing charges brought against Sergeant Brenda Cervetti, she revealed this information as part of my investigation of workplace harassment. Let me remind you, Internal Affairs is also under my auspices."

Rhodes continues, "Moving on to other matters, why did you not come forth about your meeting with Corporal Regina Boris? A meeting that took place the day before her disappearance. Even weeks later after her body was found, you still withheld this information."

Like Commissioner Rhodes, Captain Thomas Exeter also spent decades honing his skills. Whereas Rhodes developed skills based on good police procedure, constant integrity and solid leadership, Exeter honed other skills.

Opening the folder he retrieved from his apartment, Exeter begins, "As I have stated before, this whole proceeding is an outrage and merely a ploy to discredit my name. Predicated on the fear by you, Commissioner Rhodes, that I will unseat you and be the next commissioner. Here is a copy of the latest monthly report given to you, Commissioner, just last week."

Exeter flips through the pages of the file until stopping at a tab titled, Investigation of Gang Influence on the City Police Force. He turns the document around so Rhodes and Brown can read it. Then he continues, "This particular part of the report deals with corruption in the police force due to gang influence. Starting on page 4, you will see that …"

Rhodes interrupts, "I read that report. There is no page four. It is merely a three-page general synopsis. You and I went over this at last week's review session."

"I admit we only covered the first three pages at the review, but that was due to time constraints in covering all the reports. If the Commissioner wanted to go in depth on any report, I would have been more than willing …"

Again, Rhodes interrupts, "I read every page of the report after our review session. There are only three pages. In fact, I have a note prepared for the next session to ask you to give a more detailed account of what is being done to combat the influence of the gangs."

Calmly Exeter turns over the three pages of the report to reveal page four. "I must disagree Commissioner. Here is page four through sixteen of the report."

Rhodes angrily interrupts again, "Those pages are not in the report you gave me."

Exeter puts on a mock surprised look, "Oh dear, perhaps my assistant neglected to include them in your copy. I will have to speak to him about that. My apologies. However, as you can now plainly read, I noticed a disturbing pattern with raids on the Fifth Street Gang. Most of them produced little or no results.

Through an informant, Richard O'Shea, who is a member of the Fifth Street Gang, I found out that Corporal Regina Boris was seen talking with Bernie Tontas. Tontas is the alleged right-hand man of Mark Turgeson. I questioned Regina several times. Finally, she said that she made contact with the Fifth Street Gang through Lieutenant Mike Costner. The day before she went missing, I met with Regina to further the investigation.

Immediately after Regina went missing, Sergeant Lorraine Daniels started having an affair with Costner. The subsequent raid on a Fifth Street Gang hideout produced no arrests or confiscation of illegal substances. I concluded that Daniels could now be the new informant for the Gang.

That is why I met Regina Boris, that is why I followed Lori Daniels, and that is why I gave Sergeant Brenda Cervetti the assignment."

Commissioner Rhodes stares at Exeter and says coolly, "You deliberately withheld this part of the report from me, and I know why. You wanted to tout to the press that you personally brought the city's largest drug gang down. By-passing not only my office, but also the men and women of the precincts, who put their lives on the line. You have put cops in danger by not sharing this information, and you may have gotten Corporal Regina Boris killed."

With a fake look of innocence, Exeter replies, "Nonsense Commissioner. I'm sure if we get my aide, Faschnaght, on the phone he will confess to the clerical error." He then sits back and smiles.

Rhodes turns to Captain Brown, we have got to get a hold of Maylars and Daniels to let them know about Costner.

Turning back to Exeter, "You are a piece of shit for a human being, Tom," is the last thing Rhodes says as she gets up to go to Captain Brown's office.

In her office a few minutes later, Brown puts down the phone and tells Rhodes, "The raid started fifteen minutes ago. I'm on hold, being patched through to Maylars."

CHAPTER TWELVE
Show Down

As in previous raids with the task force, secrecy is the utmost importance. Only State Police Lieutenant Barbara Maylars, squad leaders, police Sergeant Lori Daniels, police Sergeant Clyde Macturner, and the driver of the lead cruiser, police Sergeant Raoul Menendez, know the location. The caravan leaves Precinct 11 through the back gate. Menendez driving the lead police cruiser is followed by two police vans and two more police cruisers.

Because the raid is at night, each team member has infrared night vision goggles on their helmets. The goggles flip down when in use and can easily be flipped up in lighted situations, another courtesy of the state police.

This target is a warehouse owned by NJDelPen Logistics. The warehouse has a large two-story annex that holds offices. Although it operates as a full functioning legitimate facility, it is actually a front for the Fifth Street Gang. Maylars is confident that this raid will be successful. The suspected gang informant, Regina Boris, is dead and the only ones who know the location are trusted officers.

●   ●   ●   ●   ●

Because Sergeant Lori Daniels is at Precinct 3 and will meet the team at the site, Sergeant Brenda Cervetti goes over the strategy one more time with Red Team. Brenda begins, "Okay, listen up red team! Our job will be to enter through the main door at the annex on the east side of the warehouse. The annex has two stories. The first floor is mainly one large area divided into office cubicles. There are two gang restrooms on the south wall. A stairway leading to the second floor is on the west wall directly in front of the main door. Also on the west wall, is a set of double doors leading to the main floor of the warehouse. The second floor has one main corridor with a shorter corridor intersecting it. Small rooms are off the corridors. We are meeting Lori at the site. She will review our assignments again."

As their van arrives, a police cruiser from Precinct 3 pulls in next to them. Lori gets out and puts on the body armor given to her by Captain Lila Brown.

Lori enters the back of the van and goes over the strategy one more time, "Sorry I did not ride here with you. Okay, Cervetti, Ramirez, and Stetzler will make their way to the stairway and start clearing the second floor, going room to room. Taylor, Morgan, Riccini, Hayden, and Scott will follow me to clear each cubicle and the restrooms. Once the first floor is cleared, Taylor will come with me to the second floor. Morgan, Riccini, Hayden, and Scott will enter the warehouse through the double doors and assist Blue Team in their sweep. At the northeast corner of the main warehouse floor is a small group of offices. All Teams will make their way to this group of offices. The goal is to trap as many rats as we can. The other squads will watch the exits to catch anyone who tries to escape.

Intel from the Staties says that they don't expect that the place will have many perps. The facility is used as a legitimate business. Most of the employees will be done with their work at this time of day. There is no suspected drug stash or lab. The goal is to confiscate the computers and files stored at the warehouse.

Listen up, Intel like this is all well and good, but we will go in expecting the worst. There may be armed gang members throughout the building. Watch each other's back and stay safe. Any questions?"

No one does.

The caravan is now fully deployed around the warehouse. Red Team rushes out of the van and gets into a defensive position near the main entrance. Lieutenant Maylars watches the screen of the helmet cams of each squad member as they get into position. Then she hears Sergeant Lori Daniels call in, "Red Team in place. I repeat, Red Team in place." Then Maylars hears the voice of Sergeant Macturner, "Blue team in place. I repeat, Blue team in place."

Maylars responds, "This is a go, go, go."

Riccini takes the battering ram to the center of the two glass entrance doors. The doors swing inward, and the glass of the right one shatters. Lori is the first into the building followed by Taylor. Brenda is next with her squad making their way to the stairway. The remainder of the team fans out across the office area.

When they reach the stairway, Brenda signals Ramirez and Stetzler to stop. She then very carefully makes her way to the top of the stairs. Stetzler and Ramirez have their rifles pointed at the top of the stairs ready to fire.

There is no door at the top of the stairway and it opens to a small foyer. Brenda moves into the foyer and uses a fiber optic lens to peeks around the corner of the corridor. The lens also has infrared capability. No one is in sight. She signals for Stetzler and Ramirez to join her in the foyer.

They stop and listen, but no sounds are heard on the second floor. After checking again around the corner, the team turns left and after a few feet come to the main corridor, which runs north and south, perpendicular to the one they are in. Brenda sends Ramirez and Stetzler to the south end to clear the rooms, while she stays in place watching the north end of the main corridor. The plan is to clear the rooms at one end of the main corridor before moving north.

Suddenly, Brenda thinks she sees a brief flash of light down the corridor. She radios to Ramirez and Stetzler that she is moving away from them to check out the flash of light at the end of the north corridor.

"That's not the plan, Brenda," Lori says over the radio.

"I'll be okay. Just want to check out a possible light source," Brenda replies.

Moving with stealth, Brenda carefully walks down the corridor. Each room she passes has a closed door. She thinks she hears a noise ahead, but with the intermittent chatter over the helmet speaker, she is not sure. Because of the helmet, Brenda is also not aware that the old floor makes a slight creaking sound as she moves down the corridor. Up ahead a door opens and fills the corridor with light. Because there is now light, she flips up the infrared goggles and readies her automatic rifle.

•   •   •   •   •

Ellis Taramelli is sitting in an office on the second floor of the rendezvous site, a warehouse north of central city. It is 11:45 PM and the facility is not active. Also in the room is the person who picked him up. The meeting is set up with very specific instructions.

Mark Turgeson, boss of the Fifth Street Gang, arranged the meeting and wants to establish a long-term relationship with the cartel that Ellis represents. To show his sincerity, Turgeson does not want Ellis to feel threatened. However, Turgeson is very paranoid about modern technology and the many ways he can be tracked or observed. He also has some old fashion, but effective means of security. No member of the Fifth Street Gang is allowed to bring a cell phone to this location tonight. That is why Ellis is told not to bring a cell phone, but to feel safe, he can bring a gun.

Earlier, Ellis leaves the hotel at 11:15 PM. as instructed, he walks two blocks up Race Street, then three blocks up Twelfth Street. He is met by a man who asks him which cheesesteak he prefers, Geno's or Pat's, another of Turgeson's security measures. The response, previously given to Ellis, is, "Neither, Steve's is his favorite."

Ellis follows the man for one block. A limousine stops in traffic and beeps the horn twice. Ellis gets into the back seat of the car. As the car cruises the city in a seemingly random pattern, Ellis is frisked by a woman, who first apologizes for the inconvenience and says her name is Joyce. Turgeson thinks that being frisked by a woman is less intimidating than by a man. All for the sake of showing Ellis that this is a friendly meeting, but security is strict.

"I will have to do a very thorough search. Please, do not take offense," Joyce says in a business-like tone.

"No offense taken, go right ahead," Ellis replies.

Joyce begins, "Please, open your jacket, I will check your upper torso." Her hands move under his clothes, over his back and neck, under his arms and across his chest and stomach. "You did come prepared in case of trouble," she adds.

"Now, please, take off your shoes."

Ellis complies. Joyce inspects the shoes. Then gets an electronic wand from a pocket in the car door and waves it around the shoes. "Checking for electronic transmitters," she says matter-of-factly.

"Please, unbuckle your pants and lean back," is the next request.

Ellis does as he is told.

Joyce continues her search by feeling inside his pants. "You can zip back up." She then takes the wand and runs it across his upper torso and legs. She then taps on the window separating the driver from the passenger compartment. The window is lowered. She tells the driver, "He's clean. Tell them we're coming in." The driver nods and closes the window. He then makes the call.

Sitting back in the seat, Joyce comments, "By the way, nice gun." As Ellis smiles, she quickly adds, "... I meant your Glock."

"That's what I thought you meant," Ellis replies while looking out the window and continuing to smile.

Joyce shakes her head and sighs, thinking, "Men are all alike."

After fifteen minutes of driving, the car stops. The woman gets out and asks Ellis to follow her. As they walk down the sidewalk, the woman puts her arm around Ellis' right arm. The two of them now simply look like a couple going for a late night stroll arm in arm. As another measure of security, all the way from the hotel to arriving at this warehouse, Turgeson has Ellis watched to ensure no one is following. The stroll is the final check to assure no one followed them.

They walk a block then turn right through an open chain link fence, past a small parking lot and into the double glass front doors of a warehouse. On the doors is a logo with a stylized depiction of a tractor-trailer and the name NJDelPen Logistics.

The woman pulls a flashlight from her purse, and the two of them walk to a stairway and go up. They then turn left and make a quick right turn down a long corridor. At the junction with another corridor, she opens a door, turns on a light and asks Ellis to have a seat. Four folding metal chairs are placed around a 3'x6' folding table in the center of the small room. A small desk with a telephone and lamp is along the far wall. At one corner is a cabinet that looks like it does not belong in the room. Ellis sits at the table facing the door, and so does the woman. She offers Ellis a drink, which he declines.

Joyce picks up the intercom phone on the table and presses three numbers. After waiting a moment, she says, "I'm here with Taramelli." She then hangs up.

The man she speaks to puts down his automatic rifle and takes off his bulletproof vest. He leaves the office on the first floor that is a part of a small cluster of rooms at the northwest corner of the warehouse. The man walks up steps to get to the room where Joyce and Ellis are waiting.

At 11:46 PM a tall man with a lean muscular body walks in. Ellis recognizes the man as police Lieutenant Mike Costner, but the man does not know Ellis recognizes him. Costner tells the woman she can leave and then introduces himself. "Hi, my name is Mike. I'll be escorting you downstairs in a few minutes to meet Mark Turgeson. He will be arriving very shortly. Did Joyce offer you a drink? Mike walks over to a cabinet in the corner of the room and opens it. This was brought here just for you. There is top shelf Scotch, Rye, Bourbon, Gin ..."

Ellis interrupts, "Yes she did offer. I said no, but thanks again for offering. How long have you worked for Turgeson?"

Costner smiles, "Please, understand until we work together for a while, it's best to keep personal information to a minimum."

Ellis simply replies, "Okay."

A noise, like a squeaking floorboard, is heard out in the corridor. "Mark must have arrived, that must be one of his bodyguards coming to get us." Costner is concerned, but does not show it. Turgeson was supposed to call using the warehouse intercom phone when he arrives.

Costner opens the door and goes out into the corridor. Ellis hears a voice in the corridor that sounds familiar. The person is saying, "Mike, what the heck are you doing here?" Ellis then remembers it is the voice of Brenda Cervetti, his good friend at the academy. He jumps up from the table and runs into the corridor.

Brenda is standing at the juncture of the two corridors in body armor and helmet. Costner in one quick movement punches Brenda in the face. Dazed she stumbles against the wall. Then Costner pulls out his weapon and shoots. The bullet hits Brenda in the side.

Before Costner can get off another shot, Ellis leaps and knocks Costner against the corridor wall. Costner pushes Ellis away and raises his gun to shoot. With his left forearm, Ellis shoves Costner's gun hand aside as another shot is fired. The bullet goes awry.

"You're a cop!" Costner cries. Ellis now grabs the arm of Costner that has the gun and slams it into the wall. As the gun falls, Costner breaks free and runs down the corridor. Ellis pulls out his gun and shoots, but Costner gets away.

He turns to Brenda. She is still leaning against the wall with a look of bewilderment on her face. She is obviously in shock. Brenda then slumps to the floor.

•　　　•　　　•　　　•　　　•

Sergeant Lori Daniels and Corporal Jason Taylor are running down the corridor towards the sounds of the gunshots. Quickly rounding the corner, what meets their eyes horrifies Lori. About 30 feet ahead of them, in the dim light coming from a room, her best friend Brenda Cervetti staggers then falls. As she falls, Ellis Taramelli with a gun in his hand can be seen moving towards Brenda. With fear for her friend combined with rage at Ellis for shooting Brenda, Lori races towards them.

Ellis hesitates as he sees Lori and Taylor approaching. Without taking careful aim Taylor fires while running. The round explodes into the wall on Ellis' right sending pieces of plaster flying through the air. Another shot whistles by his ear. Ellis hesitates a moment and looks like he is about to say something. He then scurries around a corner and is gone from sight.

Brenda is lying at the juncture of two corridors. She seems to be unconscious as Lori and Taylor reach her. Lori immediately attends to her friend. Taylor positions himself at a corner of the corridors on alert.

Lori calls into the helmet mike, "Officer down, officer down, second level, main corridor, hurry!" She takes the helmet off of Brenda then sees blood rushing from underneath her bulletproof vest. Lori removes her own helmet to better investigate the source of blood. Unstrapping the vest, she sees that the wound is under the arm on the left side where the vest does not cover. "Brenda, Brenda, can you hear me. Stay with me. Stay with me," Lori pleads.

Brenda gives a groan and opens her eyes.

Lori has tears in her eyes as she says to Brenda, "I'm going to kill Ellis for doing this, that son-of-a-bitch!"

Brenda, barely focusing on Lori, mumbles, "Ellis... why... Ellis," then swoons, seeming to fall unconscious again."

Hearing Brenda, Lori thinks, "Of course Ellis could easily approach Brenda. She would not have fired on him. She believed he would not hurt her. Then the bastard shot her down in cold blood." This makes Lori even more determined to get Ellis.

Lori rises and gives a command to Taylor, "Stay with Brenda. I'm going after Taramelli."

Taylor exclaims, "Don't do this alone! Wait for help; then we can both get him."

His exhortation falls on deaf ears. Lori is already racing down the corridor to follow Ellis. After 20 feet the corridor makes a left turn. As Lori approaches the end of the corridor, she slows, cautiously she rounds the corner. No one is in sight. She follows the next corridor to where it stops at a door. To the left of the door is an open stairway down to the main level of the warehouse.

Hearing gunfire from behind the door, Lori decides to head that way. She crouches with her automatic pistol in the ready. Quickly swinging the door open she sees it leads to a maintenance catwalk over the warehouse floor. It connects to two other catwalks intersecting at right angles. At one of the other intersecting catwalks, a set of steps goes down to the warehouse floor. No one is on the catwalks.

It is then that Lori realizes she does not have her helmet and cannot contact the team by radio. She decides to move forward anyway. Going back now might let Ellis escape even with the place surrounded by police. Gunfire erupts from an aisle to her left, but the crates are too high for her to see who is there.

• • • • •

Ellis rounds another corner and sees a stairway leading down to the main floor of the warehouse. Instead of taking the stairs he decides to go through the door. With gun in hand, he quickly opens the door which leads to a catwalk. No one is there.

Moving rapidly but cautiously across the catwalk, Ellis sees Costner running towards a small cluster of rooms. He fires at Costner, but at that instant, by chance, a door swings open shielding Costner and the bullet splinters the wood of the door.

Costner turns at the sound and sees Ellis standing on the catwalk. Two men rush out through the splintered door brandishing automatic rifles. Costner orders the men to shoot at Ellis. Being outgunned, Ellis races down the steps of the catwalk to the warehouse floor.

From the loading dock area, two more men start firing at Ellis. Skipping the last four steps, Ellis leaps to the concrete floor and rolls towards some crates for protection. The force of the fall jars the pistol from his hand, and it scatters away from him. Bullets start splintering the edges of the crate he takes refuge behind. To get away from the onslaught he moves further down one of the aisles between more cartons and crates.

Ellis knows he will soon be cornered by the four men coming after him. Without a weapon, he is as good as dead. He sees a small gap between two large crates. He slips into the gap, hoping that the men chasing him will be so intent on moving forward, they will not notice him.

A few seconds pass when Ellis hears footsteps. A tall blonde guy holding an automatic rifle walks past him. Ellis hears the steps of a second man. He takes a gamble that only two men are in this particular aisle. The second man, who weighs about 300 pounds, is even with his position. Ellis leaps out and thrusts the fat guy into a crate. Ellis bounces off of the guy, ricocheting across the aisle into another crate. He rebounds off that crate back to the fat guy. On his return, Ellis grabs the guy's gun with his left hand and quickly shoves his right fist into the man's face.

The rifle comes free. The blonde guy turns around and is about to fire his weapon. Ellis gets his hand on the rifle trigger and starts spraying bullets indiscriminately towards the blonde guy. One of the bullets hits the guy's left ear. Another gets his right shoulder. The blonde guy is thrust against a large carton.

Half stunned and half in a rage, the fat guy takes a swing at Ellis. Moving to the right to avoid the punch, the guy's fist hits Ellis' left shoulder. Ellis bounces against a crate, and as he rebounds, with his right hand Ellis brings the barrel of the rifle into the fat guy's crotch. The guy lets out a lung full of air.

A bullet whizzes by Ellis coming from the direction of the blonde guy. To get some cover Ellis jumps behind the fat guy, who is holding his crotch. Then Ellis peeks around the fat guy and fires three rounds from the rifle. The blonde guy falls.

The fat guy grabs the barrel of the rifle. Ellis simply uses the fat guy's grip as a lever and turns the nozzle into his big belly. One round does its job, and the fat guy hits the floor. Ellis rapidly moves down the aisle away from the bodies.

•   •   •   •   •

Lori hears a door open then close. From her vantage point, she sees Mike Costner, wearing body armor and carrying an automatic rifle, coming out of the office area and heading down an aisle between the crates. "What is Mike doing here?" she thinks, "Only Precinct 11 was supposed to be on this raid."

Immediately to her right, she sees two gang members running from the loading dock area and heading towards the aisle where she heard gunfire. Seeing something in that aisle, they turn and start heading for the office area. She stops for a beat, "Mike is now heading right for them," she hears herself say.

Seeing Brenda get shot and now having Mike in danger fills Lori with panic. Warning Costner becomes the most important thing in her life, but yelling from the catwalk would give Costner's position away and probably get her shot.

"Her phone, of course," she thinks. She takes out her phone and calls Costner's number. Lori does not know that Costner has no cell phone with him. It rings, but he does not answer. Then it goes into voice mail. Her heart pumping rapidly now, she runs down the catwalk as quietly as possible and takes the steps two at a time down to the warehouse main floor.

•　　　•　　　•　　　•　　　•

Without her helmet, Lori does not hear the instructions given by State Police Lieutenant Barbara Maylars to the Red and Blue teams. Through the helmet cam on Brenda, Maylars saw Mike Costner punch Brenda and struggle with Ellis Taramelli.

Maylars controls her emotions and calmly tells the teams, "To all team members, be advised Lieutenant Mike Costner is the informant working for the Fifth Street Gang. He is armed and dangerous. I repeat Mike Costner is armed and dangerous and is to be treated as a hostile.

This is for Sergeant Daniels, be advised Ellis Taramelli is a State Police Officer, he's one of the good guys."

When Maylars does not hear an affirmative from Daniels, she tells Bentley to call her cellphone. Her call goes into voice mail.

Turning off the mike, Maylars complains, "Damn, I told Ellis it would be too dangerous to go into a meeting with Turgeson without a wire or some backup. Now he's in the middle of a raid with both cops and perps gunning for him... and I can't reach him or Daniels, who is the one person who can recognize Ellis and help him."

•　　　•　　　•　　　•　　　•

At the far side of the warehouse, the controlled bursts of automatic rifle gunfire erupts. Blue Team has started the sweep and run into resistance. Lori starts to make her way to where she last saw Costner. Cautiously but quickly she moves down an aisle. At an intersection, she glances around a corner. Behind her, she hears feet running on the concrete floor. She quickly ducks behind some crates and takes a peeks over the top of one. Two gang members with pistols in their hands go running by then turn right down an aisle.

As she gets up from behind the crates and turns, her cellphone starts to ring. The two men, who just passed, turn around and start coming directly at her. One of them stops and fires. Lori jumps back between two crates for cover. Two more shots splinter the wood on the crate next to her.

She immediately dives back into the corridor and in a lying position fires four rounds at the men running towards her. She hits one in the leg, and he falls. The other takes two in the chest. He is dead before hitting the floor. The man shot in the leg takes cover behind the body of the dead man.

Lori empties her gun at the body of the dead man. The bullets pierce the stomach of the dead man and hit the other guy in the head and shoulder. Both are now dead. Lori moves back into her place of cover between the crates and re-loads her automatic weapon.

Then she hears automatic rifle fire behind her. Looking up, she sees officers Jason Taylor, Donald Ramirez, and Alice Stetzler deploy across the catwalk and start firing towards the loading docks. Lori resumes her effort to find Costner.

•   •   •   •   •

Mike Costner quickly gets to the main warehouse floor and runs to the cluster of offices where the meeting is to take place. As he passes some of the gang members, he warns them that there is a police raid and to get prepared for a fight.

Bursting into the room where Mark Turgeson is sitting, Costner yells, "This is a trap, Taramelli is a cop."

"That fuckin' son-of-a-bitch Craig Zdonskova double-crossed me. Let's get out of here!" Turgeson curses. "Why didn't the transmitter in the broad's vest let us know the cops were coming," he adds.

"Maybe Daniels is not part of the raid or she doesn't have her vest on," Costner replies as he puts on his bulletproof vest and grabs the automatic rifle he left on a desk.

Turgeson curses again, "Jesus H. Christ!"

Costner looks at Turgeson and says, "All the exits are probably covered. They'll expect us to try to leave at the exit nearest these rooms. Let's shoot our way out through the loading docks. Maybe we'll catch them off guard."

"I like that idea, boss," Bernie Tontas agrees.

"Fuck! Let's go to the docks," Turgeson commands.

Gunfire can be heard at the other end of the warehouse. Costner says, "I'll get some of the men to pull back to the center of the warehouse to protect your back while you're heading to the docks."

Costner with the automatic rifle in his hands carefully but hurriedly moves down one of the aisles formed by the crates on the main floor of the warehouse.

Tontas with two men by his side leads the way to the docks. Turgeson follows with three more men taking up position behind him. They travel halfway to the docks when gunfire erupts from overhead.

Officers Taylor, Ramirez and Stetzler are deployed at three separate positions on the catwalk. They are shooting at the group trying to make it to the docks. One guy on the left of Tontas falls. Another guy behind Turgeson yelps and hits the floor. Bullets are flying all around them from above. With his automatic rifle, Tontas returns fire to the catwalk. The two men behind Turgeson also start firing at the catwalk.

Turgeson crawls to the first man to be hit and drags him behind a crate. He sees the man is dead. Turgeson then crawls back and retrieves the man's automatic rifle. He starts to fire at the officers on the catwalk.

Stetzler gets hit in the upper thigh and falls onto the metal grate of the catwalk. Taylor calls to Ramirez, "Cover me. I'll check on Alice."

"Roger," Ramirez shouts as he switches the action on his rifle to full automatic. With machine gun effectiveness, he sprays all the positions of the men below causing them to take cover. Taylor reaches Stetzler to check her condition.

"It hurts like hell, but I'll survive. Hand me my gun. I can still shoot," Stetzler says.

Taylor reaches to get the weapon. Because Ramirez is using full automatic, he empties the rifle quickly and has to reload. When he does, the perps below rise from behind crates and start shooting. Taylor gets hit in the left arm and is spun to the catwalk grate besides Stetzler. She grabs Taylor's weapon and starts returning fire. At the same time, having reloaded, Ramirez opens fire again in full automatic.

Turgeson runs out of ammunition and ducks behind a crate just as a spray of bullets hits their position. The remaining two men who were behind Turgeson fall. He crawls to where the men are. Both look dead. This leaves just Turgeson, Tontas and one other man remaining.

The bursts of automatic police rifles and the return fire by the Fifth Street Gang is heard all throughout the warehouse. Searching the bodies of the fallen, Turgeson grabs three rifle magazines of ammunition. He crawls back behind the crate. "Bernie!" he whispers.

Tontas turns and raises his chin asking "what."

"Here, some more ammo," Turgeson throws Tontas and the other man each one of the rifle magazines. "Let's crawl to the edge of the crates nearest the dock door and make a break," Turgeson adds.

Tontas and the other man nod in agreement. By this time only sporadic fire is coming from the catwalk, but from the gunfire in the rest of the warehouse, it is obvious the police are moving closer. Turgeson leads the way as they get to the last crate before the open floor that leads to a dock door.

Turgeson, looks back at the two men and whispers, "Ready?" He is the first to rise, then the other two follow.

Lying on the catwalk, Alice Stetzler has a clear view of the floor at the dock area. When she sees three figures racing to the door, she easily is able to hit the trailing two men with two short blasts of her rifle. Both men go down. The third reaches the door and exits.

Turgeson hears the rifle fire and can sense that the other two men are down. He makes it to the door, shoves on the panic bar and is immediately outside running down the dock steps.

The high beams and spotlights from the police cruiser and van instantly turn the darkness into broad daylight causing Turgeson to stop in his tracks.

"Drop your weapon and put your hands in the air! This is the state police!" comes a woman voice over a bullhorn.

Turgeson instantly drops the rifle and sticks his hands in the air. "There won't be any trouble," he says with resignation.

Through the blinding light of the spotlights, Turgeson can make out the silhouettes of three figures approaching him. All are pointing weapons. State Police Sergeant Tanya Bentley says, "Well, well, well, lookie what we got here. Mark Turgeson. The big man himself."

Barbara Maylars walks up to Turgeson as Bentley is putting the handcuffs on him. Maylars says, "Holding an automatic rifle while fleeing the scene of a police raid. It will be interesting hearing how your lawyers are going to try to spin this." She then turns to Bentley and says, "Read him his rights."

When Turgeson has been read his rights, Lieutenant Barbara Maylars adds, "I have been waiting a long time for this, Turgeson." Then to her officers, she says, "Take this piece of shit to jail."

•　　　•　　　•　　　•　　　•

Hurrying down an aisle, Ellis turns a corner and runs into Sergeant Clyde Macturner. From the collision, Macturner bounces against a crate. Bullets start whizzing by them and wood splinters fly in all directions. Down the aisle, two gang members are shooting.

Ellis grabs the bulletproof vest of Macturner and pulls both of them back around the corner, out of the line of fire.

"Thanks," Macturner then adds, "Who the hell are you?"

"One of the good guys, sergeant. My name is Ellis," he says with a smile.

Macturner points to himself saying, "Clyde. You PPD or state?"

"State," Ellis replies. "Now let's take care of the two perps."

"Roger that, I'll take the one on the right. You take the left," Macturner orders.

They both leap into the corridor and immediately open fire. Both men shoot the gang member coming at them on the right, he goes down. The gang member on the left opens fire.

"Oops," Ellis mumbles as he re-directs his fire to the gang member on the left. The guy also goes down.

"What the heck was that!??!" Macturner cries.

"Long story, Clyde. Tell ya later. Right now I have to head this-a-way," Ellis points in the direction he last saw Costner.

Pointing to the left, Macturner says, "Well this is where we part Ellis. My squad is over on that side."

They head off in different directions.

•　　•　　•　　•　　•

Lori heads down an aisle in the warehouse towards where she last saw Costner. She is flush with adrenaline and concern for Costner's safety. Lori is relieved when she finally sees Costner and starts to run towards him. She notices a look of surprise on his face when he gets a glimpse of her. He then raises his automatic rifle. The barrel is pointed directly at her. Confusion takes hold as Lori slows her pace. She's puzzled and thinks, "Why is he pointing his gun at me?" She then instantly thinks, "Mike is not aiming the gun at me. He is aiming it at someone behind me."

From his vantage point behind a crate, Ellis sees Costner walking down an aisle and waits for him to come closer. Suddenly, Lori appears in the aisle halfway between him and Costner. He sees Costner raise a rifle and take aim directly at Lori. Instantly, Ellis moves out of hiding into the aisle and takes aim.

Before Lori can turn around to see who is behind her, a shot ring out. Instantly, the bullet whizzes past her ear. Turning back towards Costner, she sees a dark spot appear on his forehead. The spot starts oozing dark blood. Lori's mind goes blank for a split second followed by horror and dismay. She becomes filled with animal rage.

Spinning towards the sound of the shot, she sees Ellis Taramelli holding a rifle down and to the side just looking at her. Oddly, it seems to her like Ellis has an expression of relief. "Ellis shot Mike. Why is he dropping his guard?" she thinks. All of this takes a millisecond to flash through her mind, then the grief of losing Mike and the anger of shooting Brenda takes over her actions.

Lori fires in rapid succession four slugs which hit Ellis in the chest, throwing him across the aisle into the crates. Shaking with tears in her eyes, Lori walks slowly towards Ellis with the intension of putting a bullet through his head.

At that moment an explosion erupts scattering debris down the aisle. Lori is knocked to the floor. Stunned, she tries to get to her feet to finish off Ellis. The trauma of her grief and the concussion of the blast proves too much for her. She falters trying to rise. Her head is now spinning, and it seems everything around her is clouded in smoke. She is coughing and can't get her breath.

Trying to push herself off the floor, her arms give way, and Lori collapses. Lying face down, the concrete floor feels cool to her cheek. "How could Ellis turn out to be such a bad guy?" she thinks, as the fog of unconsciousness envelopes her. She fights trying to not pass out, but can do nothing to stop it. Vaguely she becomes aware that she is being helped to her feet by two people.

Officers Hayden and Scott are dragging Lori away while flames and smoke completely engulf them. They reach one of the exterior doors. Hayden and Scott take Lori to one of the police cruisers and sits her down. Breathing in fresh air brings some order to her thoughts. When an ambulance arrives, the EMTs put her on a stretcher.

In the back of the ambulance with an oxygen mask on, Lori slowly starts to come back to her senses. She is hit by a wave of grief, and her body shakes. "Mike is dead, Mike is dead," she sobs.

The EMT puts her hand on Lori's shoulder, "Maybe you should lie down," she murmurs. Willing to follow any instructions, still sobbing, Lori lies back on the stretcher.

At the hospital after a brief check-up, Lori is cleared, and she leaves the emergency room. At the desk, she asks about Brenda. The nurse says she will page the attending doctor, Roger Docent. A red-haired man about medium height and weight, wearing light green hospital scrubs, shows up. The man introduces himself as Doctor Docent. He tells Lori that Brenda is recovering well, is conscious and, yes, Lori can visit her.

Getting the room number Brenda is in, Lori takes the elevator to the fourth floor and walks in on her friend. Brenda is wearing a powder blue hospital gown, her hair is matted and needs brushing. Weakly, Brenda smiles as Lori enters. Lori leans down and gives Brenda a hug. Moving the IV stand a bit to pull out a chair, Lori sits and takes hold of Brenda's right hand.

"I killed him. I killed the son-of-a-bitch that put you here," Lori says blankly, then starts to sob. Lori promised herself she would not cry, but the emotions just pour out of her. After a few moments, she gathers herself saying, "I'm so glad you're okay, Brenda."

Even in her fragile condition, Brenda tries to console her friend, "I can't imagine what you must be going through. Killing the man you loved so much."

Lori is a bit taken aback. She then thinks that, because of the meds she must be on, Brenda is probably confused. Lori says softly, "Brenda, I killed Ellis Taramelli."

Brenda stiffens, raises herself in bed and says in a surprised voice, "What did you just say?"

"I killed Ellis Taramelli, the son-of-a-bitch that shot you," Lori repeats a little louder.

Brenda's face turns white. The look of shock on Brenda's face makes Lori sit up.

Brenda numbly says, "Oh, no Lori, Ellis didn't shoot me. He saved my life. Mike Costner is the one who tried to kill me."

Lori's brain starts to reel with confusion, but before she can say anything, Captain Tom Exeter walks into the room. Behind him are two uniformed officers holding guns and pointing them at Lori. Exeter sneers as he shouts, "Lorraine R. Daniels, you are under arrest for the murder of State Police Officer Ellis Taramelli."

Excerpt from Book Two in the Series

Lori Daniels Mystery

Lover Come Back

Captain Tom Exeter has Lori Daniels escorted out of the room in handcuffs by the two officers. He then turns towards Sergeant Brenda Cervetti lying in her hospital bed and says threateningly, "You think the cover of Lila Brown's investigation will protect you. I'll make sure you are thrown off the police force and join Daniels in jail. No one crosses me. It's too bad, you have a nice body. We could have had some fun. You stupid bitch!"

As Exeter leaves Brenda's room, he sees State Police Lieutenant Barbara Maylars and Sergeant Tanya Bentley standing at the door of a patients' room. Police Sergeant Clyde Macturner is backing out of the room saying, "You saved my life, man. I owe you big, but you got to do something about that left and right shit. That is messed up, dude."

All three laugh, then from in the room Exeter hears, "I tried painting a large "L" and "R" on my hands, but I kept getting it wrong!"

They all laugh again, then Maylars says, "Get well soon, Ellis. And I've noticed the nurses on this ward are pretty good looking, so don't think you will be allowed any long-term recovery."

Tanya Bentley then teases, "Ooo, it seems the lieutenant is jealous, already!"

Tom Exeter walks up to the group and their demeanor instantly changes. Maylars says in a not too friendly tone, "Well Tom Exeter, what brings you to the hospital?"

"I just arrested Sergeant Lorraine Daniels for your murder," Exeter says to Taramelli, who is lying in bed. "I guess I'll have to change that to attempted murder."

Ellis sits up in bed and yells, "You did what?"

"Daniels shot you. She is going to prison. End of story," Exeter says triumphantly.

Ellis thinks for a few seconds then responds, "It won't fly. I was the one who screwed up. I thought she was one of the bad guys and fired at her. She merely defended herself," Ellis lies.

Exeter looks stunned, and he says, "What are you talking about? Witnesses saw her shoot you at least four times."

"Yep, she hit me four times in the chest. Nice tight bullet pattern, too. Lori is good. My bulletproof vest saved me. I owe Lori an apology for shooting at her. Hope she will forgive me."

Exeter starts to shout, "Hope she will forgive you. What are you talking about?"

"Like I said, I shot at her; then she just reacted to my attack. Sorry, you don't have a case," Ellis says in feigned regret.

"Witnesses say you shot Mike Costner between the eyes," Exeter protests.

"Chance shot. I was aiming at Lori. I really do hope she'll forgive me," Ellis mockingly ponders.

"Well looks like your big arrest is a bust, Exeter," Maylars says matter-of-factly. She then adds, "I'll personally let Commissioner Rhodes know of Ellis' testimony, so Daniels can be immediately released."

Exeter is red with rage and barks, "You all think you're so smart. Well, you'll discover it is not very smart defying me!" He then struts away down the corridor.

Credits

1) The Dining Car, a landmark Northeast Philadelphia diner, owned by Nancy Morozin and Family
2) JD's Whiskey Buffet, used with permission of John Devitis
3) TastyKake, brand name of the TastyKake Baking Company
4) BMW, German automobile company Bayerische Motoren Werke
5) Mustang, brand name of the Ford Motor Company
6) Dow Jones Industrial Average, a stock index owned by News Corp.
7) Coors, brand name for The Coors Brewing Company
8) Carlo Rossi, brand name for the E & J Gallo Winery
9) Glock, brand name for the Glock Ges.m.b.H
10) Cheetos, brand name of PepsiCo
11) Friends with Benefits, film by Wicked Pictures
12) Titanic, film by Twentieth Century Fox, Paramount Pictures & Lightstorm Entertainment
13) Starbucks Corporation, founded in Seattle, Washington

Jacket photograph by Steve Pestrock Photography, East Greenville, PA

Thank you so much for reading one of our **Mystery** novels.
If you enjoyed our book, please check out our recommended title for your
next great read!

K-Town Confidential by Brad Chisholm and Claire Kim

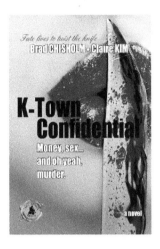

"An enjoyable zigzagging plot." *–KIRKUS REVIEWS*

"If you are a fan of crime stories and legal dramas that have a noir flavor,
you won't be disappointed with *K-Town Confidential*." *–Authors Reading*